T0197165

THE BANDANA REPUBLIC

A Literary Anthology by Gang Members

and Their Affiliates

Library of Congree Cataloging-in-Publication Data

The Bandana Republic : a literary anthology by gang members and
their affiliates /edited by Louis Reyes Rivera & Bruce George ; introduction by Jim Brown.
     p.cm.
  ISBN-13: 978-1-59376-194-3
  ISBN-10: 1-59376-194-5
 1. Gang members' writings, American. 2. Gang members—Literary
   collections. 3. American literature—20th century. 4. American
   literature—21st century. I. Rivera, Louis Reyes. II. George, Bruce.

PS508.G36B36 2008
810.8'035269—dc22

                        2007046772

Cover Design by Goodloe Byron
Interior Design by Anne Horowitz

Soft Skull Press
1140 Broadway, Suite 704
New York, NY 10001
www.softskull.com

Distributed by Publishers Group West
Printed in the United States of America

10 9 8 7 6 5 4 3 2

THE BANDANA REPUBLIC

A Literary Anthology by Gang Members

and Their Affiliates

Edited by Louis Reyes Rivera & Bruce George
with a Foreword by Jim Brown

Soft Skull Press
New York

This anthology is dedicated to all of our youth and their grand-children yet to be born. May they learn from the lives of those who once walked among us:

Oscar Brown, Jr.
Sonny Carson
Fred Hampton
Bobby Hutton
George Jackson
Khalid Muhammad
Huey P. Newton
Stanley "Tookie" Williams
Malcolm X

Greater love hath no man than this,
that a man lay down his life for his friends.
(John 15:130)

Acknowledgments

We wish to acknowledge the following comrades:

OG Ace (Rollin' 20s Crips, L.A.), Ambrose, Angelo, Africa Bambaataa (Mighty Zulu Nation), Adisa Banjoko (The Bishop of Hip Hop), Melvin Banks, Amiri Baraka, King David Barksdale, Godfather Jimel Barnes, Dwane Bell, Twilight Bey, OG Blood 40 and OG Blood Pac, Pirus Blood, OG Gator Wallace Bradley (Gangster Disciple), Jim Brown, Bruno (a.k.a. Big Man), Burner (Blood from the Bronx), OG Max Cartel (Crip), Brother Commander from Chicago, Victor "Gotti" Cherry, OG Chino of The Assassins, Chino (Godfather of La Familia), Monster Cody, Gustavo Colon, Mike Conception, Lord Cashus D (Mighty Zulu Nation), Chuck D, Snoop Doggy Dogg, Easy E., Luis Felipe, Jeff Fort, Don "Playmate" Gordon, K-So Green (of Cabrini Green Projects in Chicago), Eugene "Bull" Hairston (founder, Black Peace Stone Rangers), Umar Bin Hassan (The Last Poets), Del Hendrixson (Bajito Onda), Larry Hoover, Jay the Butcher, Cha Cha Jimenez (founder, The Young Lords), The Jungle (of the Black Peace Stone Rangers), Big Kiko (OG Crip), Suge Knight, General Robert Lee, Leibo, Willie Lloyd, M1 (of Dead Prez), Bonz Malone, Comandante Marcos, Oow-Wee, Abiodun Oyewole, Q-Bone, King Pep (founder, The Vice Lords), Pistol Pete, Big Phil, Geronimo Pratt, RBG, Red (from Hoover), Redstorm (GD), T. Rodgers, OG Madd Ronald (Rollin' 20s Bloods), Mara Salvatrucha (a.k.a. MS 13), David Sanchez (founder/president, Brown Berets), Papa Santos (founder, The Latin Kings), Bobby Seale, Sanyika Shakur (a.k.a. Monster Kody), Big Ship, Cle "Bone" Sloan (Athens Park Blood), Supernova Slom, Monte Smith, George Squeeze, Stic.man (of Dead Prez), Sureno 13s, Piri Thomas, King Tone, Kublai Toure (Amer-I-Can, Illinois), Baba Tunde (The Last Poets), Raymond Washington, Rubbin Ray Watson, Malik Yusef . . .

We thank you!

. . . As well, a warm shout-out to:

Almighty Gaylords, Amer-I-Can, Anarchist Collective, Aryan Brotherhood, The Assassins, Athens Park Bloods, Bishops, Black Disciples, Black Guerilla Family, Black Panther Party, Black P Stone Nation, Black Spades, Black Wall Street, Blood Alleys, The Bloods, Bloodstone Villains, Bone Thugs & Harmony, Booya Tribe, Bounty Hunter Bloods, The Brims, Brown Berets, The Businessmen, The Ching-A-Lings, Cirkle City Piru Gang, The Crips, Death Before Dishonor Movement, December 12th Movement, Eastside Crips, 18th Street Gang, La Familia, Five-Nine Brims, Five Percent Nation of Gods & Earths, Folk Nation, Four Corner Hustlers, Four-Tre Avalons, Four-Tre Hoovers, FTP, Gangster Disciples, The Gladiators, Grape Street Watts Crips, Harlem Diplomats Dipset, Harrison Gents, The Kaos Crew, The KAR Movement, The Last Poets, Latin Counts, Latin Disciples, The Latin King and Queen Nation, The Malcolm X Grass Roots Movement, The Mau Mau, Mexican Mafia, Mickey Cobras, The Mighty Zulu Nation, MOVE, Nation of Islam, Netas, Nortenos, NWA, October 22nd Coalition, Park Hill Bloods (Denver), People Nation, Rabble Rousers, La Raza, Rollin' 30s, Shotgun Crips, Shower Posse (Jamaica, W.I.), Six-Deuce Brims, Six-Four Brims, Spangler Posse (Jamaica, W.I.), The Stop Snitching Movement, The Taco Poets, Twilight Zone Crips, Unknown Vice Lords, Vice Lords, Watts Poets, The Welfare Poets, Westside Crips, The Yardies, The Young Lords, The Zapatistas, The Zoot Suits . . . and, certainly, all of the contributors.

CONTENTS

III—ON THE COUNT 111

IV—THE POLITICS WE SEE   153

FOREWORD

by Jim Brown

The Bandana Republic is the most provocative, researched, educational, opinionated piece of work that I've ever read. When you think of colonizing, and the effects of it on a people, you realize when you read a work like *The Bandana Republic* that it is very hard to draw any one conclusion. But I must say, just from the standpoint of research, to be able to name names of hundreds of freedom fighters, revolutionaries, and misguided individuals who appear in this work is amazing.

The one thing that I never do is look at a great book, a great anthology, and try to draw one conclusion. What you will get from this work is that the human spirit will always survive. The instinct for survival is the heart of mankind. People will always resist oppression. They will do it by any means necessary, sometimes defeating their own purpose, sometimes imitating their suppressors.

In its own provocative way, *The Bandana Republic* makes you think, reflect, cry. I saw so many names of individuals I have known personally who have sat in my home, and they all have one thing in common. They all wanted to be loved and cared for by somebody. Of all the years I have dealt with these very provocative, violent and highly opinionated people, the one commonality is that they all wanted to be loved and cared for by someone. Of course, they verbalize it by talking about being respected. The worst thing that you can ever do to a person who has been suppressed is appear to disrespect them. So much of this is not real disrespect, but their perception of disrespect. In my mind, there is no excuse to be poisoned by oppression, there is no excuse to imitate the attitudes and deeds of the master, but, unfortunately, a great part of suppressing people, controlling a people, is to create in them the desire to be just like you.

I recommend to all of you, and to all people who purchase this anthology: read it, learn from it, try to draw your own conclusions. Let it spell out your own prejudices, your own selfishness. Do not be quick to criticize the authors, because what you have in front of you is a reflection of every revolutionary, every victim that ever lived in this country. Color, gender, race, religion . . . it does not matter.

My conclusion is that the human spirit will always prevail. Only the individual dealing with correctness, fairness, love, and caring, multiplied a billion times, will ever bring about the proper change in human behavior.

Read this anthology, and then check yourself.

INTRODUCTION

*I was born
on the beerglass street,
talk that silk-jumble talk
walk that long-shoe walk . . .
say what??? . . .*

—Sekou Sundiata (FREE!)

Every child is born announcing to the world the same basic human imperative. It comes in the form of a scream to ensure breathing begins. That first cry, first shout, is not simply an ono-matopoeic device, but a complete statement that can easily be translated into any language: "I am here now! You got to deal with me, too!"

And, of course, like you, like me, every child getting past the womb and into infancy is searching and wanting to know the nature of love and life, the parameters of thought and action. Not one of us comes onto the planet wanting to hate or rob or kill. And, in order to begin to know the nature of love and to confirm the parameters of Can, we all require affirmation: "Yes, indeed, someone else believes I matter too."

But from where comes the source of that affirmation we all so sorely need? From a favorite aunt? An older cousin? An uncle who is hip enough to help add to our self-esteem? Or from neighbors and parents who watch you grow and pull your coattail to another book, another ideal, another level of thought and aspiration?

If there is no source to affirm that Yes, of course, you Can, how then do you learn to give voice to your voice, to give sub-stance to your thoughts, to shape the direction for your own sense of struggle?

It begins in the home and with the streets that confront you, as well as with the conditions you must learn to engage right beside all the other humans you meet and know as friend or enemy.

This *Bandana Republic* is the territory of our state. The folks you meet here come from the undersides of urban life. From the working poor of every ethnic group that comprises the demographics of how we've been conditioned to compete and survive inside of a social construct that pits access to what we all need against the privilege of already having more than enough. From full and broken homes these writers come, with parents who themselves have known the hard way, many of whom were barely educated and, just as often as not, hardly nurtured. Thus, in order to protect the neighborhood, the old folk and children, and to establish some form of camaraderie with one another, city dwelling teenagers learn to gather together and claim their common space.

Roving gangs, however, have been in existence as foragers for as long as humans have been walking the earth. They come with the territory of tribal conflict and human provincialism. Once the marketplace became the basis for our first cities, class contradiction and urban alienation immediately followed. And with them, total exploitation of the many who do not have access to their needs by those who claim their privilege. Those who have no privilege to claim respond as best they can.

Thug, you should know, is an ancient Hindu word first used to describe a group of religious fanatics who "murdered and robbed on behalf of Kali, a goddess of destruction." Here, in the Americas, it manifested itself somewhere as late as 1493, the year Columbus brought 1500 Spaniards to Hispaniola with the intention of conquering and enslaving the natives there. The thugs Columbus brought with him came in the form of bounty hunters, with hound dogs to help recapture runaway slaves (thus the following words entered into our dictionaries: cimarron, maroon, buccaneer, outlyer, quilombo). Those first bounty hunters laid the foundation for what we today call policemen. Needful to say, our relationship to them has not changed in 500 years.

When they took to the sea, they became known as pirates, i.e., Buccaneers à la the 16th century, U.S. gangsters of the 19th and 20th, and the gangstas of our own immediate era. And, yes, youth gangs have been concomitant and perilous to any urban landscape, often providing distorted values to the youth of the working class poor, and just as often serving as outlet for illicit trafficking: yesterday, it was slaves and gold; today, drugs and guns.

Yet inside of this phenomenon there is also the conscious compulsion to give voice to the voice, and to do so within the parameters of art; in this case, creative literature. Oftentimes, as with Miguel Piñero's award-winning play and impactive film *Short Eyes*, the aspiring writer learns to tap into that potential while doing time for street crimes. Just as often, as with Pedro Pietri's classic collection *Puerto Rican Obituary*, it grows out of the concrete reality of street life.

For despite the conditions that, with each generation, continue to confront our youth, the voices reflected in this *Republic* lay claim to their own source of strength, testifying on behalf of those who still remain voiceless. They are persistent and obviously resilient. And however the reader chooses to measure this body of work, here the voice is clearly meant to be heard.

Take J. Sheeler, for example. A young girl coming straight out of Brooklyn, raised amid the working class surrounding Coney Island, with a sensibility already hardened by her father. Notice the tone in her poem, her need to belong. Her willingness to undergo the test, and in so doing, to prove to herself (and to her father) that, yes, she can take it, she can be what she once thought was most important. Notice, too, the style of her poem, the brushstrokes in her painted lines, her potential, and above all, the fact that she controls the poem.

The battleground is always the immediate community we learn to grow through and ultimately love. Whatever its limitations, it is home, and everyone outside of it is suspect, a potential threat to the claim that because these few blocks somehow belong to me, you are a threat to it.

Dwane Bell was raised in an environment where his moral compass was in constant flux. Like everyone else in the 'hood, he learned to walk the tightrope of gang rivalry. Raised in a Chicago housing project, Cabrini Green, with family members and close friends in rival gangs, he had two options constantly presenting themselves: to take the path taught to him by his parents or learn to abide by the code of the streets. His poetry and prose were driven by self-therapy, through which he took inventory of the options before him. The fact that he engaged pen to paper helped him recognize his own potential, beyond the parameters of self-destruction.

No. This is not sociology or a collection of psycho-social profiles. No! This is not just another case presented at the bar on behalf of the defense. There's no shirking here. No cover-up. If anything, *The Bandana Republic* is a confrontation with art. Creative literature standing on its own grounds, and therefore thoroughly didactic and political, like every other sampling of fine art. The poetry, short stories, letters, essays, and interviews here presented are from men and women who have learned to stand against the limitations imposed by the idea that destiny gives you no choice. But choice and action and belief in self demand that human destiny must be shaped by the living, and not just by the manipulators of social order.

While there have been several autobiographical confessionals published from time to time, there has not been such a literary work that offers a full range of genuine creativity authored by both current and former gang members. Moreover, with the rate at which street gangs are, again, on the rise across our planet, here we have a book that serves as doorway to a dialogue with our own youth. A national dialogue that further testifies to the creative aspirations of those who first developed their own social perspective from the standpoint of street gangs. How do they see themselves? How have they learned to express their sense of politic?

This *Republic* offers teachers, social workers, adolescents, and all working class readers in search of personal direction and clarity an invaluable tool for the further understanding of contemporary urban culture, and, most importantly, an honest, upfront look at the political-economic-racial constructs that stand in the way of our capacity to realize ourselves.

Intergenerational in scope, this anthology includes such contemporaries as Crips and Bloods, Latin Kings and Mexican Mafia, Neta and Black Gangster Disciples, along with their predecessor Chaplains and Bishops and Young Lord/Familias, as well as actors, poets, musicians, singers, and activists who once walked deadly, or thought they did.

Within this framework, and in spite of the stereotypical "conventional wisdom" concerning street gangs, is ever the creative impulse that comes with breath. These folks here are not just dancing and styling; many of them read and study, learning to develop the gall to give voice to the voice—to express themselves on paper. For within those same "gang-infested" communities come the lyricists, musicians, visual artists, and writers. And they are cognizant of those who preceded them—as with James Baldwin (*The Fire Next Time*), Piri Thomas (*Down These Mean Streets*), Claude Brown (*Manchild in the Promised Land*), and Malcolm X (*The Autobiography*). The contributors here learned long ago that they were not alone, that a literature that spoke directly to them was right there, in print and in the local library. From such as Langston Hughes, Amiri Baraka, Allen Ginsburg, John Oliver Killens, Margaret Walker, Sonia Sanchez, they also learned that poetry and prose stew from within and spill out onto the page; that many of our youth are not merely Hindu Thugs and lifelong felons; that inside their communities resides a plethora of talent that refuses to succumb.

From whence the rise of the Student Nonviolent Coordinating Committee (SNCC), the Black Panther Party, Brown Berets, Young Lords, Brownstone Rangers; from where those internationally impactive Civil and Human Rights movements and, later, a Nuyorican Poetry, a Graffiti Art? Each of the above has been just as informed by urban street rhetoric as it has by our inherent will to do. How many novelists, poets, dramatists, artists, philosophers, and teachers were born and reared among the voiceless, and took to the culture of the streets, yet never turned their backs on their own potential?

It is this creative impulse that heretofore had given shape and henceforth continues to shape contemporary culture ever since the enslaved among us manifested their Freedom Songs and Spirituals, as those who followed gave birth to the Blues, to BeBop, CuBop, Doo Wop, Hip Hop, and Free Jazz, too.

This *Bandana Republic* aims to capture the fullest range of this potential drive within the genre of creative literature to document for the first time the collective conscience of street gangs, across the lines of gender and ethnicity and local border. The writers here presented define themselves on their own terms, both in the sense of human sensibility as well as in their political consciousness and in their individual and collective ability to assess the nature of the social conditions we all face.

And, yes!, this *Republic* is as much a political-historical document as it is a definitive literary work. Unlike many other books that stay within the "seedy side of city living," written mostly by social workers and missionaries looking to turn a slow page into a fast buck, or like Gangsta Rap, following behind Iceberg Slim, this collection speaks directly from the standpoint of the streets and from the need and the ability to take a blank page and create a work of art. A didactic art that truly reflects the creative and intellectual sides of those who are clear about social struggle and human aspiration.

Louis Reyes Rivera
18 December 2006

1—BATTLEGROUND

The violence that takes place in the streets between crews is no doubt displaced. But what cannot be overlooked are the African and Native attempts to reconstruct the familial in order to fortify what American colonialism has all but destroyed.

—Malachi Daniels
(former member, Black Panther Collective)

They really don't start out as gangs. They start as organizations. And for obvious reasons, the media calls them gangs. And I call GANGs, Government Assisted Neighborhood Groups.

—Malik Yusef
(spokesman for the Black Stone Nation)

Man's instinct is to survive. Body language is an important part of Gang Culture, the Art of Surviving. Your Diploma is that you survive. We had to walk in convoys because, if not, that was your ass. Society laid the groundwork for Gang Culture!

—Piri Thomas
(author/activist/ex-gang leader)

WE ARE BORN INTO THIS
Francine Rosas
(Almighty Latin King Queen Nation)

We are born into this world innocent and eager to learn
yet as time goes on society does burn . . .
our minds, our hearts, our ideals, our uniqueness,
such a cruel world
it is time we spoke up for our people
our people that cry,
our people that mourn,
and our people that are poor,
let us not fall to the ground because others knock us down
let us stand up for our people
let us speak the words our ancestors died fighting for
one body, one voice, one soul,
together we can take over the world.

SUPER TRAMP
Monte Smith

My story from child to man exploded in the face of the new south.
Disadvantaged financially, running from the insanity was a
    movement
restrained within the grip of struggle and disappointment.
An empty mind learning car lane lessons at ten
instead of the Golden Rules
resulted in my rapacious tastes and ambitions.

By day, I hustled for words, money, and any other profitable idea
that could line my stomach with the taste of life.
Musically, I was raised by urban street corner heroes.
The scenery of poets in combat
and the scent of marijuana
replaced concerts to watch and tickets to buy.

I began to look deeper inside this world scribed
on the pavement of my own feelings and desires.

Once there with my own footprints behind me,
it branded me.
Now I stood with a head full of knowledge
and an empty set of eyes to match
until that point, I rested on the thought that I knew the way.

But the wind of a new day brought word to me through song
that I was wrong.
My illusions turned on me and raped my soul
like a runaway lost in New York City.
Things had to change and this is how it happened.

SET TRIPPING
Bruce George
(Black Panther Collective, Harlem; The Zulu Nation, Bronx, NY)

Blood Killer, rise up!
Crip Killer, rise up!
Buck, buck, buck
no more toys, trains and trucks
because of Colors!

Double-Dutch
turned double jeopardy
as they jump in
to raise their chest cavities
now faces are scarred
like ancient pottery
better the odds found in Lottery
from passes going like Monopoly
but who's playing their psychology?
Go figure the trick/knowledgy!

No analytical Ink Blots
can untie the knots
of a mind on boycott
poking at imaginary dots
from stress induced blood clots.

So going bananas over bandanas
is characteristic now like gutters
running with Ruby Red Mystics
from fingers that flick
solely designed to set trip.

Their rage that's waged
is juxtaposed to the tightness of their braids
so they pass it on like AIDS.
Now streets are paved with anatomy
from being John blazed
to make splattered walls catch acne
from turf warring over stoops and lobbies
homicide is a hobby.
So finding the missing Lagos
is like counting the lines on the faces of Eskimos
might as well put faces on bottles
of Henny and Cisco
courtesy of a false bravado on full throttle.

Scripted formats
bring about tits for tats
stats and Gats
mug shots and Photo-Mats
at upstate habitats.
They're the Prison Industrially Complexed
used as Texas Instruments
such as stocks, bonds, dollars and cents
and high priced tenements
because of colors.

The old days of Peru are through
principles fell short of being
consciously political
situation got critical
from being Willie Lynched
through the umbilical.
Drive-bys to them is nutritional
like the blood that is drunk in a Satanic ritual.

We say,
don't let plaids turn into toe tags
and black veils over do rags
Like numbers pulled out of grab bags
for waxed ears
be like Australians for beers
pimped by the cheers
of profiteers!

Because to set trip
is to back flip
to shackles and whips
auction Blocks and bargain chips,
so BK, wise up,
CK, wise up
no more buck, buck, bucks,
caskets and tux
heavy is the toll
for running amok
because of colors.

INITIATION: SEVEN IMMORTALS, 1972
J. Sheeler
(Member of Seven Immortals, Coney Island, Brooklyn)

Circle of girls on the night sand,
boardwalk a glowing line behind us.
Gloria wraps the belt around her fist
as I pull my t-shirt up and off,
naked to the waist,
arms crossed,
hands spread out to cover the sides of my breasts.

Watching the dirty, undulate CI beach
roll down to the dirty ocean water,
I wait for seven strikes of leather on bare skin
to close out my individual life.

Gloria doesn't hold back,
swings like a batter at the plate,
ninth inning,
all eyes on her,
whirls into a whipping that draws out of me
nothing but blood.

To call out, to cry—that is to fail.
And to fail
is to invite the watching circle to close in,
deliver the real thing,
give me something to cry about.

That's how my father would say it.
He trained me well for this initiation.
Years of unmeasured violence honed my weapons:
blank face
bone-dry eyes.

Seven strikes across the back,
counted out,
witnessed and paced.

This is a sure thing.
A bet I have no way to lose.
The girls don't know this.
Gloria doesn't like me,
wants to stay the only white Immortal on Coney Island,
uses all her crazy white-girl muscle
to whip some kind of sound out of me
but she can't,
of course, she can't,
and the circle counts out loud,
feeds into the frenzy
—four, five, six—
a laughing scream at seven
and I swing around to face my initiator.

Welcome, Seven Immortal,
Gloria says, calm and blank at me,
dropping her belt to give me a complicated handshake.

The circle breaks up, drifts off.
I walk the dark beach down
alone
to the water
wet my shirt to wash the blood
then wash the shirt and pull it over my brand new back:
the red, the shredded black, the rising blue.
My first jacket. My primary colors.

SELF-MADE MAN
Oscar T. Lester a.k.a. Triple Blak (Chicago)

Eleven years old—on his own, his mama was always gone.
His daddy took a walk to the store and never came home. So now
it was up to him, sink or swim, what the hell couldn't excel, not
in a system that was designed for him to fail. So he just rips and
runs, young and dumb, drinking rum. Can't see straight, bailing
with a three-eight handgun. Seeking ghetto fame, trying to get a
name, learning how to slang. He claims he's true but he's really
new to the game. He's just trying to learn as much as he can. Life
has dealt him this hand, so he must play it. He's a self-made man.

Yeah, I'm a thug, but dig . . . with what I dug, I had to resort
to mugging. Because, in my household, there was no loving or no
hugging. My mama never let me know that I could grow up and
be greater. I would tell her, "Yo, hey, I'm running away." She'd
be like, "See you later." Now what the hell is that? How can she
call herself a mother when she knows that she never gave a damn
about the brother. She had problems of her own. So I guess my
problems just weren't important. She was busy turning tricks,
chasing dicks, lacing joints and snorting. But I ain't pointing no
fingers; she taught me everything she knew. Nuff respect; peace
and love, shout outs to mama are due. She said, "No need in
placing blame, because the game is hard but true. Don't try to
show no love for no nigga who don't show love for you."

So now I'm on this street shit. Don't bring me none of that weak shit. Got plugged into the set; so now I'm legit. I finally got a gang that I can roll with, some partners I can stroll with. Together we control shit. Loved by few, hated by many, respected by all! Together, we stand tall. Divided, we're bound to fall. So if I gotta kill, then I'll kill. There's not a cap I won't peel, bout it, bout it; nigga, I'm for real. Deal with this shit here, if you can. Young punk coming up, getting bucked, because I'm a self-made man.

Ten years I put in, running with that clique, now here I sit. Pulling a bit, and my life don't amount to shit. They said they loved me, then they sent me off to pull a hit. But if they really loved me, they would have let me get up out the clique. But tomorrow I'm walking out, just as free as I want to be. No sweat, my debt has been paid to society.

Parole—that's what they stamped on my paper, see. Then they handed me my t-shirt, my blue jeans, and my ID. My mama's in the corridor, waiting with a grin. My woman brought my kids, and they're all standing with my friends. It's the end. Or maybe it's the start of another trend. Go back to the strip, bust another clip, back in the pen again. Damn, where will it end? And how can I spend time playing daddy to my daughter and my son again? Man to my woman, good child to grandpops, who stopped speaking to me once I started selling rocks and licking shots, letting loose the glocks on them bumboclots. I'm just living by the laws of the land. Doing the best I can. I'm a self-made man.

THE NIGHT GOTTI DIED
Victor Gotti Cherry
(OG Gotti Valentine SMM Blood Gang)

(H)omicide sirens flashy lights people
gather 'cause of the sound of the thunder
my eyes blinked with a thought of wonder—
is this the night I may travel under 7 feet deep
soul searching for a way out of my physical

I smile but the penetration destructed my mental
(B)lood, I claim eyes steer target sky high
I question myself: is this it; am I gonna die?
Tell Teesha, Grandma, so she don't mourn or cry
I may soon come, death, I shall never fear nor shall I
run or hide. Teesha, wave my flag, protect my
honor, never let my name go down as a loser or goner

'cause our blood runs deep; even when I die may the
concrete drink the juice that flows from the veins within me
paint the town the light cherry color ashes 2 dust, dust 2 cremation.
The night I died it was for my nation 1:2:3.
The night Gotti died.

KING OF GHETTOSPHERE
(or: they killt Tone)
Avery R. Young

1.
        terry's friend
wondered why i walked

funny / said so
threw marble

cut my chin
made eyes water

swung him / lip open
befo' us bruised

runnin'
from belt / next day

we were boys
in the 'hood

2.
> keepin' folk
from sleep
> on jackson blvd.

2
3 o'clock
in the mornin' / callin'

each other faggots / slap
boxin' / thinkin'
we had ever

n 7 days fo' us turnt
old enough
to pay lynell
to remodel basement
with fiend bills

you know / *3 lincolns + 5 washingtons = 2 dimes*

3.
fount paintin' sidewalk
bloody / barefoot

all him did
was ask a muddfukka,
> *Bitch!*
> *What the fuck you looking at?*

4.
> purple brother him was
vaseline gloss
busy 4 corner

hustler / honest
daddy turnt mama
avenue merchant / crazy

bin wrist first
but him no pity statue

him was all of watchin' magic
walk n jesse white tumbler
flip pissy mattresses
olympic gold

him a sky

full of tagged walls
n kool moe dee rhetoric

a secret
best kept
too disruptive fo / classroom
                  principal office
                          punishment

      him / him only
      soothsayer / him

      a nigga you hadta beat
      to get to.

RACIAL CONFLICTS
Juan C. Valadez
(Southside L.A.)

La Raza
Que Pasa?

Misconceptions of Race.
Poison beautiful children.

Blacks/African Americans desire to fight/win.
Mexican/Chicanos desire to win/fight.

Teenagers/high school students
full of fear and pride
adolescents/middle school students
looking for a place to fit in.

The lack of historical education
slowly murdering our future
Legislators
Doctors
Lawyers
Professors
Musicians
but most of all
Our Poets!

Blood splatters
as angry children
hold on to the illusion
of Race.

Mothers cry
as their children die.

Everyone knows
that something must be done,
but no one seems to care;
they're having too much fun.

Someone,
anyone,
please do something
before
half of the precious children in this country
kill one another for a Giant Lie:
the Illusion of Race.

UNTITLED
Bmoredamu
(Member of the Bloods)

Way down in the Jungle deep . . . that's where I'm from. But my Jungle has street signs and concrete, broken bottles and burnt-out hollows from last night's beef, as we lay hungover from last night's grief. We have pride and respect . . . well, some of us do; the rest just lay on their ass and wait for a check. You say you get high to cope, and I'm trying to feel ya . . . Cops, guns, pussy, something'll kill ya. Unemployment rising, opportunity fallen, there's only two options in the 'hood: selling crack or ballin' . . . Damn! I'm tired of the lies. I'm tired of the screams, scattered thoughts, shattered dreams. It's time to open our wings. We went from Kings and Queens to Thugs and Dope Fiends. At least, that's how it seems. It took one evil white man to stop the calm, but you can't hide behind a Bush if North Korea drops a bomb. Let's re-ignite the fire and bring back the Panthers so our daughters won't have to be their Cooks, Nannies, and Private Dancers.

MARIA
Nekesha Bell

Sing: "Maria, Maria, you remind me of a West Side story."
Growing up in Spanish Harlem
living life just like a movie star.
Maria, Maria fell in love in East L.A.
to the sounds of the guitar playing.

Maria, not living life like a movie star,
Maria, trying to find her way in this forgotten place
a way to escape misery,
another generation lost.
Maria, Morena, Mestiza of the galaxies,
an eclipse of his soul,
celestial being,

Maria, a mesmerizing not forgotten memory
a haunting beauty dancing in the streets,
her hair long, frizzling in the wind.

Luna is her nickname,
her eyes are from the night sky.
"Maria, you remind me of a West Side story."
Heavenly divine, a model she could have been
then she saw him,
became pregnant.
The baby, Sol of her existence,
like Cinderella waiting for her glass slipper,
her story to change
washing
cleaning
being everything her family wanted her to be
except never living her dream,
never having a dream,
were the words on the streets.

Her perfume, a faint whisper on the walls,
her voice possesses us all,
waiting for the castillo her mujeriego
said he would build one day.

"Maria, you remind me of a West Side story."
Diego is his name.
In her twenties
and beaten down by too many tragedies,
sitting at the window in her rocking chair,
holding the baby, staring out into the streets,
remembering the fiestas, fun times,
long hours at work.
No sad face, no smirk,
giving her Papa and Mama all of her checks.
None for her.

An ancient warrior,
the only way out was him.
She a fugitive to run to something better,

"growing up in Spanish Harlem,"
anything than the mold on the walls,
the loud voices in the hall,
esta familia drinking.

The fighting,
the fire burning in the core of her soul,
the timbers simmering, settling silently.
Now all is quiet as her man tells her every day,
"Cienta en la boca."
Bound to him by marriage,
"You are my puta
to do with as I wish.
Your job is to make babies."

No amigas to call,
he cut her off from it all
the eternal essence of her existence,
as she looks at her manos, was not there,
but here, in her mind,
behind her eyes.

Maybe one day, when she can cry no more.
Sing: "Maria, Maria, you remind me of a West Side story,"
growing up in Spanish Harlem
living life just like a movie star.
Maria, Maria fell in love in East L.A.
to the sounds of the guitar playing.

She will find a way,
may the expensive pearls fall from her eyes
to escape through the door, rich or poor,
and make it on her own,
just her and her little boy,
Junior esta Diego,
and may he grow to be his own.

MACHINE IN MO-SHUUUN!
Big Kiko

C-R-I-P, C-R-I-P
CRIP! CRIP!
Minds of Steel, Hearts of Stone,
Crip Machine is moving on.
Blue Steel, Blue Flag,
Crippin' hard, no turning back.
Raise the 'C' and hold it high,
Forever Forward, Do-or-Die.
Spread yo' wings, raise yo' head,
We are risin' from the dead.
Who Say? (Ce Say!)
Who's The Greatest? (Ce The Greatest!)
Can't stop, won't stop, will not Ce stop'd.

Soldier! Soldier!
War! War!
Lose one, kill two.
Never rest until you do.
Hear the Spirit from the grave.
Got to Crip every day.
The 'C' is strong, the world is weak.
Strength and Loyalty is our Key.
Across the land, over the hill,
Strap in hand, we come to kill.
Coast to coast, state to state,
C-Machine is on the way.
Who Say? (Ce Say!)
Who's The Greatest? (Ce The Greatest!)
Can't stop, won't stop, will not Ce stop'd.

In '69 The 'C' was born,
36 years later and still growing strong.
From the East came The 'C',
From the West came the rest.
East Side, West Side, North Side, South Side,
Nationwide, Unified, Crip! Crip!
Raymond Washington did his best.

Crip'd for years, now he rests.
Big Took, Ce like him,
Dare to struggle, dare to win.
Mac and Salty, they were down.
O-G Compton, strong and proud.
Hoova Joe, he was right,
Cuttin' throats day and night.
Up the hill, down the hill,
Through the land, kill the Klan.
Kill the dog on the wall,
Bring him down, bust his crown
Who Say? (Ce Say!)
Who's The Greatest? (Ce The Greatest!)
Can't stop, won't stop, will not Ce stop'd.

Keep them Busters on the run,
If you catch him, slice his tongue.
Back him up against the wall.
To his knees he will fall.
Hold your sword, make him beg.
No compassion, take his head.
Plant the 'C' everywhere.
For we are those who will dare.
Uptown, downtown,
Blue Flags all around.
Chitty-chitty bang bang,
Nothing but a Crip Thang.
C-R-I-P! C-R-I-P!

What you want? (Freedom)
When you want it? (Now)
How you get it? (Power)
When you need it? (Now)

RIVERSIDE OUTLAW
by OG Pimp GKB G-Shyne
(Eastside Blood)

Now I lay down to rest
I pray tomorrow to do my best
to kill
to stalk
stay trill
and mack
so let these niggas know that
I Forever Rep Mine BLLAATT

So if a donut
persists on running up
let him come
and let it be done
that he will be a prime example of where I'm from
the sea is blue
which has crabs and plastic donuts that people piss in
and throw waste to pollute the earth
Blood is Red
that keeps us alive
without it we are Dead
the world needs us
in their Life
Blood is thick
water is thin
Blood keeps us alive
Shit, Blood is Alive
so next time if they run up,
Lord, let me see what keeps them Alive
and what pumps in their heart
from the start

It's me
I do
Forever I'll Stay True
Fuck Them, Crabs, Frogs, Donuts and that Ill Flue.

CATCH YOU AT THE CROSSROADS
Erica Ford
(The Code Foundation, Brooklyn)

for Tyquan Cheese Jackson, 12/29/87–11/21/03, killed by some Crips.

Life is a pleasure.
It does not have any measures.
We sit back and wonder
how did you ever go under?
Every day your mother cries.
Look at the pain in her eyes.
This reckless behavior is so insane.
Now memories are all that remain.
Just yesterday we celebrated your birth,
the wonderful days on Earth.
We will never forget you!

So many trials and tribulations,
yet so many complications.
Life is not granted
so don't take advantage.
It's time to spread Love.
It's time to promote Life.
The Life you didn't get a chance to live.

Time has come to set you free
without ever knowing the man you would have grown to be.
Today we say Goodbye
but forever your name will fly
igniting the force to change our Lives.

I DIDN'T KNOW
Eric S.

From the burst of his moans
was the clap of one's chrome
as cracks in his bones were shown
as the facts of the road
—or the streets—
things that should have to be known
as Rap set the tone
for why someone died over words that he spoke

and I didn't know
'cause, see, my skin is a little lighter than most
but far more west than the U.S. coast
where I too can relate to the ghosts
and finding ways to just cope
but nobody told me that this made me dope
'cause I struggle too
and they hustle to put some dough in a coat
I don't have

I don't bag hash 'cause the air that we smoke
isn't provoked by the wild waves of life that we boat
but rather the stinking choke
of burnt bodies from known folks

So you rock gold ropes
from rhymes that you wrote
of the thug life you promote
but one step further I'll go
with ten steps back to where me and my hope
have eloped
to where roped gold
pulls me out of trench snow
and the snow
that makes your bank roll
makes you a role
and your payroll rolls
so you can rhyme about girls looking like J-Lo

after selling Os
where someone wasted 4–0
in their nose
that I'd use for clothes
and to warm my son's toes
and have him not phat
but fat
so that his ribs don't show

And the brothers who've gotten blown
is nothing compared to the family that still hasn't shown
and the ring tones
on your phones
is over exposed
when considering the ringing tone
of mothers crying
as they bury their own

I've got war stories that can pave all your streets
and your roads
so many excuses for why from God I'm disowned
and why I shouldn't've lived the life
that I've grown into man's bones

But I won't act bold
or act cold
and die after making others low
when I'm old
'cause the king's throne
isn't shown in his gold
but how he gives to his own

And how with reason
I stole from nothing but holes
to give my children clothes
with just holes

So do I fit the description of thug life?
I don't even want to know.

SHOOTING THE RABID DOG
Marcelo

This guy I grew up with told me that he
would kill for me all the time.
I knew he was just saying this
because I always gave him his daily fix.

I was dealing at the time and would serve
him up whenever he wanted.
I felt sorry for him. I would take him to the
pharmacy to get his needles.
What could I do? I used coca to feel my
anger and let it ride, so I wasn't
in the position to tell him what to do.

I kept him up when he was too high to go to sleep,
and I would hide the needles when he would, but I
noticed that when he started looking for the needles he started
to panic and when he dosed when he panicked he would
overload and the cycle repeated.

One time, he hit the vein on the top of his wrist
and told me to take him to the doctor because his
eyes started to droop. I didn't know what he was
talking about, but the doctor thanked me for taking
him to the hospital. She said I saved his life.

It started to get so bad I could not get high—clear
my mind and flow with the powder. I wanted to
get loud, scream, feel the shield around me
and let the chemical cloud me.

He was a head rush of stress making me sick.
I was losing control and in this situation losing control
was not an option. The cops would catch on if you did
not have your head in the game. So something had to be done.

"Here, hit that. It'll make you feel on the edge of life."
He smiled and did, and when he did his eyes widened

29

like he knew that was his last high, and a sigh of relief on
his face because he was tired of the shame that he
carried for years on my back and on the backs of his
girlfriend and their kid.

As he hit the floor, I lost my friend.

ETHNIC CLEANSING
Kevin Coval

1.

last night a 15-year-old father turned swiss cheese
last breath left his body like lobsters in boiling tombs

animal Crackers assumed his identity
shot premature ejaculates into the shadows
of ghost children hung before trials

this mourning abortion cries sun over the makeshift / memorial
    arranged
before gutted sidewalks of lego mansions where the boy's body
    was found

mothers, nurses, homies, sisters, preachers, drug dealers
leave loose-leaf paper prayers, teddy bears, candles, white castles,
his graff crew's black book,
a photo album flipped open pictures of the virgin mary
and a young man in church playing christ on good friday /
back strained beneath the cross

2.

day one / poetry workshop / Wells High School /
Javier cussed me out in front of the whole class,
sayin' i didn't know shit 'bout bein' Puerto Rican from the 'hood,

nada / true / no doubt /
next day brought in Willie Perdomo's *Where I'm From* /
told students / write your own shit / where you at /
and don't be bitin' Will's style
or mimicking gangsta thug fantasies /
i mean i wanna hear your story

and Javier stuck a pen thru his arm /
tapped the blood beauty he'd written in spanglish
and struggled while reading not to cry or kill or throw himself
out the fourth floor window of our classroom

after the session i asked if he wrote a lot / said he wrecked walls and
freight trains in the hours most people sleep or sex /
when boyfriends beat
young mothers of younger children who steal spray cans /
and bomb rail yards
and yuppie condos along blue lines of Chicago El trains / said

i'm tryin' to make shit real pretty / like make bricks come alive with
colors and cartoon characters /
positive messages like crack is for plumbers
/ toys are xmas gifts
knowhutimsayin' / make shit cold like Chi winters
mad flame like Chi summers / i mean
i wanna see people seein' my shit / you know /
jus' see 'em seein' my art
/ i mean i jus want people to see how beautiful my shit is

3.

a black sedan hides the immaculate on Wood Street
searching like pioneers for the perfect raw untapped fix-me-up

white collars won't step into the street this month
too many chulos on the porch packing rat traps and garden tools
selling limonada and furniture / there is no spring in this city
only gray and unbearable heat

two days from Javier's murder
estates will be spotless / memory expunged
streets and sanitation will wash the remnants
of a boy's life into an underground sepulcher

across the street nieces and nephews
watch police pick at crime scenes
architects pick up blueprints / new mothers pick wallpaper patterns
the children pick out pages in history books
draw mustaches on Mount Rushmore
to see if the stone heads resemble the stone men
moving into the homes they've been bought out of

for only another moment will these sounds hang
in the air like bubble letters on buildings before buffing
like aerosol beneath moonbeams just after spray

the sound of boys kicking a futbol
pebbles crunching under their feet
their sisters giggling at the mess they've made
of peeled mangos and limes / sweet juices and rind
sweating down their faces / seeping into the concrete
like blood.

THESE HANDS
Joseph Andolinio

when i was born these hands were balled into fists
when i was hurt these hands my grandma kissed
when i was 15 they held her as she died
these hands pushed back the tears i wanted to cry
when i was 16 they were cuffed behind my back
7 months later they waved behind jailhouse glass
I wanted to hold my son with these hands
when i was 21 they carried my brother's coffin
these hands had fought with him
should have hugged him more often
these hands have held guns

and these hands have held ladies
these hands have been covered with blood
and they've touched my babies
but now that I'm all grown up
and a real man
i feel like i can change the world
with nothin' but these hands.

ESOTERIC RHETORIC
Abyss
(with 20-20 Down, Mack Avenue, East Detroit)

This speech is southern tanguage
deciphered from cryptic language
my verse is nothing but life's paintings
brush strokes of lost souls
this frigid world will give you a snot nose
dropping hot prose
underground like potholes
I blaze in the cold
amazing to folk
I'm a ray of hope
like a slab of coke
to a fiend on dope
this is the real no soap
these streets will kill you
no joke
it would behoove you to feel what I wrote
this is my soul on smoke
nothing but mere truth
on yellow stickies
no need to get misty
this is what happens
when your business is risky
a little more federal than icky
dem feds get picky
you can't get rid of me
I'm on this rhyme grind

funny how time flies
and how slow it is
when you're not wise
so we bake pies and carry pieces
trying to get a piece of the pie
I mean a piece of this lie
spitfire
the bluest flame
Momma said know the face
secondary is the name
because people change
but somehow remain the same
my love is your gain
anything less is pain
death numbs you like Cain
all of this shit for street fame
peep game
we speak the same
you're from New Jersey
I got throwback claim
slow dat main
we don't flow the same
you say, E.F. Hutton or Abyss
the reaction is the same
'cause when I spit people listen
I'm so Detroit they call me piston
not pistol
found God but it still feels like I'm missing
I miss Him
wishing I could clean my slate
and do it mysteriously at the same time
I'm dealt my fate
sacred death wish
lust for this street life will make you selfish
it's more than champagne, blunts and shellfish
Heaven sent acting hellish
no love for a snitch
hustling dimes out of a ditch
pitch like Tom Glavine
but we get upset when the worst happens

phone tapping
salary capping
confessing when you're rapping
your block under attack when
running your rap
about the trap
claustrophobic I feel like I'm trapped
friends don't put friends in traps
twelve can go to hell
we want the cheese but we ain't rats
just some cool cats
Zoot suits and spats
mink furs and hats
camouflage jackets and backpacks
Air Force Ones and throwbacks
is the uniform
we stand out like unicorns
rain sleet any storm
thoughts can't get a penny for 'em
so much death
the Henny stay pouring
young cheese can't grow mold
you're headed down a rough road
so do what you're told
for all of us to be 98.6
this world is too damn cold
this street life is getting old
I can't wait until these streets turn gold
the hustle era
Esoteric Rhetoric
the game sick
young soldiers take care of it!

BATTLE
Willie Perdomo

Oh shit, it's on.

DJ Cooley High got his one and
twos below the rim.

Megawatts tapped from Rosa's kitchenette,
paper plates smudged to death with cariño.

Word is out: mad beef, wild style,
beat street battle—you ready?

Don't take off your Kangol bell
if you can't spin revolutions
or turn your legs into scissors.

TCB meeting on masticated benches;
Vic Fisticuffs prepare to throw
the kind of joints that leave perfect
nautical knots on your forehead.

Who seen Moe? Tell him:
Night pool after the jam.

Fifteen of us on one nickel bag and a quart,
shell toes synchronize with atonal head nods.

Santa Barbara is rocking her eighteen karat Cuban
and Crazy Legs has just entered the playground.

Cut creator pulls out an assassin from a master-
mixed milk crate and aims toward the center.

PARTNERS TO THE END
Terrence "Kamal Imani" Oats
(formerly of the Five Percent Nation/Gods and Earths)

We were patnas to the end like Siamese twins.
Up in the attic
Droppin' mathematics
Prepared for static
Packin' automatics
Phone booking hookers
We were fanatics
We would sniff and riff and front
And roll a philly blunt
Recruit the warriors
And hunt the punks
As some of us fell and went down to the devil's cell
I fuss to say I can't trust this hell
As the angel of death
Would snuff a brother's life
I had to change my direction
Make a sacrifice
Go a separate way
And live my dreams
But we're still patnas
By all means
'Cause no matter where I go on the planet Earth
I'm reminiscing how we controlled the turf
You will always be my patna, be.
We are the universe!

RECESS TIME
John D. Evans
(Oak Park, IL)

I remember recess time with bittersweet memories
How the children played without the likes of me
How I felt out of place—in a world all my own
How I never let go of my pseudo-cozy comfort zone

On the wall where bullies made fun of my braided hair
How they teased me for the thrifty clothes I'd wear
How they mistreated a giant they didn't even know
How they never imagined the places I'd someday go
How they barked in my face and called me girly names
How they made a daily dose of ridicule their game
How my feet ached in pain—crushed in shoes too small
How my pants were high because I was standing tall
How I spent my time knowing that I was unlike the rest
How I knew that something special rested in my treasure chest
How I entertained myself by writing and singing original songs
How my weakness for poetry always made me strong
How I realized at an early age that this life was mine
Memories, just a few memories, of my recess time.

REFUGEES
Alicia Benjamin-Samuels

The Los Angeles boys are victims of a civil war
Apathy against the oppressed
Most days they dodge attacks from the wild animals
The armed forces
The hostile locals
This is the year they eat dust
Taste the sweet lick of heroin
Roll back their heads
Drift into a space where they find sanctuary

The Nashville souls are in the abyss
These boys are drowning in the families they have to cross
Many of them know their fathers are dead
Physically or otherwise
They sometimes live on their own
Knowing hunger, fear, desperate childhoods
They've been wandering
Going from home to gang to jail

The East New Yorkers are a scattered crew
Some flee the trauma of foster parents and group homes
Never to see their parents again
Buses and subways don't provide enough distance for some
They've spent so much time on the run
Finally they find shelter in New Jersey, Philadelphia or Delaware
But it's hard to leave the past behind
There's still the famine in their eyes
That won't ever be forgotten
A few feel guilty for finding the green beyond the desert

The rest remain in war zones
Ducking the demons
Looking for refuge in America

KASPER
Juan Carlos Valadez a.k.a. PeeWee
(Florencia 13 Malos)

I remember
the first time we met.
You, tall and *flaco*;
A bundle of skeletal joy—
giggling and smoking *grifa*.
I see the wicked day
you were jumped into the *barrio*.
Months later,
you were jumped into the *clika*.
Proud, indeed you were,
because you were now a *Maloso*.
You became my brother,
my shadow,
my bodyguard,
my crime partner,
my friend.
Most of all,
you were my *camarada*.

On a cold, winter night,
as I drowned into a sea of crack cocaine,
and various other drugs —
you were fighting like a *Malo*.
The bullet,
which punctured your lungs —
The bullet
which stuck to my *Corazon*,
at seventeen,
you were only a little boy,
floating in a celestial body.
The day of the funeral,
when I saw your *jefita* smiling,
I could see your multitude of freckles
cover her face like stars
on a cold, murderous L.A. night.

Today, as I reminisce,
on the day of your *muerte*,
I realize that you, more than anything —
eras mi hijo.

I RAN FROM, AND TO, HOME
Chad Marshall

I ran. As fast as I could, I ran. From the age of running fast, I ran.
The chase was on in the town of guns and knives, so we all ran.
We ran from each other, either
chasing or running to chase and dodge another day.
This was daily life in my 'hood.

They called it Frog Town and it was hard and fast.

As I grew older, my family chose to run as well, running away for
    a better life
away from the town of fists and blood, the town of fear and pain.

In my new life, in a town far away, I lived in sunshine where I
    stood uncomfortably
embraced by the calm of the sun, the calm of the wind and the
    eerie calm of nothing.
In my old life, I knew calm was just the beginning of something
    about to happen,
because in Frog Town there was never the gift of silence
without the promise of panic and pain.

As I stood in my new sunlight, I began to realize,
and soon also began to accept, that the chaos would never come.
Was it all behind me?
Was it all left in the town with no sunlight
or does it still live inside me like soil I can never wash from my
    hands?

As more people in my new town of light began to embrace me,
they also learned from where I came.
From this, the embraces became less warm
as eyes began to stare down and look away.

And like an old habit that I somehow knew I would never truly
    give up,
I began to run again.
Running from my past just as I had run from fists and knives,
I run from my past, darting through alleyways and probing
    conversations.

I used to run from painful blows
but I now run from discovery.
Has anything changed or will I only be safe where I belong?

I am an alien now,
a traitor to the land I left behind
and an outcast to those who rescued me,
adrift in the middle of 2 islands that will never be home.

HOMEBOY

K-Swift

(project coordinator, Urban Word NYC)

I'm lookin' at the directions we headed to
My man almost died over white, yellow, red, and blue
I'm try'na get it thru his head that it ain't the only life
Now I'm standin' holdin' mics in a lonely light
That's my homeboy — nearly dead in the streets
I never seen so much blood, two stab wounds deep
Both in his back, in a red shirt on top of that
Fresh from a baseball game minus the jersey, heard me?
He bled for like a block and a half
See, he Neta. Run wit' Bloods. Beef wit' Crips.
In my 'hood it's all right there
Far from a dream, sometimes I wish it was a nightmare
And sometimes I'm type scared
Like damn, what if I wasn't right there
To tell him, chill, son, sit down, just wait for EMS
My boy was a bleedin' mess, my mind is needin' rest
Can't y'all see the stress
Cuz I moved from Brownsville, the roughest ride
To the Lower East Side
Where kids cut-n-hide
Unlike my old block where niggas let the bullets fly
No slick talk or shuck-n-jive just BUCK BUCK — bye
But wit' a blade tucked inside, it's still easy to fuckin' die
Pardon my language but ain't no time for censorship
When you try'na make sense of this senselessness
Since he's just fifteen
Livin' Neta, Blood, Crip, King
I replay it in my mind and it stings
His blood ran dark on that warm October night
Nearly eighty degrees, I knew somethin' wasn't right
Nothin was
We went from all of us chillin' to
Him and a few cats illin' to
Me and his family try'na keep his blood from spillin' all over the
    pavement
To me, bein' on this gang tip is sorta like enslavement

And it just may be but it ain't no chains, kid
Still, as you bangin' and claimin'
You and the main men you hang wit' start changin'
Let's suppose there's a crew called "Soldiers"
So what you claim, soldier?
Now you a soldier and that's all
In a so-called war wit' your enemies
But y'all ain't sure what y'all fightin' for
And all sides are losin', so why keep score?
Death tolls loudly
I'm glad homeboy ain't hear it call
So he won't have to rock all black in a coffin
I prefer he wore no colors at all

WRITING INSIDE TIME
Lecroy Rhyanes

Eyes like a video game
controlling the movement of hands,
young knuckled fists hold
knowledge in a crippled mind-state.
Learning to walk on shattered glass,
we can leap by the end of the month.
Breath control asthmatic, America's air
polluting our ours, polluting
our hours. We count the days
by ones, in dash marks, pennies and
one dollar bills. Hollers cupped, wanting
more than charity but to live,
see and feel our existence,
our history, our hell, and
the creative potential to
illustrate our imagined heaven
with our colors.

Dark blood reds.
Crystal sweat clears.
Brown bruised ink.

Black scabs on the paper,
when revealed, show the flesh
of survival and the
interworkings of a mind gone mad,
happy, depressed, healed, reborn, dead
and reborn again.

DEAD ANGELS
Juan C. Valadez
(Southside L.A.)

In a state of solitude,
I often wonder why
are so many humans like I —
insane. We roam around
in darkness with sick, evil thoughts
that live in harmony —
these eat our multitude of cells.

Often,
these vicious images
are desperately fighting
to fly away into a safer place.
For some odd reason
they're unable to do so.
These wicked thoughts
of intentionally harming others —
an eternal madness — drives me
into a psychological, unpredictable rage.

Slowly,
I find myself anxious to unlock
the key to my ailing brain
but I know if I use it,
many human beings
will be in great danger —
then again
maybe they will just fly away.

WHERE THE LUV AT
Redstorm
(Chicago's Eastside GDN)

Where the love at,
when niggas be blasting Techs,
got blood draining out the next nigga's neck.
The pavement soaked and little girls choked
up about that brother they used to fuck
laying there broke up.
They say pour out a little liquor and fire up the B,
but you can't even check on a nigga's family.
Same nigga you broke bread with,
slept in the same bed with,
now your nigga dead and you ain't said shit.

Dude, how you forget so quick,
last night you had sex with the same chick.
Now you look at the chalk lines where your man once laid,
and your mind rewinds to how y'all once got paid.

But still nigga . . . Where the love at,
you didn't even make the wake,
you still on the set with a cocked hat
and a cocked gat
depending on some kid to watch your back
while you slang crack
Black, What's Up With That

Same game that got your man dropped,
and you still on the block 'cause you got a knot in your sock.
That shit ain't going to save your soul
you better wise up and roll
before you get changed like your boy.

But still, nigga . . . Where the love at,
why you still hurting your sister like that?
She knocked up with a kid
and you still selling her that shit

smiling at her mom like you ain't doing no harm.
You have become the Enemy, Nigga,
now I must sound the alarm.

THE PARIAH
Sun Ra a.k.a. Oow-Wee Shakur
(from the West Coast)

I'm not only a Brotha Living On One Destiny 4 the Struggle, I'm
also a Pariah. Pariah means a social outcast, a revolutionary, and
a nonconformist. Anybody can be a Gangster or Thug, but there
is only a handful of Pariahs who outcast themselves from being
followers. A Pariah is a warrior, not a soldier. A soldier follows
orders; a warrior gives himself orders from within, which comes
from his essence. And if he can't lead someone, he has himself to
lead. A true 100% Pariah goes to a forest where there is no trail
and carves his own path. He takes his mental tools and hacks
down all the thorn bushes, the weeds, poison ivy, and all other
poisonous shrubs, creating a new trail—which outcasts himself
from the ones who find it easy to just go to a forest where there
is already a path carved out for them to follow. It takes heart to
be a Crip or a Blood, but it takes your life to be a Pariah. That's
why only 144,000 can live that Pariah Life. So carve that "trail"—
because some become legends.

II—TELLING THE TALE

Gangbanging is not a lifestyle; it's a deathstyle!

—Cle "Bone" Sloan
(Athens Park Bloods)

The Shower Posse was created out of a need to survive in a society where the gap between the rich and poor continues to grow.

—Duane Blake
(Son of Vivian Blake, ex-founder/leader
of the Shower Posse, Jamaica)

There are only two things in a gang—cowards and kids.

—T. Rodgers
(ex-Blood leader)

FLEXING FOR TURF

Dwane Bell
(affiliate of the Mickey Cobra Nation, Chicago)

It's been one of the hottest summers on record. The truce is off and the tensions and tempers have been running high. The ready rock (crack cocaine) is relatively new to the street and it's been selling like crazy, so naturally there's going to be a beef between the brothers and folks. But no one expected that the ready rock would have them fighting amongst themselves.

It's 10 p.m. and a loud and long whistle has just sounded off! But this is no ordinary whistle. It's a warning whistle used to let the people in the 'hood know that the brothers are getting ready to put their arsenal on display. All of a sudden, the streets are empty; everyone has taken cover. Then a loud, echoing sound of gunfire coming from one of the top floors of the Rock. (That's the nickname for the two side-by-side nineteen-story project buildings that serve as headquarters for the Mickey Cobras.) The shooting goes on for twenty or thirty minutes.

Everyone waits for about ten or fifteen minutes of silence to take place before the streets come back to life. One of the main topics of discussion amongst the brothers is the types of weapons displayed.

"Man, did you hear that Tech 9?"

"Yeah, man, but did you hear that 12 gauge pump? Man, they emptied those bad boys out."

This nightly routine of displaying arsenals or flexing muscles, if you will, was done every night for the entire summer. This was the Cobras' way of letting the Gangster Disciples, the Vice Lords, and the Black P Stones know that they meant business when it came to slanging and banging.

ABSENCE OF CHOICE
Layding Lumumba Kaliba
(former Sportsmen)

It was almost a given—if you were a young child growing up in New York City in the 1950s, you had some sort of affiliation with one of its many street gangs. Just what gang you were down with had to do with ethnicity. After ethnicity stamped your allegiance, only geography played a greater role in determining what gang name would be splashed across your chest on your sweater.

My brothers and I bopped with the Sportsmen from Avenue D. Our borders were painted red with the blood of rival gang members. We controlled turf on the Lower East Side that ran north-south from 14th Street to Delancey Street, and east-west from F.D.R. Drive to Avenue A. During the 1950s, the make-up of the New York City Police Department was predominantly white—Irish and Italian males. It was rare to see a police officer of color back then. The police that patrolled our area of the Lower East Side seemed to have a laissez-faire attitude. "Let them niggers and spics kill themselves. What the fuck do we care."

The origin of the Sportsmen began in Harlem during the 1940s, right after World War II ended. City housing developments, also known as projects, began popping up like weeds, occupied mostly by returning Black soldiers and their families. Uptown Harlem projects filled rapidly, so Blacks began moving downtown to the Lower East Side developments, such as Jacob Riis, Lillian Wald, Baruch, LaGuardia, Madison, and Smith projects. Originally, federal housing projects were constructed for transient residents—a brief stop-off before moving on to claim the American Dream of white picket fences, two kids, and a dog. Suburban life. But for the overall majority of returning Black soldiers, the realization that the "dream" was not meant for them came quickly and harshly. Blacks came home to joblessness, despair, racism, and rejection, the manifestation of Langston Hughes's "dream deferred."

For many of us, housing projects became holding pens, prison camps, neo-plantations where we ended up doing life bids—cradle to grave—in red brick fortresses designed to keep Blacks locked in, not out.

There's a saying, "War is Hell." So was growing up in the projects. The Lillian Wald Projects is where my family began serving our time. It was the home of the Avenue D Sportsmen. During the 1950s, we numbered about 500 members.

Gangs were organized like small armies or small countries. There was a president and a vice-president, a secretary, and a warlord. Gangs had divisions: Senior Sportsmen, Junior Sportsmen, Sportsmen Debs, Suicide Sportsmen, and Sportsmen Tims. The Tims were a division made up of pre-teens ranging in age from 8 to 12. We were called snakes. Pre-teen Jitterbugs on the bop. Sawed-off punks carryin' sawed-off shotguns that articulated our confusion in madness and blood.

It was on a sweat drippin' August night spittin' heat in our faces as we slithered through Lower East Side streets to embrace gang wars' tragic song. But what was Mama's little angel doin' here? What about the promise to be good, clean cut, straight A? Danger awaited but I felt no fear. Just the sense of fallin' in Mama's eyes, a topplin' from grace. If I'm an angel, where the fuck's my wings? Why can't I stop fallin'? Oh, God!

So there we were: Blacks, Jews, Chinese, Puerto Ricans, Irish, and Italians. Squashed together into a volatile mix. Each group claiming its turf, fearful of the others.

The racial makeup of the Sportsmen was 90 percent Black, 7 percent Puerto Rican, 3 percent white and others. Our main rivals in the fight for gang supremacy were the Dragons, a large Puerto Rican gang whose turf bordered ours on the west. Puerto Ricans came to New York's Lower East Side in large numbers during the mid to late 1950s. We saw each other as natural enemies, competing for the same poor housing and dead-end jobs, crumbs off America's table.

My most vivid memories of those times came during the summer of 1958. Teresa Ghee, a teenage Black girl living in the Lillian Wald Projects, had been brutally gunned down on a hot August night, walking in front of her building. News spread like wildfire that it was a member of the dreaded Dragons who had snuffed out young Teresa's life. Emotions in the Projects ran the gamut, but for Sportsmen, the only thing that would satisfy the burning rage in our bellies was revenge.

In the week that followed, parents kept their children home from school. Storefronts closed and windows were boarded. The

Sportsmen had gone into full mobilization. Payback was on the mind of everyone. The call went out to all of our brother clubs, Uptown Sportsmen, Suicide Sportsmen, Morocco Sportsmen, the Royal Crowns from Harlem, the Assassins from Queens.

When the Dragons got word of what was happening, they sent out a call to all their brother clubs: the Eastmen, the Purple Gang, and the Suicide Dragons. They matched us man for man. Fear gripped the entire city. This was shaping up to be the largest and bloodiest gang war in New York City's history. All the newspapers and radio stations made it headline news. The rumble was set for Friday evening. Social workers flooded the streets, talking with gang members from both sides. They tried their best to get us to call off the impending rumble. Local police precincts were badly outnumbered by gang members. Emergency calls went out to then-Mayor Robert F. Wagner to send in the National Guard.

Forty-five years has not dulled the memory of my parents pleading with us not to be involved in gangs, to stay out of trouble. What my parents couldn't understand was, at that time and place, we felt we had no choice. You bopped with the Sportsmen or became an enemy of the Sportsmen. We chose to bop. In the world of bebaddd, Mama wanted me to be good; wanted me to behave; wanted me to become like the little white boys on *Leave It to Beaver* or *Father Knows Best*; wanted me to give up my wingtips for penny loafers, my sweatbox wee-hours-of-the-morning grind 'em ups for 6:00 to 9:00 after-school sock hops, my C average for A student honors. But in the world of bebaddd that just couldn't be.

Lower East Side streets demanded that I pledge allegiance to the flag of konked-head Jitterbug Bebop. A bandana flag that hung at constant half-mast because dreams and death had become synonymous. In the world of bebaddd, you be baddd or you be nothin'. Had to walk with skip-dip arrogance. Kick ass at drop-dime speed. Go to school strapped blue-steel heavy. But it wasn't about disobedience. It was about tryin' to be sumtin' on streets that gave up nothin'. Streets where bebadddness was next to Godliness and be cool was blasphemous.

So I shook in the volcanic eruptions of rock 'n' roll nights and street gang terror. Cursed the myth of America's melting pot theory that raped my youth with the violent thrust of its racist contradictions. And I sold my soul to the world of bebaddd.

On the day of the rumble, police and National Guard troops had set up barricades along the avenue that separated the two gang territories. The gang war never jumped off. Switchblades and zip guns versus automatic assault weapons carried by the guardsmen. It was academic. For months after the aborted rumble, news reporters held interviews with gang members from both sides and with city officials. Photos taken the day of the aborted rumble were amazing. A sea of panama hats broke ace/deuce, doo-rags and multi-colored-bandana-wearin', sawed-off-shotgun-wielding warriors. A formidable force by anyone's standards. I don't remember how long the troops and police presence remained. But I can remember my father sitting my brothers and me down that following Sunday, reading us an article from a front page *Daily News* story. It asked the question, "Have New York City Gangs Become Too Large?"

The city-led crackdown on street gangs in the years that followed answered that question in no uncertain terms. Drugs flooded Black and Hispanic communities, destroying young minds before they had time to develop. Saturday night specials could be purchased on any street corner for a few bucks. The rates of unwed mothers soared. The industrial prison complex was and still is busting at the rims due to the influx of young Black and Latino children. The once mighty street gangs—the Chaplains, Bishops, Royal Crowns, Assassins, Dragons, and Sportsmen—have gone the way of the dinosaur.

I've often wondered what would have happened had gangs like Sportsmen and Dragons been politicized and begun to move in positive, life-affirming directions. I'm sure that the City of New York, on that hot summer night on the Lower East Side, took notice and moved to make sure such a possibility would never happen.

If my friends could see me now, would they recognize me—minus the diamond-blocked stingy brim, wingtip shoes, and bell bottom pants? Could they accept the fact that in the world of bebaddd you don't outgrow it; it outgrows you? It becomes all-consuming, and you live or die on the strength of your badness. Mean streets give way to a meaner world. Raising hell pales in the difficulty of raising family. Kicking ass becomes a selective process, not always violent in nature, but lethal in its effectiveness. The blue steel of street gang youth gives way to machine gun words that blow holes in the tarnished myth of "manifest destiny," allowing our children to see clearly through the insanity of "white supremacy." You camouflage your bandana strut for freedom of mobility, but your heart still keeps time to the rhythm of Bebop. You add strings to the beat of rock 'n' roll nights to disguise the message of the sacred drums calling us to war.

If my friends could see me now, would they press their ears to my chest and listen to the chant of the Jitterbug anthem and realize it's the same song we wrapped in konked hair C averages and Mama's tears? If my friends could see me now, would they sing along: *You be baddd or you be nothin'. You be baddd or you be nothin'* . . .

UNTITLED
Jaha Zainabu
(from a section in California called The Jungle/Blood Territory)

The scene opens on an exterior daytime view of an old California neighborhood in Long Beach. Not Snoop and Warren's Long Beach. In fact, it's seventeen and a half minutes northwest of 21st and Lewis. The west side, thugly called "The Weak Side" because the drama, to the naked eye, pales in comparison to the so-called East Side (the video). Overly congested with multi-family dwellings, barber shops, storefront churches, and liquor stores.

More, Auntie's and Nana's Long Beach, where housewives still shell peas and barter sugar for apples and watch each other's children, and everyone respectfully greets Mrs. Jones whether or not she cares to respond. Indeed, all of this in the crazy '80s, and I, still a child, high school, innocent enough, was unknowingly blessed to bear witness.

At St. Luke's in the daytime, the grounds were well kept and the church secretary's blue Toyota Corolla sat parked in the same spot every day. Every day she had coffee and read her favorite passage of Psalms, all in time for *All My Children*. Then she'd begin her duties of typing reports on the church's income and expenditures, and on members who had come by later or those who sought baptism. Notes of the inside. For and by the saved. Slightly contrasting Christ's commandment to "Go, Ye, therefore . . ."

This was St. Luke's by day, but the moon brought a different vibe. Still does. Spooky. A comfortable familiar, however, to those drawn to the underground.

Brian McKinny was one. His moniker was Big Mac. Corny now, but nineteen years ago it was the name to have and Big Mac was the man to know. He could get the goods. Guns. Pussy. Dope. At seventeen and six feet, dimpled and jheri curled, light skinned (West Coast fine), he was well read for a man his age, for a cat with his rep. Big Mac, smooth and a poor decision-maker, soon to run out on his luck, traits many youngsters possessed, was caught slippin'. He, a Long Beach Crip, had strolled aware and careful in L.A.'s Bloodland. Not his first time; still, not a habit. This time he was not visiting some chick. Not seeking revenge. Not stopping for gas. This time, per his mother's demands, he was, by bus, visiting his grandmother, who just wasn't ready for him to leave yet. And she asked in a voice only poets and big mamas and ministers' wives with big hats and round bellies could muster, if he could stay at least until the end of *Wheel of Fortune*. Please. And he, looking into the eyes that had read Revelations before Genesis was thought about, could not say no to her. She wouldn't understand how those Bloods be trippin'. Bloods?

Or that he and Lil Scoops had crazy beef. She would send him to the bus stop well fed with blessed oil on his forehead and pray over with faith that in the name of Jesus and John Kennedy and Martin Luther King, Jr., he would get to the bus stop unstepped on. Even remain safe until she'd again see him Thursday after next, if God should say the same.

But, no. Brian McKinny was shot and killed that night by another man and woman's boy. That heavy on his mother's neck, somehow not being enough, today she goes about her days remembering that on the eve of her only child's services, while his body waited alone and cold beyond a comforter's cure, his murderer, captured only by karma (maybe), had tossed his body. Spray painted his casket in red letters, old English font, now tattooed on the chest of her memory, fresh until forever ends. And why? Over what?

This story is about the courage it takes to look beyond his gang status and see that he was her boy. Always kissed her goodnight. Ate greens with ketchup. Loved fish with his grits. The hole in her heart now filled only with the comfort of knowing that at least he is safe.

Return to St. Luke's.

By now, everybody knows the routine. Same show. Different star. White roses to contrast the midnight robes. Tears rioting down faces, looting smiles. For some, the air is laced with questions of the fairness of God. For others, near the rear there is a stench of doubt regarding existence. The preacher tries to preach. The deacon tries to sing. But it all seems for naught amidst the mother's screams.

From Gangs of the Ghetto to Gangstas of the Inner City
Ted Wilson

My main men and I bopped
to general agreement . . .
Down cats
we bopped to give cause to the causes
that died before they got to us.

—from *Bopping*, David Henderson

As I look back, growing up during the early and middle fifties, there were many gangs in the New York City area (including Brooklyn, which was another town in itself). These gangs had an array of interesting names: the Seven Crowns, the Englishmen, the Viceroys, the Dutchmen, the Egyptian Kings, the Enchanters, El Quintos, the Diablos, the Jolly Stompers, the Chaplains (arch enemies of El Quintos), the Bishops, the Young Sinners, and from my neighborhood, the Harlem Lords. There were a slew of other locals who never got broad recognition. There were a few gangs with citywide associations like the Sportsmen, who had chapters in various parts of the Bronx and Manhattan from end to end. The Sportsmen from Avenue D on the Lower East Side of Manhattan were extremely fierce. The Chaplains were an equal counterpart (in size and strength) in Brooklyn. They stretched into the not-so-middle-class community of Queens. Members of these gangs were called "Bops." This was short for Beboppers. This, to my knowledge, had no relationship to that form of music we call Bebop, which brought some confusion to us neophytes.

The names of some of the Bops were as exotic as their organizational names—Crazy Horse, John the Bop, Outlaw, John the Baptist, Blade, Graveyard, Tombstone, and Priest. Some wore clothing to match their names—like all black, all white, or all brown. There were certain types of hats with deep rolled brims called tip rolls. That was done by special hat blockers in the neighborhoods (back then, there were still neighbors in the 'hood). Then there were names like Snake, Pancho, The Umbrella Man, Pablo, Cisco, Deuce, Tino and Reno, Count and Lil Count, Magician, Ace, the Cape Man, Saint, and a host of others that sounded like avante garde Bebop tunes. The creativity of stylish dress was a mixture of the attire worn by R&B entertainers and nineteenth century carpetbaggers. Various colored suspenders held up chino-type pants worn with long-sleeve dress shirts and vests, making for some very interesting teenage creations. They ranged, in age, from twelve to eighteen years with a preponderance of fifteen- and sixteen-year-olds. Style was important. In some cases style was all that existed.

These were the guys, and girls too, who played behind the tougher ones who were an older brother, sister, or cousin, but there was no substance, no heart. They got over, and in some cases developed a rep, because they had family backup from a mean and respected relative. It was widely known this relative would come to the aid of the fluff and puff.

The larger, more notable gangs had uniforms or colors that unified them. This also would identify them as being down on a turf that was controlled by another chapter of the same gang. Organizations like the Sportsmen were so large there had to be some way of identifying each other. Some groups even had passwords or other little codes that made its members authentic. Serious organizational thought was put in place by the members at the top.

These gangs were primarily African American, a number of whom were first-generation out of the South. The period ethnic name was Colored or Negro. Weaved into this collective were first generation African-Caribbean, a.k.a. West Indians (a name that continues to be used, in spite of the fact that everyone knows there is no such place or person as the West Indies or a West Indian.

This is just another example of how descriptions of people are used to confuse, resulting in further division of African peoples).

There were some gangs, especially in East Harlem, that were Latino. The same was true in the South Bronx and parts of Brooklyn (i.e., Jesters, Ellery Bops, Puerto Rican Outlaws, Phantom Lords). Many of the *Colored* gangs included *Spanish* boys. This also is a period name that still hasn't gone away completely, given the oppression each group equally faces on a daily basis. *Spanish-speaking* does not make one ethnically Spanish.

Included in this amalgam of thugs were a few *white* gangs, a period name that continues because it means privilege. These gangs had names like the Golden Guineas, the Beacons, and the Fordham Baldies. There was the famous cry, "The Baldies are coming, the Baldies are coming!" forcing schools to close early on many a day to let the children get home safe, but to this day I haven't found a person yet who actually saw a Baldy. The *whites* had a natural anger (hard-on) for the *Coloreds*, a.k.a. *Nigs*, and the *Spanish*, a.k.a. *Spics*. This came out of the natural nationwide Jim Crow racial attitudes that still exist in certain urban neighborhoods as well as Southern towns. This is part of the fabric of the U.S. Where there are no African Americans or Latinos around, they would go intra-European-American (i.e., Italians against Irish or Irish versus Germans, etc.). To a degree, the same was true between the *Coloreds* and *Spanish*. Their rivalry was not as much *ethnic* as it was about turf and females, although its origins could be traced to that old toolbox of the Euro-American's divide-and-conquer principle.

Speaking of females, many gangs had sister components. In a number of cases they were called *Debs*. (Could that be short for debutantes? Yes, though not from the viewpoint of social climbing status, but from their age.) Sometimes they were more vicious than the guys toward their female rivals or non-gang girls who were considered extremely pretty. It was said once that a girl gang or gang of girls had flushed a girl's head in the toilet bowl and almost drowned her. This was on the junior high school level in Harlem. Life was tough. These Debs could be equally vicious to weak non-gang males. With all due respect, the female gangs were somewhat of a clone of the males. After all, we are talking about a time that was extremely chauvinistic.

David Henderson speaks to us again from *Bopping*: *We bopped when / about to fight / and we bopped when / happy / all in our own slight /*

*variance / known to the members / of the road / and known to the / similar
bops / of the roaming hoard . . .*

When the gangs went to war, it was called "boppin'," and the
participants would don their boppin' clothes and their boppin'
walk which went along with their boppin' attitudes. The whole
idea that these young people believed that the block or neighborhood or city housing project was a turf they owned is interesting.
They defended it like it was their own deeded real estate. What
was even more bizarre was the same attitude and enthusiasm the
guys accorded to the girls in their fantasized little empires. They
acted like the girls were real estate.

The larger gangs were not satisfied with control of the areas
where they lived. They attempted, sometimes successfully, to take
control of adjacent blocks. A higher-up in the gang, one with a
well-known name that matched his reputation, would come into
a new territory with a few associates and ask, "What click (i.e.,
clique) are you in?" If the answer was in the negative, the guys
in said blocks would be drafted into that gang. How well it was
enforced had to do with how strategically important the block
was to their home base or (here come those females again) how
many pretty, fine girls lived in the newly acquired territory. Back
then, there were no drugs or any of the other money-making
enterprises in these fiefdoms. It was all about their machismo and
rites of passage, even though I doubt if they understood it that
way.

Many of these attitudes were born out of the movies. The
popular genres were cowboys, war (recent and historical) and
gangster stories. Attached to this was the racial prejudice that
had a long history in this country with a particular slant in New
York City and other large urban areas, with people who were a
generation or two removed from the Deep South and West Indies
(English and Spanish speaking). What was seen as Southern
racial prejudice was later seen in its real form. We have since
come to understand it is systemic and thus define what it was and
still is — racism.

The gangs battled for a respect that was couched in the history
of Africans and other indigenous people and the self-hate that
had been heaped upon them. This baggage carried with it a trunk
of contradictions because these same youngsters had witnessed
the entrance of Jackie Robinson and others into major league

sports—for a price. At the same time, events unfolding, such as at Little Rock, Arkansas, or the Montgomery bus boycotts à la Rosa Parks and the freedom rides, spoke to the dark side of racial progress. This confusion left these warriors, most of whom couldn't find their way into an organization, be it sports or anything else, in a vulnerable state. A few made their way out by joining the armed forces, which made for a greater contradiction. The way out was to go deeper in and become an instrument of international racial enslavement by way of imperialism. It was either that road or the penitentiary. These young fellows were some of the toughest soldiers, with a few finishing their tours of duty and becoming police officers or some other law enforcement official. This was a win-win situation for the government.

The power structure saw and understood the force of the gangs. They saw the potential of what these gangs could become in its near future. Brown vs. Board of Education and the Montgomery Bus boycotts were now gaining national focus. The same mentality of The Institute for Policy Studies, The Kerner Commission and the NWO (New World Order) started turning its evil wheels. Along with the NAACP at one end, there was Elijah Muhammad's growing Nation of Islam on the other. These young Jitterbugs were a potential force to go up against the KKK and White Citizens councils. While the country at large was focused on a Red Menace, the government's brain trust and think tanks were looking closely at what could become a Black menace.

They brought in the dope . . . It started with tobacco. It looked hip and tough to smoke . . . *they brought in the dope* . . . next came the beer; it went with the cigs. Then came the wine . . . *they brought in the dope* . . . What went better with cigs, beer or wine? Reefer, smoke, joints, weed . . . *they brought in the dope* . . . The Bops were boppin' to another tune. Instead of warring with each other, they were groovin' to Dinah Washington, the Harptones, the Cadillacs, Ruthie McFadden, Frankie Lymon and the Teenagers, the Chantels, the Moonglows, etc., and . . . *they brought in the dope* . . . Smoke was for squares, chumps, or at best junior hipsters. Sniffin' scag was what was happenin'. Turf was no longer important. Who had the dough for a nickel bag? *They brought in the dope* . . . no more uniforms, passwords, codes, or other special unifying symbols . . . *they brought in the dope* . . . Sniffin' went to skin-poppin', but you were not a junkie, you just had a chippie . . . *they brought in the dope* . . . The boppin' walk became the junkie nod. It was like a contest to see who could nod the lowest and longest and not fall over. *They flowed in the dope and the rest is history* . . . Down went the Mighty Chaplains. Down went the Mighty Sportsmen, the Corsair Lords, and the Seven Crowns. The Black/Latino army gave way to the smoothies, hipsters, jazz aficionados, boogies, intellectuals, and again, interestingly, some of the ex-military men who had gained some clarity about who was the true enemy.

This configuration evolved into another movement that fought for a real purpose, in another kind of way. The movement that took place ushered in young men and women who understood that things could not stay the same. Instead of turf wars and battles over women (now *sisters*), neither of which they owned, the energy was directed into equal accommodations, voting rights, and various forms of affirmative action, at least on the surface. Simultaneously, a sense of self was beginning to take form. The battle for self-worth and recognition of people throughout the African Diaspora and the African continent itself began to rise from the level of venting local neighborhood frustrations to a national Civil Rights Movement to a worldwide Human Rights Movement.

A coming together and a bonding of youngsters from the North and South by way of sports and higher education brought a burst of energy the think-tankers could not anticipate. In *Negro* colleges throughout the South, debates and discussions moved into full force. In the North, cultural groups and organizations began to examine their African selves, re-examine and redefine beauty. Out of the Southern colleges came SNCC (Student Non-Violent Coordinating Committee), and in the north CORE (Congress of Racial Equality) and NSM (Northern Students Movement, closely aligned with SNCC), along with various nationalist groups. The gangs were now organizations of diverse thought and approaches but with a focused purpose. The liberation of all oppressed people in general and African People in particular was the aim and goal.

There was a recognition of the destruction of the fifties generation, its potential and illness. Brothers and sisters started reaching back to help those who had been damaged by the drug plague. It was first done on a broad level by the Nation of Islam. Other organizations, such as US in Los Angeles, the Black Panther Party, the name of which came out of the Lowndes County

Freedom Organization, grew to national attention. Locally, in New York, the Young Lords became the Panthers of the Latino community in the South Bronx, East Harlem, and Loisaida (a.k.a. Manhattan's Lower East Side).

Culture played an extremely important role. There were the cultural nationalists who greatly influenced and gave an image to this new movement of thought and action. Just as the gangs of the 1950s had their rituals and dress, so it was with the so-called cultural nationalists, who very much gave shape to the overall movement. The music began to take on another character. It was the 1960s and a conscious clarity was growing. There was relevance in R&B, Jazz, and Gospel. They all merged with their diasporic relatives and found a relationship to their mother, Africa. As drummer and activist Max Roach often said, "Everything is socio-political." The music was being written, arranged, and performed with the movement in mind. This carried on into the early 1970s with an emphasis on electing people who were supposed to carry the movement to another level.

For some, it provided the sliver of light to move forward and upward in ways that, in the previous generation, one could only dream about. For the offspring of the Harlem Lords, El Quintos, and others, along with their Debs, the new era gave birth to a generation that was now growing up without the ethics, morals, and respect that even those Jitterbugs once possessed. The desire to rise and respect those who had pushed forward, or attempted to, eroded. This erosion continued to spiral down to the following generation, now two generations removed from the Jitterbugs of the fifties. Many of the children and grandchildren of the junkie generation had actually raised themselves. They became the pur-veyors of inner city degeneration.

As the nouveau revolutionaries became leftists, Pan-Africanists, and general Third World activists, that old New World Order raised its head again . . . *They flew in the coke* . . . as children raised themselves into crack/cocaine dealers and users, bodyguards and killers . . . *They brought in the Uzis and Glocks* . . . murder became the order of the day. Human life lost all value. The word *respect* became a reason to try out these new toys of destruction . . . *they flew in the mules* . . . turf wars resurrected, this time for control over the sale of death . . . *They flew down the fools* . . . young girls and not so young, with babies to take care of, from young men who call themselves and each other "dogs." Chaplains became Bloods and Sportsmen became Crips (on the West Coast) and El Quintos became Latin Kings (on the East Coast). Life deteriorated to a jumbo cap of rock, and females of any age became a slab of meat and were treated as such.

From the boogie-down Bronx came a new art form that created a new culture. Just as bebop jazz had created a new culture, by the late '70s, so did rap music (the music part is debatable) descend upon the culture and "blew up" in the 1980s as a key component of hip hop culture. In the beginning there was relevance and consciousness from people like African Bambaataa and the Zulu Nation, KRS 1, Public Enemy, Melle Mel, and a few others. As time progressed, what was positive, conscious rap, which had started on the East Coast, became the negative but conscious gangsters like NWA from the West Coast, which was initially tolerated. From there it all went downhill. Foul, vile lyrics became and still remain the *odor* of the day. This offspring known as gangsta rap became the lyrical expression of the Crip/Blood crack world permeating an African/Latino view in every low to low/middle class community of its inhabitants. Just as the crack/cocaine industry started on the West Coast (as per Gary Webb, reporter on the staff of the *San Jose Mercury News*, who investigated and reported on the U.S. government's involvement with the Colombian drug cartels to purposely target these same communities on the West Coast and move East), so too did gangsta rap.

They rose up rap and promoted it highly . . . So went the new warriors and their consciousness raising lyrics in the 1980s . . . *in come the Bloods and Crips from West Coast to East* . . . Never before have neighborhood gangs become national in scope . . . *They took the neighbor out of hood, made prison dress the style and convicts the trendsetters in style and language* . . . The queens are now called shorties, the warriors have become dogs (mad ones at that), and race pride has been reduced to *Nigs* . . . *they brought in five-o and these children have become the fuel for the prison industrial system* . . .

The question is: will there ever be Peace in the East as long as there is Unrest in the West? They claim "they know what time it is." Do they really know it is time to look in the mirror, look inward, see the damage and move to repair it—which is what Reparations Time is about.

GHETTO NOSTALGIA
T. Rodgers
(B.P.S. L.A. via Chicago)

It was a time of Ed Sullivan and the Mickey Mouse Club was in Black & White, Superman was in Black & White. The whole world was in Black & White.
Yet I never saw Black & White in America.

It was a time when you could smell the summer. I mean, one could really smell the colors. You could taste the sunshine and feel the air.

It was a time of discarded wine bottles, free-flowing wind-riding multi-colored butterflies, flowers in bloom, ladybugs, grasshoppers, dragonflies, mosquitoes, and lightning bugs.

It was summer nights of catch a girl, kiss a girl, hide and get it, pulling butts off of lightning bugs and putting them in a jar.

It was a time when you could hear the grass grow in the morning and listen to it die in the night.

It was that time when you could hear the distant pounds of a basketball sound the plea to get out of here.

It was a time of girl talk and boy talk. It was a time of playing the Dozens; just don't talk about my mama.

It was a time when I can remember sweat so sweet, it was the first time that I had broke a sweat. Man of man, it felt good. To feel my young, strong striving, driving, pulsating, rheumatic body living, breathing, and whining! My God, I am alive and nothing can stop me. This Planet is Mine!

Hugo, Mary, and I would run behind the Watermelon Man trying to get just one piece of that sweet red meat. No one ever told us about Horse Shit on the Run.

There were times when we would be so close only to slip and fall and get up with the whole front side covered with horse's shit.

Man, those were the days, ha! The good ole days! From sunup to sundown, you could always hear the cry of the peddler half singing and half crying, "W-a-t-e-r-m-e-l-o-n, w-a-t-e-r-m-e-l-o-n! Fresh and ripe! Watermelon." And his counterpart, the Rag Man, making his rounds, singing, "R-a-g-s and ol' Irons, Rags and ol' Irons."

The crack of his whip, the crunch of those big wood rotten wagon wheels rolling over broken pavement and worn cobblestone patches that peak-a-booed through the asphalt. If I was to believe in Magic, that alley was full of it.

In the summer, it traps all the sounds of the city and I was the Prince of that alley. The sun had a funny way of showing you happiness in the summer, the smells, the sounds, and the colors belong to me. And in the winter the sun, the sun beamed down on rotten wasted garbage along with broken glass that shines like diamonds, rubies, emeralds, and pearls. Ahh! Yes, that alley that separated a red-gray brick Catholic Church that had a wrought iron fence around it that looked like something out of the . . .

On the other side was home. A three-story tenement building . . . Well (Slum). Regardless of the rat bites and their size, as big as cats, the junkies that died and pissed on the stairs, and the fence that didn't work. The one bathroom shared by the rest of the floor. Those alleys that led to the backyard where we had rock fights and bottle fights, where Harry hit me in the head with my own toy gun.

That backyard was a world in itself. This is where my training began, and I have the scars to prove it.

OUR CHILDREN ARE SCREAMING
Gino Morrow

Shhh! Listen!
Do you hear 'em?
Pay attention!
Now do you hear 'em?

The children. They're screaming from the streets. Maybe it's too late. Maybe we've missed them. They aren't as predictable as they used to be. But if you listen closely, you might hear them.

On any given Saturday, in the morning, at approximately quarter till eight, little Tommy and Darnelle would venture from the courtyard of their apartment building to this one spot directly beneath the window of Antoine's bedroom. Antoine lived in a brownstone high-rise. His window towered three floors above the spot where Tommy and Darnelle stood. Darnelle stared up at the window, using one hand to block the sun and the other to secure a basketball to his side. He wore cut-off shorts that sagged, and when he walked, his shoestrings dragged behind his high-top hand-me-downs. Tommy, knock-kneed as well as pigeon-toed, placed his tiny boom box on the loose gravel and stood—back fully arched and hands surrounding his mouth, creating a fog-horn, so that he might be heard when he was calling. And from the deepest recesses of their ten- and thirteen-year-old souls, they would simultaneously bellow:

"Antoine, can you come outside? Antoine, come outside, man."

I would watch them from my window across the courtyard. Antoine would poke his head out of his bedroom window, plant his elbows into the window's paint-chipped frame, which encompassed him like a caged bird, and with pouted lips, respond, "Naw, man, my mother got me on punishment!"

"Aw, man, you always on punishment. What you do now?"

"Yeah, what you do dis time?" Tommy and Darnelle respectively shouted. The sound of their high-pitched adolescent voices echoed between project walls, waking Ms. Hughley (an elderly woman who occupied the apartment space two doors from Antoine's family).

"My stinky sister told my Ma I drinked her pop," said Antoine with a hint of embarrassment.

Tommy and Darnelle erupted into laughter at Antoine's all too familiar reason for being punished. "Man, you stupid," said Tommy.

I laughed, thinking how these young boys constantly referred to one another as "Man."

"Shhh, man, y'all gone get me in trouble," shouted Antoine. "Be quiet."

"Yeah, Tommy and Darnelle! You two boys don't need to be up dis ully hoopin' an' hollin', wakun' evr'body unda Gawd's green auth. Shut up all dat noise, y'all heah me?" shouted a voice coming from the window of Ms. Hughley's apartment.

"Yes, Ms. Huge, I mean Ms. Ugly," mumbled Darnelle.

"Keep it up and I'm a tell y'all's momma . . . lil smart asses."

"So, she ain't gone . . ."

"Hey, watch ya' mouths. Y'all know better than to talk back to ya' elders," I replied.

"Yes sir, Mr. Davis," said Tommy.

"Sorry, Ms. Hughley," muttered Darnelle almost reluctantly.

"Antoine? Ask your mother if you can come outside, man."

"Okay! Hold on a second," Antoine said, ducking his head back into the window and out of view. Within seconds he'd poke his head out and shout, "Meet me at the poles."

The door to Antoine's apartment building swung open by the sheer force of this eleven-year-old's newfound freedom. His mother's demanding voice followed, "And I want a two-liter Pepsi or you gone be on punishment tomorrow."

"Yes, Momma," he would say.

From there, Tommy, Darnelle, and Antoine headed off into the day. And although their weekend activities seemed as sporadic as the beer bottles, broken glass, and crack vials that shrouded the streets they played on, their days were as planned as the seasons, and as timely as the poplar blooming in the spring or the earth's course around the sun.

The world was truly their playground, and weekends provided the opportunity for those three boys to find out just how large the world was — or at least the East Side. They played with boom boxes and basketballs and, in unison, they spat rap lyrics to songs like Run DMC's "You be Illin'" and LL Cool J's "My Radio."

Darnelle would start:
My radio — believe me I like it loud.
I'm the man with the box that could rock the crowd.
I don't mean to offend senior citizens,
but I push my volume way past ten . . .

And again and again and on and on and you don't stop. So the three boys continued. But before they carried out their ritualistic two-mile hajj to downtown-area hotels where they robbed quarters, dimes, and nickels from the fountains that decorated the lobbies, they would walk through the park at Lanigan's to see Taka Molson break a few ankles on the basketball court.

"Antoine can do Taka Molson better than anybody," said Tommy.

"Yeah, Antoine! Do Taka! Do Taka!" said Darnelle as he passed Antoine the ball.

"Shhh. Listen, y'all. Can you hear 'em?"

"Taka Molson brings the ball in-bounds, dribbling through all defenders until he finds an opening on the right side of the court. He drives to the lane; he squares off, takes aim, and fires."

"Shhh! Listen . . . Can you hear that?" whispered Antoine.

"Hear what? Hear what?" said Tommy and Darnelle, anxiously anticipating the culmination of this street ball scenario, just as they did the week before that, and the week before that.

"Shhh . . . Swiiish!"

"All net, boy! Yeah, in yo' face, in yo' face!" yelled Tommy and Darnelle.

"Call the psycho ward because the crowd is goin' insane," Antoine shouted. I still remember.

Back then the world was their playground. And while at play, they made the most of it. And when the streetlights came on, they made their way home, talking about movies, their favorite automobiles, and girls, of course. All the while, divvying up the candy they had bought with the change stolen from hotel fountains. From this window here, I watched them. In no time they would grow to be young men. But they no longer called themselves "Man." Instead they called each other "Nigga."

How strange.

Yeah . . . things changed!

The boys made new friends and grew in different directions. Tommy traded his boom box for an I-roc with Alpines and a sub-woofer that warned people ahead of time of his arrival. The game was no longer basketball, but rather survival.

Antoine was more than an eye-full as he held down the corner of his block with a nine millimeter glock in his pocket to ensure fair trade. His stock in crack-rock kept him paid. And how can Mom say anything, sporting a complimentary three-carat diamond ring? Just one benefit—being the mom of a pharmacist.

Darnelle made good on his promises of expanding his playground around the earth. In each bordering neighborhood, he demanded large shares of his enemies' turf. Paying debts in cold blood. Killin' time with white girls, white lines, and bud. And the rhythm on the streets—repeat—the rhythm on the streets repeats like a scratched forty-five playing over and again through the years.

Sounds of our babies crying fall on Def-jammed ears of folk who deny they hear the desperate acts that call for help.

Remember, "One for all and all for . . . self"? Unwritten street code leaves the weak with their feet cold and hands extended to passersby who'll act offended or pretend that they can't hear, so they veer away. They fear that they may be infected by the struggles of the less fortunate. Lost peers and lost years from rival clique warfare. Uncles, brothers, and sons with guns. Mac10 rounds emulating the sounds of rapid-fire drums.

Periods of violence produce moments of silence for lost souls of loved ones. Echoing voices of distress playing a game of high-stakes. Is this the world our parents left? Maybe it is too late. Maybe we've missed them. They aren't as predictable as they used to be. And now our next generation of young black boys looks up to Antoine, as Antoine did Taka. Carefully studying the details of his handle. Driving by defenders, squaring off, and firing.

Shhh! And if you listen closely, you can hear our children . . . you can hear them . . . screaming!

TODO POR MI FAMILIA
An interview with Chino Familia, Godfather, West Side Familia
Cherryl Aldave

To friends and family, he's simply Chino, *though others know him by the title he's held for over twenty-five years on the grinding streets of New York City—the Godfather. Chino Familia is a Puerto Rican OG who rolled with the Sandmen and the Savage Nomads before founding the Manhattan-based La West Side Familia in 1979. His family, as Chino refers to them, rose to prominence in New York at a time when crew culture was king. Today, due to what some deem overzealous efforts by government agencies to infiltrate gangs and destroy activist movements, Chino's tight-knit, multi-cultural crew stands as one of the few remaining "families" in New York.*

Growing up on Manhattan's Westside—the area La West Side Familia is named for—Chino stomped with one black boot in the street and the other in the struggle. Once part of the Black Panther–influenced Young Lords Party, Chino has championed causes from tenants' rights to Cuban autonomy and Puerto Rican independence. He's also spearheaded community clean-ups and led anti–police brutality protests, balancing activism with the life of a Godfather and the responsibilities bound to that title.

In the early 1980s, when crack had New York in its grip like a two-dollar stem, tensions between La West Side Familia and a notorious crew called the Ball Busters escalated to a deadly confrontation between Chino and one of their leaders, Robert Matos. Chino took Matos's life in an act of self-defense, for which he served five years in prison.

Today, Chino still lives on his beloved Westside, and can often be seen wearing his crew's black and white beads and their official jacket, which features the words "La West Side Familia" in black letters over the head of an Indian chief. Chino and his family were the subject of the early '90s documentary Family Values—Gangster Style, *by filmmaker Crystal Moralas. They are also featured in the forthcoming* Apache Line: From Gangs to Hip Hop, *a documentary from Jorge "PopMaster Fabel" Pabon on the foundations of Hip Hop as it emerged from the mid-1970s Spanish Harlem gang era.*

In this interview, Chino discusses activism, the slaying of Robert Matos, his relationship with King Tone and the Latin Kings, and the trials and triumphs of being the Godfather.

Cherryl Aldave: Chino, when La West Side Familia first started, what were you guys about?

Chino Familia: We are from 93rd Street and Columbus Ave., and at our headquarters we used to party and everything, but we had a policy that we didn't want people from the outside to do things like breaking into cars or robbing people. We didn't call the police or any of that. We would just beat your ass and it's over. But that's how wars started. The real beef was with a crew called the Ball Busters. They were Dominicans from Washington Heights, from about 135th to 181st Street. They were almost like . . . untouchable.

CA: Were the Ball Busters your biggest rivals at the time?

CF: Yes. And one of the leaders was [my] cousin, and I never knew it until we had a confrontation and it came down to the last wire. Then one time we took two of them to a place. We said, "You're not leaving here until we know who is the head of [this whole crew]." And when they left just fine, the next thing you know they were found somewhere beat down, and they ended up in the hospital for two weeks, but we never knew who did it.

Then one day, the fellas grabbed one of them on the train and took their sweatshirt and brought it to the block. I stuffed it up with paper and put it up on the lamppost, and they came in a car and opened fire. We returned fire. They wanted the shirt 'cause that was embarrassing. They didn't get it. A couple of weeks later, it got escalated. [They] beat up my boy's brother in the train station, then they came to the neighborhood and started shooting. We shot back, but then the people on the block was like, "Well, if you guys didn't just hang out on the corner, they couldn't come shoot at you." They wanted to have a neighborhood meeting because they wanted to invite the Guardian Angels to patrol.

CA: Did they come? What happened?

CF: Well, this white lady from one of the private buildings got robbed before this, and when she turned the corner screaming, two of my friends ran seven blocks and got the guy, beat him down and got her purse back. At the meeting, everyone was talking about, "My car been broken into," or, "I got robbed on

95th." This white lady said, "I was robbed on 95th and when I came to 93rd, I saw that group. You say they hang out and drink, but they chased the guy and got my purse back and now I feel safe."

Then she told them about me and I came forward. They asked me how I felt about inviting the Guardian Angels and I said, "I reject that completely because we can set it up so we patrol the neighborhood." After that meeting I got phone calls from people who wouldn't even look at us before and they were like, "We didn't know you were like this. We thought you were just hangin' out with your boots and chains and killing people." It was a whole change around.

CA: Some people may be confused about the difference between La West Side Familia and La Familia. Are the two groups affiliated?

CF: We don't have no affiliation. My little brother, Guillo, had a crew called the Chillout Family . . . and when he got a little older, I said we should just make one crew and become La West Side Familia. That was '79. Around that time, Brooklyn had a street gang called La Familia. They were at war with the Dirty Ones, the Chosen Ones, the FMD (Filthy Mad Dogs) . . . We had a meeting like in 1998 or 1999 with Khalid Muhammad (RIP). He wanted to bring the gangs together so there wouldn't be no more war. At that meeting, there was the Bloods, the Crips, La Familia, all of us, and when I got up to speak, someone said, "And now we have one more member of La Familia."

At the second meeting, like a year later, I got up and said that I wanted to set something straight. I said, "We are La West Side Familia from Westside Manhattan." But when we came in with our jackets everyone was [looking at us] and some of [La Familia's] members were saying, "They're giving you the best props and we're La Familia too." We agreed to have a meeting in Queens because we weren't gonna settle the thing with the name there. That was everybody's forum. Then at the meeting in Queens, they said, "We have to be one, La Familia." I said, "No, and if it comes to that, we will go to war for the name because we are La West Side Familia. We don't want no one to mistake us."

CA: The government funds anti-gang initiatives, but little if any money goes toward training gangs to work through their existing structure to uplift communities . . .

CF: They don't want that. They think if they do that we're gonna "get all together" and they fear that. That's the thing with the Latin Kings and all these crews. They want them to be at war so they have a reason to say, "This is why we don't want the gangs."

CA: We need more community centers too.

CF: Yes. We had a community center at Goddard Riverside, and that was a big part that helped me in organizing and things like that, because we were all involved in the center. Now you have to pay five dollars to be a member of the community center; then staff was being cut; then they started putting people in there that wasn't so comfortable with us. Once there was this man there, Bernie Wolf, who did everything for everybody. He was director from the '70s to almost '95–'96. Now there is a new director. There used to be a counselor when Bernie Wolf was there, and when they did the [*Family Values*] documentary, they found him and he talked about me as a nine-year-old kid being influenced by the squatters' movement. This group called Operation Movement, they used to take over abandoned buildings and redo them so people could live in them. The city would just say, "You cannot live in there," so now you have thirty families who live in the shelter. There's a book called *The Tenant Survival Book*, by Emily Goodman, and there's a picture of me in that book as a little boy with three other kids from the neighborhood in front of their building.

CA: How did you get involved in the Operation Movement?

CF: I used to come by their office on 87th and Columbus sometimes and do my homework. One day, I had come out of school and went in the building and they were barricading the building up. There were six or seven families in there. The police were coming and it took them a while to come. When it was time for me to go home, everybody was like, "Whose kid is this?" Then one of their organizers was like, "What are you doing here, Robert?" Then the police came and shut the block down. They came with a truck and started breaking the whole front of the building. Two or three hours later, they found everybody in the basement and led everybody out to the paddy wagon. My father had to go to the precinct to get me. He said, "You ain't going out for a week," but after that I just got more involved in protesting and going to demonstrations. That documentary has this picture of me when they was taking over the building, and it showed me demonstrating when I was like twelve years old. But I've never influenced any of my people to do these things. I explain to them what's going on and sometimes they go, but usually I go by myself. If my whole group gets involved, next thing you know we're labeled a "terrorist group." This one's involved in the independence of Puerto Rico . . . this one's involved in the Black Panthers . . . so everyone does their own thing.

CA: What are your feelings about King Tone and the Latin Kings?

CF: When everything had started going down, I told him, "When you knew they were trying to frame you, you exposed yourself to the media and they nailed you." When we had the first meeting [with Khalid Muhammad], that's when that big investigation came down, and it was like, "What's going on?" Tone changed. *[Interviewer's Note: In 1999, a sweeping joint investigation* (Operation Crown) *by the Brooklyn DA's Office, the United States Attorney's Office, the Bronx DA's Office, and the NYPD resulted in the arrest of Antonio "King Tone" Fernandez and over 100 members of the Latin Kings in New York and New Jersey. Charges included narcotics offenses and murder. King Tone is currently serving a twelve-year sentence in a maximum security prison.]*
We had sat in panels and been at demonstrations and he never brought this up, but then he tells me, "I feel like you starting something up to take my nation," because his lieutenant always looked up to me and listened to me. I said, "I wouldn't want your nation. I have my nation." After that, I still went and vibed with him and supported him when he went away.

CA: Why did you continue to support King Tone?

CF: It was not because of him only; it was his council, the Crowns. The guys from Brooklyn, Bronx, Manhattan, Queens.

La West Side Familia still kept a bond because we're involved in organizing anti–police brutality demonstrations and that type of thing. The Latin Kings, La West Side Familia, the Bloods and all that, all these meetings we used to have like the meetings on 125th with Khalid Muhammad . . . every meeting there was a big impact because it became like a bonding thing. And in the summers following, incidents in the city were reduced because you didn't have so many people just picking up the bandana, claiming crews they were not a part of, then doing crimes. All these leaders, when I speak with them I say, "What are you doing to organize in your neighborhood?" All these meetings definitely have a big impact.

CA: Tell me about your involvement in the fight to send Elian Gonzales back to Cuba.

CF: When they sent Elian back to Cuba, I was on one of the main organizing committees. The week before Janet Reno ordered the raid [to retrieve Elian from his family in Miami], we went to Washington to demonstrate in front of her office, and about eight of us went in. I was one of the translators, and I asked her if she was gonna go forward to get Elian. She said, "I have a press conference to give today; tomorrow's Good Friday, but I promise you by Easter Sunday he will be in the hands of his father." From there, we got on a bus and went to the Cuban embassy and we had dinner. This thing was a challenge because the public didn't know the background of Elian's family in Miami. They were into drugs and a lot of bad activities, but people didn't know that. And they was just using Elian as a propaganda tool against Fidel, but when the smoke cleared a lot of people found out the truth. That house was armed to the teeth. That's why Janet Reno did everything, so they would not make a mistake like they did with Waco.

When it was over, we met with his father, Juan Miguel. I got pictures with him, but not with Elian. He said, "When you come to Cuba, you are welcome in my house, but today no one is allowed to take pictures with him because of the way they parade him all over." It was right to send him back, and on that Friday before the raid, I bet that by Sunday Elian would be in his father's hands. I made $1700. Everybody was saying, "How the hell do you know that?" I was like, "Don't worry about it!"

When Fidel came to Riverside Church *[in 2000, during the United Nations Millennium Summit Week]*, I was one of the security. I shook his hand and got pictures with the President of the Cuban Parliament and had dinner with him. There's something I admire about Cuba. When you go to Cuba, one flag flies over Cuba, and that is the Cuban flag. Puerto Rico is not what it was years ago. Now you go there and it's the American flag everywhere. I don't agree with that.

CA: You told me once that you've served time . . . For what?

CF: For an incident that happened April 28, 1984. I just had my anniversary. I got out in 1989.

CA: What happened?

CF: These guys from the Ball Busters, they had someone's jacket for two days before that. It was a friend of mine . . . his little brother's jacket. The fellas went back and got the jacket from them. Then the oldest one of them got involved, and they came to our block and there was a confrontation. That's when I went back to their neighborhood and said, "I want to speak to the one in charge." That's when the oldest one, Robert Matos, came down and we spoke. He was the head of them from 109th Street. I said to him, "As of today, if any of my friends disrespects any of your people, come to me. And if any of your people disrespects any of us, I'm coming to you. Now it's between you and me."

Next thing, we were down on Broadway and 93rd Street, hanging there and drinking beer. He was coming like a block away with two guys. I turned my back and kept talking to some fellas that were there, and one of them was ready to pull out. I said, "What are you doing?" He said, "He's coming." I said, "I don't care; let him go by." My little brother was standing on the side of the store, and he turned around and said something. I don't remember exactly what it was. But I just kept talking to the fellas, and I was looking at this glass in front, and I could see behind me when they was walking by. That's when he reached to his waist and I pulled out and opened fire. The other two guys took off, and he ran across the street and collapsed on the other side . . . I walked in the store and the people in the store said, "Get out of here before the police come!" and I walked out and took off and got rid of the weapon.

CA: What did you shoot him with, and where?

CF: A .38 Special. I shot him with a dum dum bullet *[a hollow point type of bullet]* and hit him one time in the chest. You can get five years extra now just for having those bullets. He just ran and I didn't see no blood. I found out in the police report the next day that the bullet had exploded. I had come to my house and got a vest and two more guns because I thought, now they're gonna come, so I gotta be ready for them.

A week before this happened, this man got fresh with a lady at the store, and I was outside sitting with some fellas. When the lady came out all nervous, she said, "This man just tried to grab me in the store." So when he came out I beat him up. His wife was coming and she tried to hit me with a bottle, so I pushed her. This same lady, his wife, was in the store when I went in there with the gun in my hand. So when the police came she said, "The one who killed him is the one from the gang. The one with the beer."

CA: Did they come to your apartment and arrest you?

CF: No. I went away that day but came back. A friend had called me from the hotel right in front of where I had shot [Matos] and said he didn't have no food, so I took a cab and came back. The detectives were going around with my picture, asking if anybody had seen me. That's when that lady told them it was me. The "one with the beer." When I walked in the hotel, the girl at the switchboard gave me a look, but the manager was standing there and I just went upstairs. The detectives had been there, and when they came back the manager told them, "He just went upstairs. He's on the 11th floor."

[The police] blocked off the whole street; the SWAT team was getting ready, setting up ropes to the window in the apartment. I just told my friend, "I'm going out, but don't go with me." I went out and that's when I heard the clicks. I put my hands up and I was not going to put them down for anything. All their guns were drawn at me. I told them, "I have two guns and two full clips," and told them where they were.

The next day I went to jail at Riker's, but I kept fighting for better deals for almost a year until they came with a [good] offer. Then I went to Sing Sing.

CA: How'd you keep yourself together during that time?

CF: The first year? Forget it. I was in a lot of trouble, and I was in the box for like ninety days. Then I got involved in the law library; then I started working and moving around so I wasn't isolated in one block. Then I went to Mercer College. They transferred me to Clinton twice after I [got in trouble], then they shipped me back to Sing Sing because I was in college. When you're locked in your cell and those bars close, that's when you have time to think about how you're gonna make it tomorrow. But when you have people that have that communication, that's what keeps you going. My family would write and visit all the time, but there's people in there right now, they don't go down to that visit room. They don't get a letter. Those are people that get in there and tend to snap.

CA: Were you ever under threat of being executed in prison?

CF: When I was locked up, they put contracts out, but at that time I wasn't worried about it. Then, when I came out, I let everybody know where I was gonna be and what I was gonna do. One day, I'm gonna go see God so I don't fear anything like that.

CA: Did the killing of Robert Matos help lead to the end of the Ball Busters?

CF: Oh yeah. When I got out and saw most of them, they were grown up, and when they saw me they were like, "Oh my God, it's Chino," and they shook my hand.

WITH ALL DUE RESPECT TO BIG TOOKIE
Big Kiko
(118th St. East Coast Crips)

With all due respect to the Homie, my friend and co-founder of the Crips Organization, Stanley "Big Tookie" Williams.

The Crips was formed in 1969, as a direct result of racism, police brutality, and a lot of the adversities that still exist today. At the age of fifteen to sixteen, Stanley Williams, a.k.a. Big Tookie, and Raymond Washington put their minds together in hopes of counteracting these atrocities and injustices they were witnessing throughout the confines of the 'hoods. Big Tookie led the whole West Side while Raymond ran the East Side.

The foundation of the Crips was based on a positive movement: the betterment of self and our people as a whole. But our struggle has ultimately deviated from those elements over the years because the Crips still exist, consistently growing in numbers. It's not too late to return the Crip Movement back to its original course.

As we mourn the millennial lynching of one of our founders at the hands of this twisted Amerikkkan government, let's not allow our emotions to cloud our intellect! Without a doubt, I'm mad as hell, and the eye-for-an-eye mentality is right at the cliff of my thinking. Yet, on the other hand, we must not allow ourselves to be put in a trick bag by reacting with anger to this killing of our Big Homie. Instead, we must unite and take this giant step right here, right now, and stand in strength in honor of Big Tookie, and others like Raymond Washington. May they rest in peace!

Homie, let's not continue to be misled, manipulated, and just straight out brainwashed by the powers that be. We've always posed a threat to their establishment, which is why they've assisted toward our destruction for decades.

The creation of the "Gang Modules" in the Los Angeles County Jail System's 4700–4800 was for nothing more than to breed that hatred for fellow Crip Brothers that still exists today! There was a deeper plot by the powers that be when they created the Gang Modules. They wanted to have us Crips under a microscope to pinpoint our leaders and make it possible to pursue the Crips like they did other organizations, like the El-Rukens, the Black Panthers, and the Mob, and apply the RICO Act and other harsh prosecution methods on the Crips! So we must break the chains and regain the momentum to our movement: Crip— Community Revolution in Progress!

It starts with us, and once we get us together, those who ultimately come behind us . . . Remember Locs? Crips Don't Die, We Multiply!

So plant your feet on concrete and be proud to be a Crip, because real Crips' Pride Will Never Die! Until this thought is linked with purpose, there's no intelligent accomplishment. Aimlessness is a vise. So such drifting must not continue for those who wish to steer clear of catastrophe and destruction.

The course is yours!

Big Me, CA'RIPPP! Machine in Motion. Rest in Peace. All Homies, keep on Crippin'. One Love.

18th STREET SHOWDOWN
Johnny Berger

Walking through the access road that leads to Venture at Melrose Crossing, the new shopping mall in Melrose Park, that's when I saw it: the Nova. It was flat and shineless and had a few bondo spots by the wheel wells. The Nova that creeped behind us: me, Dave, and Eddie. It must have been in the fall of my freshman year. I was selling weed and these guys rolled up to us, the window already down. It was one of my first lessons in the business.

"You guys got any weed?" the one in the passenger seat asked while the driver and the dude in the back looked. Dave and Eddie looked at me.

"Yeah, whatcha want?"

"Lemme see a quarter."

"All I got is eighths."

"Lemme see two of 'em."

I had a weird feeling about these dudes and leaned into the car, letting one eighth unroll to a visible baggy of nice green bud. I held on to it, 'cause, again, I had a bad feeling about these mutherfuckers.

"That's what I got."

"Well, lemme check it out!" He smiled as if to tell me not to worry, and I reluctantly let it go. He showed it to the driver, the three of them grinning as the car chirped out of my reach along with my bag.

I still, by instinct, tried to grab hold of the bag, but my arm caught the door jam as it ripped away, leaving me with a pain in my arm and worse — the feeling that someone ripped me off. Worse than that — I was stupid enough to fall for it.

Lesson number one: get the drugs, get the money, whatever the transaction may be, but the exchange should be at once — otherwise, bend over and grab your fuckin' ankles.

The car sped off in the distance as I feebly jogged behind it for a second. I stopped and turned around, my friends staring at me. Dave looked at me, shaking his head. Eddie chuckled, the fuckin' prick. After I got him high all night, the guy has the nerve to laugh at my misfortune; however stupid I was for it, it was still misfortune. Fuck him.

"Who the fuck were those guys?"

"I never seen 'em before," Dave replied.

The conversation was futile. I just wanted to see if I could grab a name and get some retribution. These dudes were definitely older, but I had a lot of older people who backed me up — I wanted payback, revenge, or just plain equality. But there was no fucking equality in this business; it was who was stronger and bigger and, as I later learned, who had more guns, and many times that didn't even matter — still no one won. Me being a scrawny little fuck of maybe 110, I didn't stand a chance, but I still wanted these fuckin' assholes to pay.

As we got to the sidewalk of Venture, we saw a familiar face. In a beat-up hatchback, an older buddy, James, drove up. I was in no mood to talk, no mood to tell this dude who I didn't know too well how stupid I was a second ago. Dave did.

"Some dudes just ripped off Johnny for an eighth of weed," Dave told his buddy.

"Really?" He looked at me.

"Fuck it, it's only an eighth." I played it the only way I could, like I was so bad ass that it didn't even matter, a fuckin' eighth. It cost me around five bucks. Who gives a fuck?

"Who was it?" James asked, leaning across his empty passenger seat.

"Some dudes in a black Nova," Dave answered, not taking my hint to drop the subject.

"I just saw some dudes I know in a Nova."

All of a sudden, my eyes shot up from the ground as I leaned into the car. "You know them guys?" I asked.

"Three of 'em, right?"

"Yeah."

"Yeah, they're from over by 18th," he says with a serious look.

The three of us stand on the sidewalk for a minute; my head is pounding, my stomach filled with butterflies. This is the kind of shit that, if you don't take care of, could lead to a short career or a career of everyone in the fuckin' neighborhood ripping you off, not to mention everyone in the surrounding neighborhoods. Reality sets in as I know I got to take care of this or I'm fucked. And I'm fucked anyway because we were about fourteen and they were about nineteen and big, or eighteen and bigger. Fuck!

We roll down 18th in James's piece of shit. We weren't from this 'ville, and everyone on the street is looking at us like we're intruding on some sacred shit that only assholes from their neighborhood know about. We do the same shit when they roll by us in our neighborhood; everyone does it—I have no idea why. This was not our stomping ground and we knew it. We knew dudes from here, but we were the outsiders today, here and now.

18th is a long street that runs the length of Melrose Park, a highly dense town on the edge of the Chicago city limits, mainly consisting of Italians and Mexicans. Originally Italian, it was where the outfit guys lived—not the bosses, but the workers, the earners, the head busters, the bookies, the drivers and entry men that made the mob what it was. Slowly, the Dagos moved out and Mexicans moved in. This part of 18th was the first part they'd invaded. It was north of North Avenue, nestled in between the factories. Three streets that were two long city blocks each, jammed with six flats, three flats, and long unit buildings with small parking lots in the back.

Everyone was on the street 'cause there just was nowhere else to go, no parks, nothing but factories and busy North Avenue surrounding it. The street bustled with people on nice days and nights; kids would rush out from between tightly parked cars, chasing balls as cars would screech to stops. Nobody gave a fuck; nobody watched their kids; nobody watched themselves. Occasionally, someone would get into a screaming match and get their face split open on the grill of a car, and occasionally worse things would happen, but that didn't concern me right now—I wanted my twenty bucks, and this was not going to be an easy task.

It was dark and all the kids were in bed, maybe. All that was out were small crews of guys standing in front of their buildings looking hard. A few chicks lingered around, looking hot in their shortest skirts and highest heels and reddest lipstick, talking about who's gonna beat whose ass and who's pregnant.

Our target was just up ahead, almost at the end of the block by the Jewel Food plant. James pointed at the building. "Is that them?"

I see a group of guys standing on a one-step concrete porch. I couldn't tell and wasn't sure if I wanted to tell or just keep driving.

"Fuckin' right, that's them!" Dave chimes in from the back seat.

James doesn't even hesitate and pulls into the skinny blacktop driveway that runs the length of the building leading to the back. Immediately, the guys take notice and stroll up to our car.

"Hey, what's up, James?" one of the guys asks.

I couldn't figure if he was driving or sitting in the back, but I remember the fuck that grinned at me as he snatched my bag a dope and drove off—he was right behind this asshole, glaring at me.

"These dudes wanted to talk to you about something, so I drove 'em over here."

"Oh yeah?" The one with the mouth leans down and pipes a look to me. "Well, we're just hanging out, so jump out if you wanna talk."

The crew walks back to the porch, snickering and smiling; my blood boils as I spin around to the back seat.

"What's up?" Dave asks.

"Whatta' you think? You guys got my back?" My eyes are shifting from Dave to Eddie. Eddie just shakes his head, a scared smirk on his face.

"Man, I'm not getting out of this car."

"Fuck this. I'll get out. Johnny, I got you."

While Ed's eyes are averting my attention, Dave's are like two daggers stabbing right back at mine—his bottom lip tucked tight in his teeth. "Fuckin' right! They came to our neighborhood to rip us off, so we gotta do this."

"Fuck right, dude."

"James, you gonna help us out, man?" Dave persists from the back seat with balls of steel, putting James right on the spot.

"I told you guys, this is your deal. I know these dudes and I'm cool with everyone here, so, ya know, this on you."

Dave don't bat an eye, turns to me with a look of death. "Fuck it, let's go."

That was all I needed to hear from him as I got out of the car, not knowing if my legs were going to drop out from under my body. He popped out behind me as we walked across the drive-way to the grass.

They walked right up to us. They were each at least a head taller than us, and they were ballsy mean fuckers from 18th. There was no way they were going to puss out and come up with some money 'cause they didn't want to throw fists in the grass. These mutherfuckers lived for scrapin' and we were fucked.

"What's up, man?"

"Dude, ya owe me some money."

"How's that?"

"Dude, c'mon. Ya drove off with my eighth a weed. Ya owe me twenty bucks."

He chuckled and looked back at his friends, now five of them. I wasn't smiling at all and I could see Dave out the corner of my left eye, ready to go. Then the amazing happened, a miracle, a divine intervention, a little help from the Lord, if you will.

From the back of the house appeared this dude, a stocky fucker, but not huge. They all seemed to jump when he appeared, like he had some lease on their existence, or at least the grass they were standing on.

My eyes were on the grease ball in front of me. I didn't hear what was said at first, but he busted his way into the middle of the confrontation, if you could call it that.

"What's going on?" He looked down at my scrawny frame, almost exploding with laughter. "What's up?"

"This dude owes me some money."

He looked back at the group. "What?"

"He asked me for an eighth over by Melrose Crossing, then did a snatch-and-grab with my weed. Dude owes me twenty bucks."

Silence hung in the air; the fuckin' street didn't move; nothing was alive but my pounding heart.

"Is this true?" He looked at each of the three that had been in the car, then back at me. There was pity in his eyes for me and Dave, then a wash of respect came over him as he looked back at his crew. "You ripped off these little fuckers? Is that true?"

They all began chuckling and laughing, even he was smiling.

"I can't fuckin' believe you guys." He looked at Dave, ready, looking like a pitt bull with zits. He poked me on the chest as he began addressing them. "You took this dude's weed?"

They all nodding, laughing a little harder now.

"Where is it? Alright, that's it. Give this kid his weed back, right now."

"We smoked it, remember?" one of them piped up. "That was the shit we just burned with you."

"Oh, my God!" He looks at us and back at his crew, now embarrassed, pissed, and God knows what else.

Then it happened. "That's it! Everyone pull some fuckin' money out right now!"

The entire crowd hopped as he said it, fumbling around, digging in their pockets, pulling out wrinkled or rolled-up dollar bills and piles of change. He circled every guy, collecting from each one. All I could think was that for a bunch of tough guy Dagos from Melrose Park, they sure were a bunch a broke ass bums. They were like scolded kids, apologizing to him as he shook his head, mumbling at them for what they did. They hung their heads; all that was missing was a spanking.

Stocky walks me and Dave back to the car, putting his hands on our shoulders. "I took up a little collection from the boys. What did ya want for that eighth?"

"Twenty."

"Well, I don't think there's twenty here but there's some cash. Are we cool?"

I looked back at the crowd of hang dogs who stood with their hands in their pockets. "Yeah, we're cool."

As we rolled out of the neighborhood, back onto North Avenue, past the Zenith Plant, up the 25th Avenue Bridge, I counted my money.

"How much is there?" Dave asked.

"'Bout thirteen bucks."

"Assholes."

"That's alright, I still made money on it. Fuck 'em."

The car was silent except for James's laughter as he dropped us off in front of Dave's house. My boy Dave. The backup, the nigger on the trigger, the pitt with zits, the man. All I could think of that night was how big of a beating that guy saved us from. I could think of the guy who lipped off to some Melrose guys at the Dago feast, and about ten of them beat him to death with bottles. I thought of how they never fought fair, always in groups. How they were all connected and never got in trouble for anything. I thought about a lot of things as we sat in Dave's backyard and got high.

✦   ✦   ✦

At present, many friends and partners have graduated to bigger and better parts of the business. Today, they deal in truckloads that come up from Florida or Arizona. Some are dead and some are doing bits in the joint, while others are still growing bigger and richer. Some, like me, wised up and moved on to regular boring jobs, runny nosed kids, and girlfriends who know our past and put up with who we are. We tell them war stories at 3 a.m., after sex, about how we could get them anything they want, and how maybe I should start up again and give her a life she deserves. She knows the temptation and struggles I go through as she tells me not to worry about money—that it doesn't matter.

As I try to stay away from anybody who may suck me back into being a career again, there are a few of the boys that are still my blood, my people. To this day, twenty years later, I still talk to Dave, almost every day. I couldn't tell ya where to find Eddie, though.

INNER CITY DISEASE
Twin Poets Al & Nnamdi, Sons of Hicks
(founding members of Blackie Blacks, Delaware, Chester, and Philly)

Infected with the inner city disease
It's doubtful I'll see tomorrow
Sleeping with my sorrows
I wake up with my mind unraveling

Traveling at the speed of thought
I try to run away from my life but I wasn't fast enough
My past keeps catching up
I keep messing up on life's exams
Every question is multiple choice
But damn, they so confusing
The devil's like, "Look, MF, just choose one!"
God says, "Be patient, son, ain't no re-test today"
Too much stress, so I take recess
Go to my old elementary school
And watch the children play
Their smiles make me feel a certain way
I grieve, can barely breathe
As I watch them run
'Cause my younger brother never made it to 21
Instead of tasting death
I wish he never left my Mama's breast
Stress builds in me
I'm wondering why the devil acting so friendly
Making me my own worst enemy
They say the journey of a thousand miles
Begins with the first step
But so often it's my own feet
That impede the path of my own progress
I guess it's easy to see why we are victims
To the devil's inner city disease of confusion
The devil's illusion
He got inner city slaves
Believing they're being paid
The devil will sell you anything
That you're big or bold enough to ask for
The price, your life
And you won't believe
That you've been deceived
Until you've been diagnosed with the inner city disease.

WHAT BLOOD MEANS
OG 40 Dogg

Most people have the wrong idea as to what blood means. To us, it is a way of life. It is something that is lived, not done! They call us thugs and hoodlums, and, indeed, there are those of us, just like in any organization or lifestyle, who don't live according to our rules of loving your brothers, sisters, and family members.

A lot of us are very intelligent and skilled and some have been formally educated, but most of all we are all willing to bring movement to the stagnant. What people should try to remember is that we were born into a society that treated us like subhuman second-class citizens. We didn't ask to be beat by racist cops then railroaded by a polarized and biased "just us" system.

It is not our fault that the revolution is not being televised in a fair and equitable way; it is not our fault that we were forced to fight back; it is not our fault that we brought fear to the so-called fearless; it is not our fault that as a consequence we brought laws and rules to the lawless and unruly and gave a sense of family to those who, for whatever reasons, didn't have one. All in all, no matter how we got a bad wrap, it's all about showing love to the people and showing extreme prejudice to those who go against the people.

We look out for our 'hood. Ain't no old ladies getting robbed in our 'hoods and no one is scared to walk down our block. There are elderly people who shout to me, "What's popping, 40?" and little kids who run up to me when they see me and say, "Hi."

The negative element is the fact that the majority of us don't have jobs and the ones who do are grossly underpaid; so some of us sell drugs to help feed, clothe, and house ourselves and our DNA (i.e., "blood family," not "blood brothers").

D.T.K. (DOWN TO KILL)
Ron King
(Quincy Chaplain, Brooklyn, NY)

"Don't wear that kind of hat!" DJ, my older cousin, shouted at me on the corner, his eyes glued to my deep-rolled Stetson brim with a diamond-shaped crown that matched my birthstone.

The hat had come from my grandfather's collection of unwanted ones. I now wore the crown of a Chaplain. My hat block signified that I was a Jitterbug, which reminded DJ of the "knock-knock," when rival Bebops would come to each other's homes.

There's the story of Beavers who had knocked on Tom Sawyer's door and said, "Miss, can we see your son?" Then, bang! They shot him.

My cousin knew the consequences that went along with gang membership. Even his last name, Bishop, often brought Bebops to his front door, causing him to assure them that he wasn't in a Click (i.e., *clique*). You could get hung like Luther by the El Quintos. He'd been hung from a tree in Tompkins Park (now Vonn King Park). Only the cries from a mother had stopped the Robins from hanging her son on a lamppost.

Back then, my cousin DJ knew that those who chose to Jitterbug would not be safe, even in their homes. In those days, a bullet might come through your window. There were several "ride-by" shootings by rivals who rode the elevated train along Lexington Avenue, taking potshots at Big Nut and Little Nut's window. But DJ was no longer my babysitter. I was now a teenager myself, and he couldn't tell me what to do. Later, it dawned on me, he may have wanted me to be more like him, the lover who'd give a girlfriend a slight slap across the face with his black leather gloves. But I was now Shanghi, War Counselor for the Quincy Walk Chaplains. The "Walk" part never suited me. I associated that word with the Corsair Lords from the Kingsborough Projects. They had Walks, namely Seventh Walk, known as the hill, their stronghold. But I did accept the Vice President's decision for our name.

In later years, I would meet a Boys High School alumnus, Spade of the Buccaneers. He would recall my whole gang's name. Outside of school, we had been enemies, yet here we were, holding nostalgic feelings for our school colors. Whenever we'd meet, he'd say, "Red and Black!"

I'd repeat his words, at first with a puzzled look. Then he'd add, "Boys High!"

Those words would lead my lips to sing our old school song. *"The morning sun greets many banners . . ."* There had been many Jitterbugs from different parts of Brooklyn who went to "The High." And we had rules for no fighting in school.

"Deno, you run out with the bologna and cheese. Supe, get the mustard. Mingo, take the bread. Chink, sneak the mayonnaise. Tate, stand outside the door and play chickie [be the lookout]. Shanghi, don't forget the Sandwich Spread. And I'll sneak some soda," Junebug would say. That's how we all contributed to our communal lunch whenever we played hooky.

It didn't matter that teachers and students in Alexander Hamilton High School could see us from their classroom windows on the roof of the apartment house across the street, eating and drinking wine. Rooftops were our getaway from the hustle and bustle. They were also the firing ranges we used for zip guns or Molotov cocktails.

There I'd sit with the other hooky players shrouded in secrecy. Our code of honor for not telling on each other was stronger than a son's love for his mother. Rather than expose one of the People, Junebug would let his mother believe a lie. "Why don't you be like him (meaning me)," she'd say, "and don't play hooky."

He never told her otherwise. We were family. These were My People. We fought together, sometimes each other, but still family. We slept at one another's homes, sharing homemade biscuits and Great Northern beans, or fried fish offered by one of the mothers every Friday. Many times, Deno's dining table served as our Knights of the Round Table for playing Bid Whist.

Before I turned fifteen, we had started out like "Our Gang" — young boys in a clubhouse made of wooden planks for the roof, with the different types of wood we found used to make the walls. We would roast marshmallows and sometimes franks that could be snuck out of the home. From time to time, the clubhouse became a refuge for an unwanted dog. We first learned about territorial battles and rock fights by fighting for a hill in a vacant lot on sun-parched dirt, broken glass, and weeds. Now and then, a white moth, mistaken for a butterfly, flitting here and there, came to symbolize peace between battle lines in those tenement back alleys and deserted lots.

We followed in the footsteps of older Chaplains, which had been so named by a teenager looking up to a church's steeple one day around 1950, saying, "We're gonna be Chaplains, the Little People" for the Robins. During the era of the Robins, gang fighting was called Bebopping, naming their behavior after the new style of jazz. I came to believe that I was born to Bebop because I was born in 1945, the year that both bebop jazz and "Bebopping" had officially begun.

By the time I was fifteen, I had deserted my Boy Scout troop without any notice that I was leaving. My merit badges found themselves in the bottom of my dresser drawer, along with the Star Rank badge and the feather that stood for the troop's scribe. The Panther Patrol was now left with no patrol leader. The Explorer rank I had earned was forsaken in favor of exploring neighborhood streets. Instead of walking in an erect way, I now walked with a bop in my step. But I was not Bebopping; by the time I came along, it was called Jitterbugging. It meant wearing white schoolboy caps or a short brim cocked to one side.

"For the boys upstate!" is what we ritually said whenever we chipped in for a bottle of wine to share. A bottle cap full of cheap wine would be poured on the ground, a libation for The People who'd been locked up in upstate reformatories. That first drink at the age of fifteen, costing forty-five cents a pint and seventy cents for a fifth, along with the meeting in Chink's house, changed my personality, my whole way of thinking. That night, we climbed down the rear fire escape of our tenement to formally organize our gang. Jumping over rooftops to avoid the nosy neighbor downstairs was much like our childhood days of following the leader. That was fun. This was something else. It was time to choose the leaders for our gang.

I had to have a nickname. Before settling on Shanghi, I'd been laughed at for changing nicknames so many times. I'd be teased with, "Who are you now?" followed by constant riffing behind all of my undecided names.

We had our own drinking hideout, down in Little Paradise, our small maze behind the apartment buildings we lived in.

"First!"

"Second!"

"Third!" was what we shouted to determine the order in which we would each drink. If you didn't want to be last or near last and have to drink the bubbled saliva at the bottle's bottom, you had to be quick. The wine could have been any of the many brands that we drank on weekends. It could have been Five Star North America or Sneaky Pete or Thunder Bird ("What's the word?" "Thunder Bird." "What's the price?" "Thirty cents twice."), even

Hombre, Swiss Up, or that "Gitty-Up" Golden Spur. Depending on our taste buds, a half gallon of White Port and orange Kool-Aid would satisfy all.

Whatever coins we could get from our parents or hustle up by stationing ourselves on different corners to ask strangers for change went toward getting someone old enough to purchase the wine. Some of my chipped-in change came from shining shoes in the shoeshine parlor or from what I had after cleaning fish in a fish market after school. Other times required a little more imagi-nation for getting drinking money, like going upstairs to the pool room on the corner of Nostrand and Gates and taking the Coca Cola bottles from the machine to cash them in for change.

Of course, there were consequences for drinking, an omen of what was coming. "Don't take me home! Don't take me home!" I said to My People as they struggled with me, lugging me up through the front door before falling and crashing down on my mother's brand new French Provincial bed. "My mother's gonna beat me!"

And Mom said, "You're damn right!" She jumped on top of me like, as they used to say, ugly on an ape, punches coming from everywhere. Who's to say that Vic the Cop was wrong for taking our wine from us because we were underage and had violated the law? There was never an arrest, unless you didn't want him to drink the evidence. We learned to obey the law: run and hide that wine bottle. Getting drunk, like everything else, for the most part, was about the weekend. And when it came to Jitterbugging, we were "weekend warriors."

Our first encounter with rivals happened one night when we crossed the border of Bedford Avenue into Bishop territory on Franklin Avenue.

"Who y'all?" a group of bigger and older boys stopped us. One identified himself as Killer. A partner of his stood with one hand shoved inside his shirt, indicating the place where a gun was hidden.

"Coolies!" we answered.

"Well, y'all drafted into the Bishops!"

Mingo shouted, "Chaplains!"

"What?" They took off running one way and we ran off the other, laughing and calling them punks. Since we had identified ourselves as Chaplains and had survived the confrontation, we felt a little more seasoned. We bugged harder now, but soon other lessons would come with Jitterbugging.

That Halloween of forty-five years ago we knew as the night of the Goblins. Chaplains from surrounding blocks had amassed on the four corners of Quincy and Nostrand, packing weapons, hoping, waiting, sending a couple of The People as bait, trying to draw Bishops into our trap. Prowl cars crept up the Avenue and kept an eye on the overwhelming number of Jitterbugs. DeKalb Chaplains (DKCs) came up the Avenue like storm troopers, bopping in step, shouting cadences, wearing black hats with white hat bands, and led by its president, D.M. No Bishops showed, though.

Laws had recently been enacted against us: no more than three people could assemble together on any corner. But that didn't stop us. Whenever a squad car would stop or slow down, we would just walk away in different directions.

My lessons in weaponry started with how to make various types of homemade zip guns, single or double barrel .22s. My former hobby of putting plastic boats and jet planes together, plus the workshops at school, gave me the know-how to be a gunsmith. Knowing how to assemble zip guns increased my rep with the Fellows. In making a single shot, I needed a piece of wooden coat hanger for the stock, two car antennas for the barrel and the bullet, a sliding door latch, some tape and rubber bands, and sometimes a cap gun that I would convert into a zip gun. My own arsenal included extra bullets, a bayonet, a meat cleaver, and various types of knives, particularly the K-55 that would lock the blade once it opened. In immediate situations, a car antenna would do as a whip, and a metal garbage top was good for a shield.

"Pow! Pow! Pow!" All that Saturday afternoon the zip guns didn't misfire. We had bottles propped up on the rooftop, our firing range, and every shot went without a misfire during target practice.

Later that night, we planned to go down on the Latin Crowns on Myrtle Avenue. Nightfall came and we faced off against thickly accented and slick-haired boys who had gathered on their corner, shouting at us, "Click! Click! Click!"

Mingo aimed his Derringer zip gun toward the sky and fired. "Click!"

"Give me the gun!" I yelled as I snatched it from his hand. Someone else snatched it from me and lowered the barrel at the crowd, pulling the trigger to no avail. It was an act of fate. The gun didn't fire, but the cops rolled up in their squad cars and we ran. We had what we called "guns-for-the-run," meaning that we could take them apart while in flight—no evidence.

In the lull of no fighting, sham battles among ourselves served to keep us in shape, fist fights in the summer and snowball fights in the winter. We'd split up into teams, boxing or bombarding each other with left hooks or snowballs, depending on the season. Our form of make-believe war games.

Since we were considered the "Baddd Boys" on our block, whenever we didn't get invited to a party, or were told we couldn't come in, our response would be, "If we can't come in, then nobody can come out!" And we meant it too.

Jitterbugging sometimes required playing different roles, or having a power of suggestion. In some ways, it's like the poker games that we played for change. You had to bluff to fool your adversary. A small restaurant, a few blocks uptown into Imperial Lords territory, where we went for knishes with cheese and mustard, brought a run-in with the Lords. When we spotted them coming at us, Chink reached down into a brown shopping bag and pretended to have a shotgun. They believed him as he charged at them, chasing behind the fleeing gang, shouting, "We're burning!"

Similarly, that following week on Memorial Day, we'd been bluffed when three teenagers walked through the block and put their hands inside their shirts, announcing, "Bishops!" in response to our asking, "Who y'all?"

That same night, a mixture of anger and wine spurred our demand for free rides on the B44 bus. Since we had already spent our money on booze, we didn't have bus fare to ride up Nostrand Avenue and hit the Ringo Bishops who had jumped a few of the Fellows earlier in Prospect Park.

"Where's your fare?"

We took seats and said, "We ain't got no carfare! Just drive the bus!"

The driver was at our mercy since, back then, he didn't have a radio-phone to call the police.

Our clothes were as contrasting as the day was. We wore black pants, black and white checkered shirts with a white rayon sash. The sash came about due to Supe's heroic act of taking a roll of material from the fabric store on the Avenue (Nostrand, that is), then ducking and dodging people along the sidewalk during his getaway. We wore black and white.

Brew had passed out on a park bench along Eastern Parkway from too much wine and heat. Adding to the contrast, Clint rubbed vanilla ice cream all over Brew's face, which was the same color as the Ace of Spades.

Dressing was important, so we had to find a cheaper way for buying clothes. On a given Sunday, we would walk from Bed-Stuy to Williamsburg and across the bridge to shop along Orchard Street for five-dollar pants, and then walk back.

Back then, you had to have a pair of Kangaroos or Split Toe shoes. Shoes had their own value because they cost more than the other garments.

One night, I had loaned Deno a pair of my shoes, but they were too big for him. However, since his shoes were in the shop, he had to wear mine or not go to the party that night. Anyway, we were walking on the Avenue, and I turned to Deno and noticed that my shoes had slipped off his feet. So I said, "Deno, go back and get my shoes!"

Just then I saw this dude who had pulled a knife out on me a few days before and started chasing him. I turned and shouted back at Deno to get my shoes and continued chasing this other boy up the Avenue, catching up to him and whipping him with a car antenna. Deno was running behind me all the time, the shoes slipping off his feet with a rhythm of their own. I stopped and again told Deno to get me my shoes. Then I started the chase scene again until, somewhat satisfied, I let that other dude go.

We also wore each other's clothes. At times, we'd go out on a shopping spree for hats from other boys. In times of need for money, we'd shakedown passersby from other neighborhoods. "Jump up and down," we'd order them. "All the change I hear I keep," one of us would add.

Caps also drew attention. Our division's white schoolboy caps mixed well with other Chaplains'. Or that's how it turned out one night as we were en route down the Avenue to the Marcy Projects for a rally before going down that night on Buccaneers in the Sumner Houses. We looked good, in our opinion, probably too good because the police had a way of identifying you by your hat. They also practiced putting gang members in their car for a drive to a rival area. Deno and Superman found themselves being driven up Myrtle Avenue and past a slew of Buccaneers shouting threats.

There was a romantic side to being a Jitterbug. You belonged. And if you had a reputation with fists or knives, you were recognized. A rock 'n' roll music station would take requests on Saturday nights. Gang members would make dedications by nicknames and gang membership, and these would be announced. Often, we would sit around Deno's hi-fi radio, waiting for our dedications and hearing our names called out on the radio.

It had been a long time since we had shot marbles or slingshots together. Now we were getting shot or shot at. Heavy from the Corsair Lords was shot. His death led to the breakup of the alliance of the NCC (Nits, Chaplains, Corsair Lords) at Junior High School 35. Times were changing, getting more serious.

China, the leader of the Fort Greene Chaplains, along with Piza from the Bucs and Bomber of the Tiny Tims, had shot three DKCs with a shotgun. Cheyenne Chaplains and Renegades from the next block from us had joined with China and the Bucs. Now, DKCs decided they were coming down on our block. But all of our main People were in upstate reformatories. It was just Superman and me left to defend the block.

I was the War Counselor and loyal to my title, so I decided to go meet the DeKalb Chaplains down at P.S. 54. Superman said, "I'll go with you."

It was a hot and humid day when we bopped down to the schoolyard's basketball court. "Who's the president?" I asked.

Their basketball seemed to stop in mid air. You could feel the tension. "Who are these guys?"

Because Superman had formally attended this school, he was not completely unknown. Everyone he recognized he spoke to, which made our cause a little more agreeable to them.

After introducing myself as Shanghi and meeting Saint, their Vice President, Superman and I were invited to come later that night over to P.S. 56 to meet other DKCs.

As far as my grandmother was concerned, me hanging out down there was too depressing a fate. We were actually drinking down from the corner where she had lost her first grandchild to a stab wound. Now I'm in the same area. When she found out about it, Gram tried to protect me by following behind me whenever I'd go to DKC to hang out.

"Stop following me!" Eventually, she gave up.

Going down with them made me better understand the expression "going to the front lines." I wanted action and action is what I got. I joined the SS (Suicide Squad). A few of us would go behind enemy lines for a snag, better known as an ambush. Of course, it worked both ways.

One night, I got caught up in it. We were working on a snag when, all of a sudden, we were under attack. Snake of the Buccaneers had spotted me. Bricks rained down from the roofs, putting dents in car tops. Threats were heard. "We're gonna surround you on the block!"

I got away, but the incident woke me up to the fact that this was war and could mean death. Death was no stranger to anyone, especially the Bucs. They had previously ended the lives of two Stompers, so this was not a game. Superman and I were the new blood into the DKCs because we were always ready to go down. New tactics were learned.

"Shanghi, since they don't know you, go up on Troop Avenue and count how many Bucs are up there." There I was, scared as hell, walking like a boy scout with my cap hidden in my shirt. It just happened that there was nothing to report.

After a while, a lull in street fighting had started to take hold. It was time to call it cool, no more "The Shit is on!" Finally, one day, Mojo said, "Let's go see the Bucs. DKC ain't Jitterbugging no more."

That Saturday, Mojo, Superman, and myself, along with several others, took our last steps as Chaplains as we walked over to Hart Street and Troop Avenue. We were greeted by a small mob of Bucs turning the corner with a taller teenager in front, sporting a long peacock feather in his hatband. Their numbers took us by surprise. A natural reaction was to take a step or two back, but as I did, Mojo shouted, "Don't run!"

We stood fast. It was on me to speak. After exchanging some words between me and them, we decided not to fight. Rivalries were coming to an end as old friendships were renewed. After that, Buccaneers started coming down our way and we hung out up their way. Eventually, I got arrested and found guilty of shaking other boys down for money. The judge sentenced me to Riker's Island Reformatory. As I was led out to the bullpens, Superman yelled, "Shanghi, throw me your hat!"

I took the straw hat and slung it across the courtroom. He snatched it from the air as it sailed toward him. We smiled and the door closed on my days as a Jitterbug.

BIG TOMMY, LITTLE TOMMY
Johnny Berger
(Franklin Park, Il)

Mannheim Road, the armpit of the Northwest Side. Every kind of fuckin' loser you could imagine crawled this street. When I was a kid and I would tell my mom I was going bike riding, she would say, "Go wherever you want, but stay the hell away from Mannheim Road."

I never understood it as a child but knew what she meant as I got older. Strip clubs, junkies, perverts, hookers, head busters, hustlers, pimps, faggots, transients, cops. That pretty much summed it up. It was its own little disgusting subculture. Close to O'Hare, so you always heard about some dead mule found in one of the hotels with fifteen balloons of heroin in his gut. It happened every season. Someone was always getting shot or raped behind somewhere. Most of all, what you really noticed when you drove down Mannheim was the overabundance of cheap hotels. The Argon, the Lido, the Regal 8, the Tokyo, the Air Host, the Sky Box, the Melrose Inn, the Country Club, the Americana, just to name a few. These weren't the kinds of places you took your family to stay at when you went for fun-filled weekends in Chicago. These were the kinds of places that people rented for a quick crash or a quick fuck. We used to set up shop for a weekend at some of them, so we had a place to take phone calls and peddle dope. But if you were really lucky, you resided at these places, you lived there. Fucking disgusting.

I met Little Tommy as I was walking down my block on my way to sell a half ounce a weed. At that time, I wasn't that hot, meaning the cops didn't know who I was — yet. That meant that I also had more shit on me, bagged up and ready to go. In later days, I would only leave the house with what I intended to sell; nothing to get busted with.

An old brown beater pulls up alongside me as I'm walking to meet my connect. Two shirtless scumbags slow down and look out the window at me, glaring. So I look over, and one of them is smiling at me; I got no fuckin' clue who these assholes are. "Johnny," he says.

"What's up." I looked at him through squinted eyes.

"You got any weed?"

I looked at him like he was nuts. "I don't know you, man."

"It's me, Jeff. I live down the alley from you. Me, Jeff, man." I looked closer at him, and it slowly creeps back in my head. No shit. I hadn't seen this guy in ages. He was even older than my sister, so it wasn't like we grew up together; he was always old. I start nodding as it all comes back to me.

The guy riding shotgun isn't saying a fuckin' thing; he's just smiling, a big scar by his good eye and one fucked-up eye. I walked to the car as it curled to a stop, the warm engine idling on the hot summer day, reeking of gas.

"Yeah, whatta you guys looking for?"

Scarface looks at me, still grinning and making me nervous.

"Whatta you got?"

Now I ain't the sharpest pencil in the box, but a question like that usually comes before someone ganks your shit. I look at Jeff, not answering. I may be young but I'd be gone before these guys can catch me.

"Don't worry about him, Johnny, this is my buddy, Tommy," Jeff says. Tommy offers his hand as I shake it reluctantly. "Get in," Jeff says.

Tommy lifts up his seat as I crawl into the back of the piece of shit and we roll off. We rolled off, alright. Man, it was hot that day, my legs sticking to my jeans which stuck to the hot vinyl seats. We did our business and all was cool.

Tommy is in the front seat rambling about his old man. My dad this and my old man that, he says. "Whatever you want, we can get it. You want coke? My old man gets the best coke in Chicago. You want pills, whatever." He taps a bowl with a lighter and takes a hit.

"How 'bout Vs, can you get any Valium?" I ask him as he passes the pipe to me.

He points at me as he holds in a large hit of weed and grins. I had a thing for Valiums at the time; I loved them and they were great to come down off a coke jones. Plus they sold like hot cakes. I don't know why, but offer a kid who's never done pills in his life some pills and they buy them. Probably because they were cheap.

I sold five-milligram yellow Vs for fifty cents and ten-milligram blue Vs for a buck. I think they went because most of these assholes were used to buying crappy speed out of magazines, but here I am with pharmaceutical sedatives. Fucking beautiful.

Tommy's mouth opens as smoke pours out. "Fuck yeah, anything," he turns back around and watches out the car window. And so began my relationship with Big Tommy and Little Tommy.

They were a dysfunctional bunch even to us in the neighborhood. Little Tommy worked for his old man, peddling and going on buys; he was also the muscle. Big Tommy hung out in the hotel room where they lived. And I mean the seedy little dives on Mannheim Road, not the Ambassador East or anything. Usually they had two rooms, one for sleeping and living and the other for the shop. Big Tommy's wife, Betty, took care of the details, all the bullshit they didn't want to deal with. I later learned that he had another son who was younger than me, but he didn't show up in the picture at this point.

It was after a few weeks went by, as Little Tommy made sure I was cool, that I could be trusted, that I wasn't some little bonehead. That was when I got to meet Big Tommy.

Big Tommy was a great guy. I have had many mentors in the different careers I've chosen over the years, but I have to say Big Tommy was like a mentor to me in the world of drugs. He taught me a lot. A lot I knew, a lot I figured out the hard way, and when I met Tommy, he taught me the rest.

Tommy moved coke, but he loved to smoke good weed, and I had good weed. It almost seems like when people get on certain levels, they can't connect with the simple things of life. And here's where my little, simple, reefer-selling ass comes in.

The door swings open as Little Tommy walks in. I follow him cautiously. As I get into the room, it is ice fucking cold. They got the air pumping, and this is one of those brutally hot and humid Chicago summers.

Betty lies on the bed watching the TV. She eyes me and goes back to watching her show. A warmth of panic seeps into me. Who are these people? How do I come in? I ain't seen Jeff in years, and he pops up, and here I am. Jeff is nowhere in sight. Is this a fucking set up? Are they MEG agents? Are they gonna burn me and kill me?

"C'mon in," Tommy says as he walks in.

My eyes check the room out as I see Big Tommy for the first time. He stares at me with a respect that most older people don't give fourteen-year-olds. He wears black dress pants and dago T; his head is cocked a little with a smirk on his face. This guys is old, I mean in his fifties, and I'm still under the adolescent frame of mind that no one over thirty parties.

"Sit down, Johnny," Big Tommy says calmly as he motions to an empty chair. His voice is low and raspy but friendly.

"This is my dad, Tommy."

I reach out as Big Tommy rises halfway and shakes my hand. "It's good to finally meet you."

"Good to meet you," I reply.

He reaches over and lights a smoke as Tommy stands nervously by his side. Tommy's disposition had gone from dope-moving street soldier to scolded child, all in the second it took us to pass through the door.

Big Tommy looks at Little Tommy. "Go down to the Steak and Egger and get some dinner, huh?"

"Sure, Dad."

Tommy reaches in his pocket and pulls out a wad the size of his fist. He peels off a twenty and Little Tommy disappears out the door.

"So," he smiles. I smile politely back. "I need some weed, and I need it on a regular basis." He holds up a bag with a couple buds in it. "Is this the shit you get all the time?"

"Yeah, unless my guy is out."

"Good," he nods. "Did you bring some with you?"

"Yeah. What do you want?"

"I'll take whatever you got." He smiles.

I look him in the eye. "I brought a z with me." I notice he doesn't get what I mean. "An ounce, an oz. I just say 'z' on the phone in case, ya know."

He smiles. "You're smart for being so young."

I grin at the compliment. I hate it when people treat me different because of my age or size. As far as I was concerned, I was on the same fucking field as anyone in this business. We were all colleagues in my eyes, and that's exactly what this guy was treating me like, a colleague. "I don't like to leave any loose ends," I tell him, as I reach into the crotch of my pants and pull a bag filled with weed. "And I hate cops."

"Me too," he chuckles as Betty looks over at me. She smirks approvingly. He picks up the weed and looks at it; he nods at me. "How much?"

I pause for a second because I know this guy isn't a sap, but I know what I need to get for it. I put the price right in the middle. "A hundo," I say, knowing that he could get me down to ninety or even eighty at the lowest.

Big Tommy doesn't bat an eye. "That's fine." He reaches into his pocket and pulls out the wad, then he pauses. "Do you want cash or do you want to get paid in coke?"

Now here's an interesting proposition. "What will you give me for this?"

"Well, I charge a hundred for a sixteenth."

I'm quickly doing the math in my head. It all floods in— weights, measurements, and my bank roll. I never learned math and measurements quicker than when I was selling drugs. I instantly realize that if I sell five quarter grams at twenty (the regular price) I would have a half gram for free. This was about the small amount I was doing on the weekends at this point. Yeah, it amazes me to think that I did that little and was happy.

"That's cool. Let me get the sixteenth. Betty!" he calls, as she gets up and opens a drawer. She hands him a small case. He opens it and pulls out a small corner of a baggy that's twisted and tied at the end. In the corner is a little pile of white goodies. He hands it to me as I feel it. It's nice and rocky, big chunks of beautiful cocaine. I never had this much before; not that it was a lot.

"You want to do a line?" he asks as I look at my bag apprehensively. When you sell weed, it is common courtesy to smoke a joint with the guy that sold it to you. I didn't want to share this because I was a very organized dealer. Dipping in would throw off my whole system of breaking it into seven equal piles and recouping my profit. Also I did not yet have a good scale for small amounts, only a shitty little hanging scale, not the three beam I later came to depend on.

"Johnny," Tommy said, as I looked up and saw him dipping a key into a bag of coke and dumping it on the table.

"Oh, yeah, I'll take one."

The guy was partying with me on top of it. What a class act, I thought. I know I'm in and begin my jump in the industry from weed peddler to coke dealer. From that day on, the path would get stickier and stickier . . .

THE DARKEST OF KNIGHTS
John E. Marshall III

As I represent Life
I also represent Death

Funny how brothers
will talk violence trying to intimidate others

But, you see,
intimidation to me is an insult
and insults bring out my alter ego
The Grim Reaper

Reaping of Souls
too ignorant to value their lives
though so easily they speak
of robbing the lives of others
yet not willing to pay the piper
consequences for every action
there is reaction

They cry out my name
trying to Reap my Fame
but when I come to claim my seat
you can hear the scattering of feet

Some even amuse themselves
with Rap and Rhyme
up comes the Reaper
Rocking and Clocking
Brother's Rhyme has been timed

Funny how brothers talk
for The Grim Reaper has a silent walk
I, The Grim Reaper,
am my brother's keeper

I, The Grim Reaper,
Reaper of souls tormented

by anger uncontrolled
Reaper of lost words
lost in the last calling
of your Lord
like a fallen chord
Reaper of Peace.

I, The Grim Reaper,
am my brother's keeper

ELOQUENT HYPOCRISY
Jesús Papoleto Meléndez (East Harlem, NYC)

We come to the Courtroom,
             the room
                 where Court is to be heard—
                 where Justice
                         supposedly, will get a word
To see Ourselves
         en*Slaved* again
 answering to a System
   that professes Justice
             while knowingly
                     owing Us
             much more
             than it is willing
                     to pay;
                         the cost of
                             lost human lives,
             unwilling to admit
                         to its crimes . . .
Here we are,
         the beautifully arrayed
         Latino-Africano faces
         of beaten, torn
                 men & women,
                         some with
                             their children
         Torn, from our native lands,
                             distant
                                 as memory
             Forced by the slick trickery
                             of democracy
             to bow & cower
             to a bunch of lies
                         told
             by a bunch of liars—
                         Be they Black or
                                 White
                         who told them.

105

Oh, Yes!
  They have Us on their sides, confused
    into believing
        that because they let us
     now wear their uniforms, dressed
             in the plain clothes
                 of Them

    We are one of Them, are
      with Them;
        Loved
     by them —
         A Credit to
       our Race,
          in Complicity
      with the Crimes
         of their hate.

Look across the rows
   of the calmly seated
      falsely accused gathered here,
               Today

  And you just
     see Us;
        Once proud warriors
      sitting with our arms
        folded across
          our Eurocentrically dressed
             Chests!
           Gone are the handmade
                trinkets
          that protected Us once;
         Gone are the beliefs
       that held us in a united
       song
             of a Spiritual
Truth.

Instead, now
   our minds' eyes
are focused on
    the Idolized ideals
    of other men,
Who used them
   to capture
   & shackle Us, even
    unto this post-modern day —
         as it nears
         the ending of
     another millennium-year
       of Man's Life on
          Earth;
      Ruling over
       the dominion which God
           himSelf
         has given him,
          so say *They*
        who oppress
        as they pray,
         while their morals
              collide
      with the face of the Truth.
Why are we here?
  We ask of ourselves, aloud
   & in the privacy of our minds,
        we think
The subtle reason,
  as bright as a new falling star
       :Because of who we are!
We failed, they say
  to pay our way
   into the subterranean death of Their way
          ,a theft
      of a measly
      dollar&50cents
        — SmallChange
         conSidered
     anyWhere in this world
        toDay . . .

But, Where, O Where is the compensation
　　for the cost of
　　　　　　Their Crimes,
　　　　　　　　　　Committed
　　　　throughout ancient
　　　　　　　　& now modern times?
　　　　　　　　　　　Nowhere
　　　　　　　　　　　　to be seen
　　　　　　　　　are their tears
　　　　　　　　　for their suffering peers —
　　　　　　　　　　　　　Just the panic of
　　　　　　　　　　　　the rest of the world
　　　　　　　　　　　　living in fear
　　　　　　　　　　　　　　of eXtinction!

Make clear the distinCtion —
　　　　　　　　　Who lights the candle
　　　　　　　　　to light up the way?!
　　Who Is It Among Us,
　　　　　Who burns frankincense & myrrh
　　　　　for the memory of
　　　　　　　　our elders & ancestors;
　　　　For those
　　　　　who suffered before Us,
　　　　　For being just like Us
　　　　　　　　:Black as the Day
　　　　　　　　　　　begrudgingly
　　　　　　　gives way to the Night.

Woe!
　　Surely, Not Those among Us
　　　　　　　　Who
　　　　　have given up
　　　　　　　our Cause
　　　　to wear Their shields
　　　　　　without honor
　　　　& take pride in
　　　　　Their red badges
　　　　　　of cowardly courage —

Not They;
    The lost warriors
        of our tribes
   Who are now
    forever on Their sides/
          Against Us,
       Who arrest Us;
            Who
        bring Us
        In,
       handCuffed,
             bearing
        FalseWitness
      of the Justice
         they Serve.
            No!
            They have lost
              the Know-how
                To *Bow*
              To *Our GODS!*

III—On the Count

*Sometimes
the brightest minds
are behind bars
blinded
because brilliance
misdirected
is lethal . . .*

—Leila Steinberg
(hearteducation.org)

I AM WHAT IT IS TO BE
Richard Gonzalez
(member of the Bloods)

I am what it is to be. I don't talk much, my hunger talks for me. Boxed in 22 hours, almost 23. Fear nothing in sight 'cause I love death just as much as the next one loves life. Look around me; only a chosen few could survive in my surroundings. Those with a big mouth mostly wash laundry. Silence is as much a virtue as patience. Show signs of weakness and the wolves will be waiting. Evangelists call us Workers of Satan. I call us survivors of the American matrix. Society sets up the crimes we commit. I call it routine; the system calls it a glitch. The world actually believes we are to blame for the malice that actually exists partially dead to the outside world. Correction officers don't correct shit; they submit to oppress those who need to be helped, not given more stress. I don't usually deal with emotions, but anger is always at my surface. Cowards who don't stand up for the cause get treated like they're worthless. We will never let the system win in this abduction 'cause Brotherly Love Overrides Oppression and Destruction.

AS I LAY IN MY LONELY AND COLD BED
King Blood
(Godfather of the NYS Almighty Latin King Queen Nation)

As I lay in my lonely and cold bed, with no other company than my pillow, I feel the hurt in my eyes for the troubles of today.

I try to look out my small window and I see the police lights flashing in the city. I hear the cars roaming all around; everything is possible in the concrete jungle.

I hear the helicopters and sometimes the gunshots too. I lay here thinking which one of my homies may have gotten smoked today.

I have been praying every night, asking God for another day, and to be true to the only thing that's keeping me awake, the hope of seeing just another day.

Oh Lord, Father, King of Kings, our gutters flood, our streets are full of our Latinos' blood, our people are so torn apart that my hopes seem lifeless.

The man came into my 'hood with a trunk full of guns and drugs and acting like a white Santa; to my homies he sold his goods.

What can I do? What can I say, if I know that tomorrow everything will be the same?

Our homies are dying so young, God, they all feel cold. The majority of them are not even eighteen yet.

They gave my homies a TV, and a gangster movie is shown. All the violence heard on the radio got my homies dying like cats.

Oh God, let me see another day. Probably tomorrow my boys will think straight and their lives may be spared.

Maybe tomorrow it will rain; maybe we'll never see the sun again. Maybe my homies will all die trying to reach a hollow dream.

God, touch my homies with your blessing and make them all understand that only through the love of our brothers and sisters may our Latina Raza live.

I come and pray because I don't know what else to do. I just ask you, dear Lord, why so many of my homies have to die so young.

I'll lay down and my eyes I will force shut, but I will not try to sleep because my hopes of seeing another day, with my dreams, may go away.

A LETTER FROM THE INSIDE
Jay the Butcher
(Sharkcity Records)

I'm sitting here in prison with a pen in my hand
where I spent most of my life trying to understand
the meaning of life and love
and if it is true that there is a god above
how should I put this, how should I start
to express it straight from my heart

I woke up this morning in a prison cell
it was dark as a cave and it was cold as hell
I looked into the mirror to see what I would find
And what I saw looked back; it blew my mind

There was an old man standing where youth once stood
and I finally understood how I got so old
why my face was so bitter and my eyes were so cold
I started thinking about all the years gone by
and all the times I laughed and all the times I cried
I started thinking about my family and wife
and how I let them all down when they depended on me

And if you listen to me
real close, you will hear
the wisdom of an old man through a young man's tears
so don't act a fool thinking that you're cool
you're better off living by the golden rule
I tell you once; I won't tell you twice
you play with crime and you will pay the price

You see, I live in a world where death is a test
where you got to be deadlier than all the rest
it's a dog-eat-dog world where the strong survive
and there are fools walking around taking good men's lives
I only tell you this 'cause I know it's real
you will find one day that you just can't feel
nothing but your own hate and your own despair
you will find yourself knowing that you just don't care

My neighbor got bad news from his wife
he tied a sheet around his neck and took his life
all is well, ashes to ashes and dust to dust,
for a man will do what he feels he must

You see, I feel no grief and I feel no pain
all I hear is the pouring rain beating against my window pane
filled with sadness and filled with gloom
it won't be long now, I heard them say,
they'll be coming to my cell soon
to take me away down to the end of the hallway
where a priest will tell me
I will soon be free
There waits a chair for me
They will strap me down and my eyes they will hide
as I take a breath of cyanide

With all my love I send
tell my family that I am sorry this is how it had to end
as the final tears fall from my eyes
perhaps you could hear me say goodbye

Listen
as the final tears fall from my eyes
perhaps you could hear me say goodbye

A PRAYER FROM HELL
Kakamia Jahad a.k.a. Jackie Henderson

Dear God, Allah,
Look into my brown bloodshot eyes.
See how cops brutalize
cross color lines to confine
and minimize the bearer of universal minds.

Why was I sent to hell
transformed into a jail
a black face given life
stripped from my wife
while 2 whites regain their rights?

If this is a test of loyalty . . .
I've failed!

Here I sit
in the belly of desperation
seeking salvation
begging for universal rest,
take me to the revelation.

But yet you let me grow old
barefoot on hell's coals
but I'm gonna ride
till the earth's blood spills,
die on earth's soil
while man lives on death row —

Fuck it,
God, you're too raw.

If your journey is to crucify
those who cry in your name,
then bear witness:
You are your own shame.

WHERE'D HE LEARN IT FROM
Kakamia Jahad a.k.a. Jackie Henderson

Ebonics, slang, a slip of the tongue.
11 years old, 1st degree murder tears
and blood-stained pride . . .
caught with the gun.
Incarceration with no one to back

his side of the story.
One lost his life
for 50 seconds of criminal glory.
He will grow up in the earthly hell of corruption
because of society's neglect to care.
He was not told of life's ups and downs
and is among the living dead because of a dare.
From having the world and being set for life
to becoming a prison bum
and I can't help but to ask . . .
Where'd he learn it from?

THE CAGE!
Charles Bronson
(infamous gangster from the UK,
armed robber and serial hostage-taker)

A hole in the ground
There is no sound
A blanket of silence
In a room of gloom
You're a zombie
Forgotten
Beyond touch
Like a hollow tree
Empty
And waiting to die
Even dreams are dark
A big black cloud
The lights gone out
Goodnight.

HAVE YOU SEEN THE SUN
Rolando "Clever" Ortiz
(Eastside Choppers; Twelve Gangs, Bristow Park, East L.A.)

I haven't seen the sun in six months
No warm sunrays upon my face
No walks on the yard to free my legs
No sounds of birds chirping
Or the wind blowing upon my face
No idea what the outside world is like
Just cell doors and guards and inmates getting shanked.

With all this on my mind
I asked the guy across the way
Have you seen the sun?
He said,
"I haven't seen the sun in two years, six months, and twelve days."
So I asked the guy next to me
Have you seen the sun?
He said,
"Yes. Last month and nothing has changed
but the time wasted away in these cells for living the gangster life."

JAILED
Alicia Benjamin-Samuels

Her garden is no longer Eden.

I'm on the auction block

An inmate
A prisoner
Men eyeballin' me
in the shower
on the toilet
I can't even relieve myself
without bein' assaulted
by eyes

travelin' my Temple
My crime?
armed robbery
My punishment?
rape
by guards
who go unpunished
for defilin' me

She is the earth/soiled.

Now I'm pregnant
with the seed of a man
who stripped me of
my freedom to choose
who I let inside
my Paradise.

THE GAME
Don Babatunde
(The Last Poets)

Hip Hop flashes as Ego clashes
Red versus Blue
The honey bee gashes
Born in gangster bonded in blood
Generations dying
Baby's daddy gone
Population behind bars
As a rite of passage
No responsibility
Shows no compassion
Sleeping away one's time in brand-named blues
Words of power creates the fool
With rhymes and no reason
Hip hop's the news
Immortality is the Oscar
As death presents the trophy
For how many bullets

And the nominees ARE . . .
A time for peace can be had if egos have an open hand
Where's my hoe to plow the land
The Fertile mind of a dying man
Fire against water a cloud is formed
Fire with water an island is born
Hip . . . Hop . . .

EXCERPT: "DOWN FOR REVOLUTION"
An Interview with Clyde Young, a.k.a. Comrade X

Ed. note: The following is an excerpt of an interview with Clyde Young, a.k.a. Comrade X, conducted by members of the Revolutionary Worker *(Issues 569–57), the official newspaper of the Revolutionary Communist Party, USA. Reprinted by permission of the author.*

From Part 1: "Coming Up: Fried, Dyed and Laid to the Side"

Revolutionary Worker: You spent a lot of time in prison when you were coming up and you became a revolutionary in prison — and a revolutionary leader. So we'd like to get down on that whole story.

Comrade X: . . . I can remember when I was arrested for the first time when I was nine years old. It was a situation where I was in a five-and-ten-cent store. I stole something . . . and I can't even remember what it was but it was something really petty. And I was arrested and taken downtown and put in jail. I was in a cell by myself, but I was actually in the jail for men — when I was nine years old. And they held me down there and tried to intimidate me — and succeeded — until my parents came and got me. This is the kind of thing that happens growing up Black in this country. Had I been white it probably would have been resolved a lot differently, just by either taking me home or telling me not to do it anymore. But, in my case, right from the beginning, it was resolved in a very harsh fashion.

The first time that I was really convicted of something was a very minor and petty offense — I stole a pound of hamburger. At the time when I was coming up we were very poor, so I had a scheme that

I would work. My mother would send me to the store with a dollar or two, and I would steal what she wanted me to buy, and then I would keep the money to have some spending money. And this one Saturday—I can remember it very vividly—I stole something and I got busted. And once again, right away they took me downtown. But this time it wasn't even a question of my parents coming to get me. They put me in a juvenile detention center for a couple of months, and then I was put on probation. This was when I was twelve years old.

When I was thirteen, I was arrested again for shoplifting and riding in a stolen car . . . which was a violation of my probation stemming from the previous incident of stealing the hamburger. So I was sentenced to the reform school (or boys' school) for a period of time. Actually, the way they did it at that time was they sent you there indefinitely until you were eighteen years old. At that time I was not really conscious of how to understand all this. There were some ways I knew that this shit wasn't right; some things were wrong, and I had some sense of how Blacks were oppressed. But it wasn't any kind of put-together understanding that I had at that time. So I went off to reform school for nearly a year, and I would say that, through all of this, I was beginning more and more to get an understanding of some things.

RW: A lot of times the youth are caught up in it, but they don't see that it's the whole system coming down on them.

CX: Of course. Looking back, I can see it much more clearly now. When I was growing up in the South, Black people still had to sit in the back of the bus and were subjected to all kinds of Jim Crow shit. And that was not only true in the South but also in the North. In fact, Malcolm X made the statement at one point that the South begins at the border of Canada. In other words, it was the whole country, because in the North some of the same stuff went on, but it was more disguised. Because . . . I can remember, when my family moved to the North, even where I lived, which was in the North, Blacks couldn't sit at the counter in some of the drug stores and restaurants to eat—the same way it was in the South. But the whole system, the whole penal system . . . was set up in such a way that everything was aimed back at the oppressed people. And this is the same kind of thing that you see coming down on the youth today in a lot of ways.

You'd go in to see your probation officer or social worker, and the interviews a lot of times would consist of: "Were you fed well? Did your parents abuse you?" Here was a situation where we were very poor and a lot of times it was a question of not having anything to eat, of having fuel or coal. I would have to go out and find wood so that we could stay warm, and I would eat sugar sandwiches because we had no food . . . In other words, we didn't have shit. This was before there was a lot of openings in the 1960s where Black people began to get into better-paying jobs. And instead of that being looked at as the source of the problem, the authorities, the social workers and such, would ask you: "Well, do you think you're a kleptomaniac?"

And, ultimately, I came to see it as a bigger problem—that capitalism and imperialism was the source of this and the whole character and nature of the oppression of Black people in this country, having been brought here as slaves, forced into slavery, and then even after slavery, being forced into a state of virtual slavery in the South. And that oppression in a different form has continued right down to today. All of this had everything to do with the contradictions that I was facing as I was coming up as a kid.

RW: What happened when you went to boys' school?

CX: When I went to boys' school, it was a very regimented type of situation. The boys were in cottages which were like small houses. But first they kept you in what they called quarantine where they oriented you to the rules and basically began the process of breaking your spirit, which is what it was all about. I can remember being in quarantine. The floors were just spotless; you could almost eat off them. And largely what we spent our time doing was mopping and waxing the floors and walking around with pieces of cloth under our feet so we wouldn't scratch the floors. We couldn't wear shoes or anything.

It was also very segregated. The Blacks were in certain cottages and the whites were in different cottages. And the whites, to the extent that this could be the case, had more privileges than the Blacks. When I got out of quarantine I went into this cottage—and everybody was going into what we called the scullery—I guess it's some English word for the kitchen—and I was the last to go in.

As I walked past the cottage supervisor, he said something to me and I said, "No," and all hell broke loose. He knocked me down, threw a chair on top of me . . . pulled out a whip and whipped me, and all of this was because I didn't say, "Yes, *Sir!*"

They only let you wear your hair so long, so in order to keep your hair long you had to put on a woman's stocking. You'd take it and put it on your hair so that it would be pressed down and it wouldn't be too long. Otherwise they'd make you cut your hair, because when you first go in there, it's just like the army. They cut your hair off; it's very regimental, very humiliating. They make you march in formation and say the Lord's Prayer and pledge allegiance to the flag and all this kind of regimentation and strict control over everything you do. There were certain areas of the cottage where you could talk and others where you couldn't talk, and if you were caught talking you would be punished. There were snitches who would report violations of the rules to the cottage supervisor who was your surrogate parent. And if your name came on the list, then you would get the strap. For all this talk about child abuse (and I don't think kids should be beaten or otherwise abused), they would make you lean over a chair and make you pull your pants down and beat you with a razor strap. For talking in the dining room you'd get ten licks—but if you let go of the chair before the cottage supervisor got to ten then the supervisor would start all over again, so this could go on for quite a long time. If you were in isolation for some infraction of the rules, you would be forced to sit in a corner with your nose to the wall for eight hours while the other inmates worked (guess they wanted to make the point that isolation was for punishment), and if you were caught in some position other than sitting in the corner with your nose to the wall, you would be beaten in the way that I have described.

It was just very fascistic in that kind of way. And it wasn't all that inconsistent with the atmosphere in the country in the 1950s and early '60s—that was the way things were carried out. Later on, when I got out and got a little older and then came back, I rebelled against some of that—including challenging the cottage supervisor himself.

RW: Where were most of the guys from, what kind of background?

CX: Overwhelmingly proletarians. A lot of the guys that I met in reform school—and these guys came from throughout the state—I was later in prison with when I was older. This was the track you were on, and the people you met in reform school were often the same people you met when you got to prison later on in life.

RW: Some people treat the whole question of crime in the inner cities and youth gangs like it never existed before, when in reality the oppressed people have always been in a situation where it was allowable to brutalize each other, but crossing that line to fight the system was something different.

CX: That's definitely true. In fact, that was a point the Chairman *[RCP's Bob Avakian —ed.]* made in the interview about the Black Panther Party . . . And also, this whole point of youth gangs being allowable in a certain sense if you are fighting and killing one another. It is different than if you start committing violence and violent crimes against whites, to say nothing if you begin to go over to become a revolutionary and start attacking the system. That's a whole different ball game.

RW: Getting back to your story. Clearly when you were in the boys' school and they ran this whole discipline trip on you, it didn't work. It didn't achieve the desired results.

CX: No, it did not. I would have to say before I began to take up revolutionary ideas, and especially before I began to take up Marxism-Leninism-Maoism, that they could confuse you. They never really succeeded in breaking me and a lot of the people that I grew up with, but they could confuse you in terms of your understanding. I used to think: Why am I getting into this shit all the time. I don't want to get busted all the time, but here I am. I made a promise to myself that I wasn't going to get into this situation again, but there I was again. In other words, there was a whole thing of making you think it was really you that was the problem rather than that there's a whole system and the whole setup. Like when I was young and used to shoot dice, we used to have different kinds of fake dice we could put into the game, six-ace-flats and so forth . . . And that's the way this system is: the dice are loaded. They're shooting loaded dice against you.

It wasn't like I really had it together in terms of why all this shit was happening this way. But like a lot of youth, I not only had dreams but I also thought about why shit was this way, and why it was that people over here were poor and people over there were just born rich. Where I lived, the whole area was all Blacks and extremely poor, but then not far away from where we lived it was like a whole rich section of town. And you'd think about these things. Why was it that way? Why was it that people had to go hungry and go without the basic necessities that it takes to live? And, on the other hand, they were mocked and surrounded by all this wealth. That was a thing I did ponder when I was a kid before I came to understand fully what this was all about.

RW: Who were your heroes?

CX: As I grew older I wanted to be a hustler, I wanted to live by my wits, and I wanted to be in the streets. I didn't see much of a future in working like a slave eight hours a day like I'd seen my parents and other relatives and other people do. It just didn't seem to be heading anywhere. It didn't have any attraction to me. What attracted me was this other kind of life, where you are more in the streets and living by your wits and hustling. And that's the sort of thing I got into.

When I was coming up, a lot of the people that I admired were the older brave elements — the brothers who stood on the corners and wore their pants high. They used to have a style where you wore your pants all the way up to your chest. And they wore their "Kadies" and they had their switchblades. It was just a certain style of going up against things, not in a conscious way, but there was a certain style in opposition. And it was what it meant to be a youth at that time. Those were a lot of the people I admired and later ended up in prison with.

Those were the kinds of people, the people who had their hair fried and dyed and laid to the side, with a part not too wide. Back then, it was called a Process. There was a certain edge to that style that was not respectable, that was in your face. Black people who were respectable or who were into entertainment might wear a process, but to wear your do-rag and to have your do-rag in your pocket and that sort of thing, there was a certain unrespectable edge to it that sent the other side up the wall.

They were the outlaws. They would wear their outrageous clothes, and they would stand on the corner, and they would croon and those kinds of things. And that's who I admired and who I wanted to model myself after. And later it was me that was out there like that.

RW: In opposition to the treatment you received, you developed a certain contempt for death which is similar to the attitude in the lyrics of the NWA rap, "Fuck the Police":

> *They have the authority to kill a minority.*
> *Fuck that shit, cuz I ain't the one*
> *For a punk motherfucker with a badge and a gun*
> *To be beaten on and thrown in jail.*

CX: I think early on a lot of this contempt for death and a lot of the way the stuff came down was against one another. There was this whole thing about who was bad on the corner, and you weren't gonna let anyone get the better of you.

But there was also contempt for the pigs. When I first began committing robberies and burglaries, I would go into a place and start burglarizing it and just in terms of the fearlessness I had, I would go in and start cooking myself a meal. Like I figured they had the same thing that I had, and I probably had more heart than they did, so if they came, I was ready for them. And that was the spirit that I had and, in fact, a lot of the youth had, and it's not all that different than what exists now.

I was just not long ago rereading some of Malcolm X, and he talks about when he was coming up — this whole thing about face. It's like a street code and also it's a similar type of code in prison. In other words, the way he puts it in his book is that for a hustler in our sidewalk jungle world, face and honor were important, no matter. No hustler could have it known that he had been hyped, meaning outsmarted or made a fool of, and worse, a hustler could never afford to have it known that he could be bluffed, that he could be frightened by a threat and that he lacked nerve. It just basically comes down to being macho — that you can't let people do anything that would offend your manhood or offend your face. And if that happened, then you had to go down or you weren't down.

A whole part of existing on the streets, that you had to have that heart, have that nerve, not be backed down by someone else if it came to a confrontation. That's part of the whole psychology of the streets that goes on, and some people from the 1960s who are now getting down on the youth today have forgotten that. This is not something that just existed in the '60s; Malcolm is talking more back in the '40s, that same kind of code of the streets and also something that exists in prison. This is something that I've struggled to rupture with as part of becoming a revolutionary and a communist.

RW: Looking back on it, you said you see positive and negative things in it. What do you mean by that?

CX: On the negative side, I can say that the street and prison code has a lot of individualism mixed up with it—to say nothing of macho-ism and male chauvinism. I've been there; I know what it's all about. And I've come a long way in breaking with that kind of outlook. That's The Man's way. Our way is: Brothers rising up with sisters, strong, proud, and with equality. That's our way, the way we all get free. The youth today (and here I'm speaking especially of the brothers) have to be struggling over that kind of thing, that kind of macho outlook. The revolutionaries have to have a first-string orientation and all-the-way revolutionary politics in command, uniting with the anger of the people and striving to direct it in the most powerful way at this cesspool that they call the greatest system on earth. And we got to make that part of preparing to bring this system down. As we've said: while we're battling them back, politically like that, we've got to make this part of getting ready for The Time—and it can come soon—to wage revolutionary war.

On the positive side, when these youth begin to become more conscious and that same fearlessness and anger and contempt for death begins to be directed at the system and the powers that be, then you have a whole different ball game. All that is a necessary part of what we have to do in bringing this whole thing down; you need that spirit. You obviously need a lot more than heart, but you do need that. So that's how it divides into two. On the one hand, the way it plays itself out in the streets and in prison and all of that is a reflection of macho-ism and gangsterism and that sort of thing. But, on the other hand, there is the situation that when that attitude gets transformed through the leadership of a party and people begin to take up the science of Marxism-Leninism-Maoism, it's not like you lose that fearlessness and that hatred—it's just tempered, if you want to put it that way.

I can remember having a lot of hatred, but it was not focused, not directed, and oftentimes it would be focused in the wrong way and in the wrong direction, but it's not like I've lost that hatred and that anger. I still have a monumental anger and monumental hatred for imperialism; as the song says, "Deep in my heart I still abhor 'em." And after all these years, I still don't fear them. So the question is: how do you lead that, how do you have a first-string orientation?

When I was coming up, there wasn't a party, there wasn't a party that was based on Marxism-Leninism-Maoism in this country that could give some direction. And later, as I got into my teens, there was the Black Panther Party, which played a vanguard role and made tremendous contributions. Today there is a party, our party, the Revolutionary Communist Party, USA, that is preparing to make revolution in this country as a component part of the world revolution. There is a party with the line, leadership, and battle plan to lead things all the way this time around.

A whole generation of youth came forward in the 1960s who wouldn't be intimidated and weren't too impressed with the power of the state, and we need to bring that forward again and take it all the way this time . . .

RW: The rap "Black Steel in the Hour of Chaos" tells the story of a brother who refuses to join the army and ends up in the joint. You almost joined the army once. What happened to change your mind and how do you see it now?

CX: There was a time when I was under the gun. I knew that it was a turning point in my life. I had been repeatedly in lock-ups and jails, and I had just recently gone through a whole situation with a stolen car where I was being chased through woods and shot at and dogs were after me and all of that. And I knew the likelihood that within a short time I would be dead or in prison. That was the terms of things. There weren't any other terms I was looking at . . . I was not so politically aware at that time. So I was going to join the Marines, become a man, that sort of thing. I was desperate.

RW: This was during the beginning years of the Vietnam War?

CX: Right. It's kind of ironic, because here I was into all this shit with the pigs and the system and had pretty much grown up in penal institutions, but at the same time I was caught in a trap of their ideology—you become a Marine and go overseas and all that, and you become a man. And that's the sort of thing that the men in my family—especially those who had served in the military and fought in Korea in particular—had talked about for years. So I felt that this was my way to get on a different track. But as it turns out, a few months later, I was in prison, which, in the final analysis, was a much better resolution of the contradiction.

RW: Some people would be shocked to hear you say that you thought being in prison was a better resolution than being in the army.

CX: In hindsight, in looking back, yes. I had an uncle who struggled with me not to join the Marines. He was struggling from a Black Nationalist position. But later on, when I got into prison and as my outlook developed in terms of taking up revolutionary theory, I became an internationalist. There was a certain sense in the '60s, a certain aligning of oneself with the enemy of your enemy. So there was a whole thing of identifying with the struggle that was going on in Vietnam from the standpoint of the Vietnamese people and identifying with the struggle that had gone on in China and Korea. Some of the things that were really exciting and liberating to me when I was in prison was studying about how the U.S. had gotten their ass kicked in Korea and how they were getting their ass kicked in Vietnam. Here was a country with peasants who were able to defeat one of the most powerful countries in the world. That was tremendously inspiring. So I think that going into prison was in a certain sense going into school, for me. I had been schooled through my life experiences, but in prison I was introduced to revolutionary ideas. And that's why I would say, looking back on it, that going to prison rather than going to Vietnam to fight my sisters and brothers who were oppressed just like me was a better resolution to the contradiction.

RW: What were some of the early incidents you remember when you started to have more of a revolutionary awareness?

CX: I was beginning to put some things together that had been occurring to me throughout my life on what the fuck was going on, and one of the things that began to strike me was how many poor and oppressed people were in prisons, both Black and white, that if you had money you were able to avoid going to prison, and overwhelmingly it was proletarians who were sent there.

The robbery that I was involved in netted $140. And here I was marching into prison with twenty years. The deck was stacked, so to speak.

When I went in, there was this one guy I had been in jail with for a period of time, whom I had grown up with, and by the time I got to prison, he was already into Black Nationalist politics. So he tried to turn me onto those politics. But I kept my distance. Then there was an event that had a big impact on me and began to change me.

A year or so after I was in prison, some of the more politically conscious prisoners—who at that time were into Revolutionary Nationalism—they had a protest. These guys came out and they had some demands that they were going to present to the warden. And the prison authorities immediately sent guards armed with shotguns to quell the protest. A lot of times in prison, that's what happens when you protest; right away they bring out the guns and they use them.

So my fear was that they were just going to blow everybody away. Things went back and forth for an hour or two—a very tense situation—where the prisoners clearly weren't going to give up, but at the same time it seemed like they were just going to get massacred. Ultimately, the protest was resolved in a way that nobody was killed; they just put everybody on buses and transferred them to another prison. But what had a very big impact on me was the courage of the prisoners and that they were willing to risk getting killed for what they believed in. It created an interest in me for where they were coming from. So that's when I began to start reading some things.

First, I read the *Autobiography of Malcolm X* and *Malcolm X Speaks*. And in a very intense period of about a year I went through a lot of changes. I joined the Nation of Islam and was a member for a couple of months, and it wasn't long before I became interested in the Black Panther Party.

RW: What was the turning point when you first started to consider yourself a revolutionary?

CX: Within a couple of years after I was in prison I considered myself a revolutionary. I had become familiar with some of the most advanced revolutionary leaders and thinkers in the country at that time. I had studied and become aware of the Black Panther Party, and I would have given anything to have been right there with Huey and Bobby and others in the Party when they were facing down the pigs. It was very difficult to be in prison at that time, you know. So I got into the Panthers and through the Panthers I met Mao.

I had also tried, at that early stage of my development, to read things like the *Communist Manifesto*, but it was just over my head. Mao was something that I could really understand. I continued to struggle with things like the *Manifesto*, and later I got into much more difficult things, like Engel's *Anti-Duhring*. But I was really into Mao, and I could relate to some of the ways the Panthers were promoting Mao and to some of what I had learned about the Cultural Revolution in China. I did not have a full understanding of the Cultural Revolution from where I was sitting, but I was really inspired and excited by what I learned of it and heard of it. You know, people throughout the whole world, including people in our international communist movement, a lot of us were brought forward by the Cultural Revolution and Mao in terms of becoming revolutionaries and taking up the science of Marxism-Leninism-Maoism . . .

RW: Were there certain individuals who played a key role in the revolutionary movement in the prison, or was there a group? How did that come down?

CX: At the time in prison, people would get together in groups and collectives and study. There was a core of people who had more revolutionary consciousness, and we would study together and work out together. What we envisioned in that period was that there was going to be revolution. And we were going to be ready. So we were studying and we were training physically and all of that.

Then at one point some Panthers actually came into the prison, and that was quite an experience in terms of beginning to get more of a sense directly of where the Panthers were coming from and what they were all about.

. . .There was also another thing that we used to do for recreation a lot of times—instead of playing basketball, we would sit out on the recreation yard and study. And that was another thing that was forbidden. So there were all these kinds of repressive measures going on. And they ended up putting those Panther brothers and some others in solitary confinement for some of their revolutionary activities. By that time, I had developed into a revolutionary and a revolutionary leader. Placing the Panther brothers in solitary confinement basically precipitated a rebellion.

RW: Tell us about it.

CX: It sort of played itself out over the course of two days. The first day we sat down in the prison yard and submitted some demands to the warden. The warden said he was going to review them. Of course, we had a plan of action if the prisoners weren't released from segregation or solitary. After we presented these demands to the administration and they said they were going to take certain steps to release these brothers and deal with the other demands we had presented to them, we basically dispersed. But at the same time we were very skeptical that this stuff was going to get resolved. So that night we began making backup plans, so to speak. We were trying to figure out how we could really hurt them if they didn't concede to our demands.

On the second day, the prison authorities said that they would consider releasing these prisoners who had been put into segregation. This was the central demand that we had. I wrote about the rebellion in an essay a few years later while still in prison: "By the time we were released from our shelters for recreation that day, most of us anticipated a confrontation with the prison guards but few if any anticipated the tragic consequences of that confrontation. Before we assembled on the recreation yard, we received word by way of the prison grapevine that the prison officials had not acted in accordance with their promise to release two of the brothers from administrative segregation. Instead, they had placed the brothers in the hole. Segregation is a situation where you are confined to a cell twenty-four hours a day except for showers and whatnot. And these cells are separated off from the general prison population. The hole is like when you are put in there, you don't have any blankets or any bedding, you just sleep on the concrete floor and it's dark. So they had been put in the hole . . ."

I also wrote these lines in the wake of the rebellion: "Frustrated and angered by the treachery of the prison officials, approximately thirty of us decided to burn down the prison's furniture factory, as had been planned on the previous day. Although the furniture factory is the source of a considerable amount of the state's income, prisoners who work there are paid a meager salary of approximately fifteen cents an hour. Therefore, we felt that the destruction of the furniture factory would constitute a powerful blow to the bureaucratic state and correctional officers who were responsible for the oppressive conditions which then prevailed at the prison." So that was our orientation.

RW: Do you remember that day; could you describe it?

CX: I remember it very vividly. It was very tense when we came out of our cells that morning, like you didn't know what was going to happen. You knew that something serious was going to happen, but you didn't know what. We were confronted with the prospect that many of us would probably be dead. There was tremendous anger. Things had mounted up, and locking up these prisoners who we saw as our leaders was like the culmination of a whole number of things.

So when we went out that day, the plan was that some people who were working in the furniture factory were going to supply the flammables that were necessary. And some others of us were going to come into the furniture factory and carry out our plan. What happened though is that we were repelled. We got shot at from the guard tower, and we weren't able to get into the furniture factory to carry out our plan. So, after being fired upon, we retreated back to the drill ground (recreation area).

The prison authorities ordered everybody to leave who wanted to leave, and there were about 450 prisoners who left. That left 212 of us. One of the lieutenants ordered a Black guard, like a token sergeant who was out there, to leave. He was unarmed. He had promised us that we wouldn't get shot. So the lieutenant told him, "Well, walk around the corner and you won't see it." All the guards remaining behind were white.

The prisoners remaining on the drill ground were overwhelmingly Black, with two white guys and one Chicano. And there was something that I learned in that particular battle in terms of uniting all who could be united against the enemy. Because we hadn't succeeded in doing that. In other words, it wasn't like the white prisoners couldn't have been won over—at least some of them—to what we were trying to do, but there hadn't been sufficient effort to reach out to them.

The guards surrounded the drill ground, and I can't remember the exact words, but it was something along the lines of, "You niggers have five minutes to leave."

So we said, "Fuck you! The five minutes are up; we're not going to leave."

And from what I can remember of the sentiment, it was like that point Lenin talks about in his writings about those times when the oppressed have contempt for death. That's what we had . . . utter contempt for death.

It was clear that some of us could likely die, but we were determined that we were not going to back down, that we would see through what we had set out to do. It wasn't like we had this Martin Luther King sit down and turn the other cheek kind of thing. We were just fucking angry, and at the same time it was a tactical miscalculation and illusion on our part that because we were not engaged in any violent acts, their hand would be stayed, that they wouldn't actually kill us. But that was like a really violent introduction to what these people will do to you.

After the five minute period was up, they opened fire on us. We were lying on a volleyball court. It was like a fenced-in recreation yard, and the volleyball court was like five or six feet from the fence. The guards were immediately in front of us outside the fence. And they had shut the door to the fence and stuck their shotguns through there. And some of them were pumping and shooting so fast that one of the guns began to malfunction.

But one prisoner just wouldn't sit down. He remained standing and shot his fist into the air, and he didn't sit down until they shot him down.

So I learned more from that than I have learned from many books about the nature of the enemy. Two people were killed and forty-five were injured. The brother who wouldn't sit down was not killed, but he was seriously injured.

And even the events that occurred after were an indictment of the system too. A lot of these prisons are set up in these rural areas that are mainly white—and the hospitals in the surrounding area wouldn't take people. So the prisoners had to be taken several miles away to a major city to be hospitalized because they just wouldn't take them in the local hospital because they were Black.

RW: The Chairman has said, if you want to be bad, the revolution is the baddest. Reflecting back, you had been faced with death before in your life. How would you compare the difference?

CX: The whole point about dying that Mao made in the *Red Book* is this: to die for the people is heavier than a mountain, but to die for the imperialists is lighter than a feather. And there was a whole spirit in that period that captured all of us, about the willingness to put your life on the line for the people and to die fighting imperialism. And we not only felt it then, but we have not given up on it. And I think that's a lot of what the youth have to get down on. The courage they have in one context has to be translated in terms of going up against this whole system and bringing down this whole thing. Because one of the things we understood then in a basic sense is that without power, everything was an illusion—that once we could bring these people down, then we could perform miracles.

RW: You mean state power, taking on the whole system, not just having a piece of turf.

CX: State power, taking on the whole thing, not just having a block or having a corner or having part of a city, but taking on the imperialists, overthrowing them in revolutionary warfare, establishing socialism and beginning to move on towards communism. That's the whole vision that I began to develop back then. And that was a whole different kind of thing . . .

RW: Do you remember the first time you realized that it was going to take a revolution against the whole system to deal with the problems coming down on Black people and all the other social problems?

CX: The murder of Fred Hampton had a big impact on me. And it was obvious to me, knowing the nature of these people, having lived in the belly of the beast, even within the belly of the belly, it was obvious to me that Fred Hampton was assassinated. Some things came together. There were many things that I understood about the system, but some things came together on a much higher level around that time.

Leading up to the prison shooting, on one level I looked at myself as a revolutionary. Those events, combined with the Fred Hampton murder, were crucial things that played a certain role in terms of what I had to do with my life. That was the most profound turning point, if you want to put it that way. There was no turning back. Mao says that the oppressed are oppressed, and in fighting back against their oppression they search out a philosophy. I hadn't really been that interested in school when I was growing up, especially a lot of the history they taught at that time. When you read history, it was the slaves picking cotton and that sort of thing which was just humiliating — you were just glad when the class proceeded past those pages. But when I got in prison and got affected and influenced by all of what was going on in society and throughout the world — I began to take some steps to try to understand the world better.

RW: So it was like Mao talks about learning warfare through warfare.

CX: Very much so, very much so. It was just being thrust into the struggle with the other side and a lot of it raising questions about what kind of society you would replace it with. And I can remember being just excited and thinking about not only how they can be defeated, but also getting a beginning vision — from what I could understand of things like the Cultural Revolution in China under Mao's leadership — of what the society would be like; after having overthrown the system, what kind of society would it be — that we can deal with a lot of these problems in terms of the oppression that the masses of people face, the humiliation and degradation, the rich over the poor, men over women, whites over Blacks and other oppressed nationalities and, in a word, wiping out all exploitation and oppression and classes themselves. And that overthrowing them would be a big step in wiping this shit out, not only in this country but throughout the entire world. And that vision was very inspiring to me when I began to take up and study Marxism in a serious way—and it has been deepened and enriched over the years since that time.

RW: That's the strategic Double C—contempt for the enemy and confidence in the masses that the Chairman talks about.

CX: Right. It's based on something; it's based on the party, which is armed with the most revolutionary science that exists today. And I learned this through the crucible of struggle against the enemy. I explored a lot of different philosophies, but I came to see that this was the most advanced philosophy that exists. This was controversial. Some people said back then, "Well, that's just for the white boy or that's the white man's philosophy," just like some people say that today. In fact, one of my best friends stopped talking to me because he disagreed with my insistence that we had to unite all who could be united against the enemy, including white people. That was very hard because we had been through some heavy struggle together. Later, he came around. But for some months he wouldn't talk to me. But I stuck with it because this science is the revolutionary philosophy, the most advanced philosophy for people all over the world because it is a liberating philosophy.

RW: You know, I've noticed that among some male revolutionaries who've been in prison there seems to be more of an understanding about not treating women like sex objects and property. And I was wondering if this was because men in prison actually go through some of the same abuses that women do—where power relations actually take the form of sexual abuse—and the whole question of being treated like a sex object is so intense. Speaking of going against the tide, this must have been a big topic of struggle.

CX: When I was a kid, some of the people we admired were the pimps. In fact, there is a series of books written—I was in a bookstore the other day, and I see that they're still out there—a series of books written by this guy called Iceberg Slim who was a pimp. And the young brothers would read those books and admire his style and where he was coming from. And thinking back, you can see how far some of the brothers had to come. I'm speaking now of the period of time before I became a revolutionary and started taking up revolutionary politics.

On the streets, it was considered hip to be a pimp, or a player, which was a term for a guy who lived off women. To have a Cadillac and to have several women, that was a goal to aspire to. And those very brothers who looked toward the pimps and admired them and in some cases did actually do that themselves, if they had been forced into some form of servitude in that kind of way, they would have been totally outraged about it. But in this case, it was something that was part of being cool, and it was considered part of being cool to dog women in this way and to actually end up being a slave master in this type of way. And that's the screwy relations and contradictions that you actually get under imperialism.

Men can't say that we're against imperialism but at the same time carry out the imperialist/male supremacist mentality in relation to women. There's no way that you can carry through a thoroughgoing revolution without "breaking the chains and unleashing the fury of women as a mighty force for revolution." You cannot have an all-the-way revolution without fighting for and realizing the emancipation of women.

RW: This sense of preparing to take power is a theme that runs through your story too.

CX: There was a sentiment in the prisons at that time. The events at Attica, George Jackson and the Soledad Brothers, and all of that represented a very advanced current of what existed throughout the country. There was a whole attitude and a whole sentiment that there was going to be a revolution and people were getting prepared, and when the prison doors were opened, people were going to be ready to come out and play a role in being able to bring this whole thing down. That was part of the whole climate and the whole atmosphere, and once again it brings me to the point that Chairman Avakian has stressed about the importance of a revolutionary movement and a politicized atmosphere—what that can do, not as an end in itself, but as part of preparing for revolution and preparing to bring this whole thing down. And what that can do in terms of bringing out the best in people. I think a lot of the best in people was brought out in that period. And the point is not to look back on it just to be nostalgic and to talk about how things were when we were young, but to look back on it precisely for the purpose of learning as much as we can in order to go forward, and we just might have a chance to go for the whole thing this time. That's what we are working for and that's what we are preparing for, and those opportunities could very well come, and soon.

On a personal note, having had the opportunity to work with the Chairman in the past in a number of situations, including going into housing projects with him before he when into exile, I can say without exaggeration that our Chairman too has given his heart to the masses, to the oppressed, not just in this country but the world over. And this comrade is thoroughly intoxicated with the revolution. His leadership has been decisive at key turning points in the revolutionary movement in this country—going back to the '60s—and it is crucial today and looking ahead to the future. As we have said, our ideology is Marxism-Leninism-Maoism, our vanguard is the RCP, and our leader is Chairman Avakian.

MIND GAMES
P.J.S. 1
(former president, Brotherhood of Roots)

Behind these walls it's clear to see
    This isn't what our lives should be
Mistakes have been made; must we be unforgiven
    With success we'll be blessed if our talents are driven
Are we stars behind bars; is this where we belong
    Let's look in the mirror and see where we went wrong

Reflections and images all seem the same
  Ideas are enhanced; we're entranced by mind games
Thoughts of quick money we all should dismiss
  Because of such thoughts I am here writing this
Make the best of the grim situations you're in
  And stop playing games you know you can't win.

THEY GAVE ME TWELVE YEARS ON THE WAKE-UP
Shaka B. Shakur a.k.a. Sherrod DuBois

They gave me twelve years on the wake-up on my first ride; forty-eight behind the wall and eight on the outside. I came in a buck-fifty, soaken wet and scared to death—now a two hundred pound souljah down to ride to the last breath.

For every day that passes another part of me gets colder. My only regret in this shit is that I might not live to see my kids get older. Somehow, though, through all the madness there seems to be a justification for my moves. Am I a victim of this sickness or a young brother paying dues?

A friend once told me I think too much about my time, but it is hard to forget what lies in the front of my mind. I was spawned from an urban complex similar to the one upstate, and often I ask myself, was that a practice for my fate? As I walk the prison yard contemplating my reality, I am met by many stares and cold faces. Around here, love ain't got no places. I'm sending flicks home with poses to let you know I'm gonna make it; but if you look deep into the eyes of the face in the picture you can see I can't take it. Behind these walls is where I'm surrounded by stress and asking questions like, why they wanna flip on me for premeditated aggressions? I'm sending kites to my people only to get no reply. I swear if it wasn't for the anger in my heart I'd probably die. They gave me twelve years on the wake-up on my first ride, forty-eight behind the wall and eight on the outside.

I'M JUST WAITING
Noel Rodriguez a.k.a. King El David
(Almighty Latin Kings & Queens Nation)

I'm just waiting
waiting for that knock on my door
Federals coming to seize me for no wrong
but cuz I was willing to fight that which was wrong
waiting for my home to be violated once again
my personal life legally put on display
my words recorded and my movements filmed
I'm just waiting

Waiting for that false testimony of a tecato whose hunger was fed
those tecato's words that land my ass in a room under hot lights
surrounded by pigs that work hard to break me,
waiting for that moment that I am alone
and the easy target of those same pigs
to plant some shit on me, or even just around me,
so that the people I worked hard to gain trust from
see me as a betrayer of the community, a false prophet

I'm just waiting
waiting for that gangsta who wants my crown, or the respect I earned
to creep from the shadows and put two in my head
never looking into my eyes,
but looking down at my body, face to the floor
Brrra! Brrra! "How you like that power, nigga!"
I'm just waiting

I'm just waiting for that sexy mami to seduce me with her eyes
her walk and the fruit between her thighs
showing me a world of lust that is so addictive I become her slave
and she becomes the black widow that devours me,
sells me out and kills my soul

I'm just waiting
waiting for the reality television show that I'm the star of
the exploitation of just another Latino,
seeing nothing but interpreting a vision of hell
all justified, all access granted, all freedom lost

Hey, it's just the Patriot Act,
what are you complaining about, you let it happen?
You're just waiting too, like me . . .

I'm just waiting
Waiting for that final check
when the big business I work for has made so much dough
they need to let me go to make even more dough
waiting for that excuse that they will use to relieve me of my duties
knowing it's just that I am not a part of their bigger picture,
Nah, I'm just a pawn, only here to be taken

I'm just waiting
waiting for that rear view picture of my home fading away
while red lights flare and sirens cry
my wrists embraced by cold steel
tears falling from my daughter's eyes
she, having no idea why,
she'll be forever asking . . . why?

I'm just waiting
waiting for my mother's pain, her tears and shame
waiting for the "I told you so" and the "Why didn't you listen to
    me?"
and my menz from the 'hood saying,
"See you shoulda' deaded all that revolutionary shit
and chilled with us smoking trees."

I'm just waiting
waiting for my own brother to spread some lies so that my people
    divide
waiting for my reputation to be destroyed and my name to cause
    disgust
waiting for that pack of wolves when I'm alone in the cut
waiting for that final blow,
that taste of blood,
that sigh of relief from my enemies . . .
Thank god that nigga's gone

I'm just waiting
waiting for that bus and that bright orange suit
waiting for the first pen and pad to write my fam'
waiting for that first fight where blood is splashed
waiting for that kiss from my wife from behind a glass

I'm just waiting
waiting because there ain't no clearer picture than the one of doom
because without you, fighting for me, while I fight for you
there ain't shit to expect but that very last breath
So I'm just waiting

BEHIND PRISON BARS
LaRonz Murray

   The spirit of my hustla's soul yells out mad as hell, locked in this cold cell, dressed in prison wear. Icy-glazed stare showing no fear; hardened grill froze with the Real Thug Pose, doin' time for managing hoes, keys sold. I am what I am, another Black Man, a statistic doin' 25 to Life in the can from a broken hustlin' plan. Yo, son, the street life was so sweet, mad paper buildin' week to week, pushin' drugs, pimpin' freaks before it all ended, lifestyle suspended. One dude broke the rules, got knocked when I was playin' pool, gun tool to my head, one false move I'm dead, rights being read. Knocked, 'cause a nigga snitched and told the feds. Should've made him bleed red, instead I gave him a break and let him go. Now I'm being handcuffed out the ghetto.
   (*Pause*) . . . Flashback to 4 kids in a sack. We was too poor to eat off Mama's faith. Father we hate. Took a chance on an early wake for the cake. I couldn't live life to the minimal; that's why I turned into a criminal. So, I paid da cost to be da boss, had the projects and block on lock, hoes hoe'n, dough's flowin' non-stop. Gucci painted Benz, drop top. Extra cake got from my hot club brothel spot. Twenty-four hour clock, glocks cocked with 1 in the chamber.
   (*Pause*) . . . Throwback to the remainder of how I flipt the script from a PJ's misfortune to a *Ghetto Fortune 500* millionaire 'bout to exchange my pimp wear for Riker's gear. But don't knock

da hustle, street game hustle, take the bitter with the sweet. Did I question The Word the preacher preached? Da game's made for the Strong, not the weak. Yo, son, it's a cold cold world living in darkness. Everyday I wake up to fight this. Do I regret being unrighteous, ignoring *The Light*? It was my right, choosing temptation.

(*Pause*) . . . Taking a thought visitation, staring at these prison walls I'm facin'. For my seeds, I'd end the money chasin', change my situation, stop being a devil's creation to start a Christ relation. My divided soul's torn, born the son of a poor righteous mutha' straight from the gutta. Yo, all this grimy brotha ever wanted to do was be a Paid-in-Full ghetto superstar pushin' exotic cars. I chose to be Thug Hard, played the Hustla's Card, street dreams only took me so far. Now I'm doing 25 to Life behind prison bars.

(*Pause*) . . . Throwback to when my life was a Curtis Mayfield soundtrack, *Superfly*, dough stacked, Free & Paid with the Blue Print laid. Back in the day, I was makin' mad bread as the Head, runnin' organized crime in my prime. Then fatherhood started sinkin', mentally thinkin', one last hit, go legit, but who would've known we would've blown ten million from my dealin' with a childhood friend who dimed, confessed the crime. Now, I'm doin' time 'cause that nigga Rick snitched, could've been filthy rich instead of a convict. But don't shed no tears. I had my years, Big Bossin' Flossin', Money Tossin' like I was a Rockefeller dashin' thru the city with a N.Y. State of mind, in the grind. Pushin' on the gas. Flash! Picture on the cover of *Felon*, tellin' my story how I grew up a juvenile delinquent, frequent, gave Mama stress, first got arrested when my manhood was tested. I was brought up fatherless in violence, heard my first whistle blow, murdered dude in silence. I barely escaped an early wake, fled the scene, heavy breathin' heart beatin', jeans full of cream.

Cash rules everything around me, chasin' that dollar bill, niggas getting killed 'cause it's real in the field. The Street Life kept callin'. Wanted to be Big Time, ballin' like those stunnas from New Orleans. Yo, I'm telling the truth. I was an impressionable youth, just a Ghetto Boy, when my mind started playin' tricks on me, thinkin' about my dead homie.

(*Pause*) . . . Flash forward to the present with the book I hold. God saved this soul, broke the devil's hold. No more contradiction, soul division.

(*Pause*) . . . Reflecting, dissecting my life: drugs, money, murder & mayhem, killing our people like the Son of Sam, just for the cause with every pause, I had sleepless nights, ignored *The Light*. Caught up, I fell into the hands of the Unrighteous. Been re-enlightened by the Righteous.

Was this all worth it? For my Moms to die with pain and hurt, for me to go from bad to worse, to break a generational curse, to be Spiritually Rebirthed. Heedin' to the scriptures of this book that comes first: the Basic Instructions Before Leaving Earth. Now, I finally see *The Light*, doin' 25 to Life behind prison bars.

LETTER TO MY SON
(Incarcerated in an Illinois State Prison)
Luis J. Rodriguez
(Chicago)

December 20, 2003

Dear Ramiro:

It's been seven years, *mijo*, seven years without your presence for holidays, birthdays, talks, hugs, and hanging out. Another seven years—if the Creator wills it—before you're released. With good time, that's fourteen years of a twenty-eight-year prison sentence. You'll be thirty-five then. Your three children will be in their teens, but you understand that. Despite all this, I've seen you mature in prison. I've seen you embrace your own conscious powers. I've seen you begin to understand the gifts of *palabra* and nobility that you've possessed to impact this world — although for the longest time those gifts and powers fueled a destructive life on Chicago's brutal streets.

Even in the cells of your ordeal, you've found the keys to your freedom, the innate dream of a child born into a man with society's misplaced judgment at your window. Look out now, son, the world is not all cruel.

The long fingers of a wanton life, from the ends of a twisted road, pull at us with the perfume of the streets and its myriad romances, all intoxicating, gripping at our skins, as the blasts of late night shoot-outs, the taste of a woman's wet neck in a dark alley, and the shatter of glass free us from the normal world, yet chaining us to the warped cement walks of our diminished existence.

The gang—the Nation—with its symbols, stances, hand signs, and language, so potent with meaning that many of us sacrificed everything, including our actual lives, to be held in its steely arms. I recall the barrio of my youth in L.A., the *clika*, the *carnales*— brothers in the flesh—that gathered all our religious upbringing, the street's passion, and our parents' own harrowing journeys through rivers, fences, cultures, and hatred to create the rush of the exhilarating genius of our rage. It's called *La Vida Loca* for a reason. It was crazy, the only way to live when the "sane" world is unbalanced and crazed at the root. In Chicago, the Nation was "insane"—you had to be just to be noticed, to be alive, to be dealt a different hand because all the good things, the polite things, the respectful gestures never got you anywhere. Be crazy and then people would see you—finally, they'd see you.

I run with you inside me entering layers of darkness, blankets of night, with accelerating thoughts in the velocity of the city's demands, constantly moving, but inside standing still, searching for words to cut through the nonsense, the screams around my ears, the pain of neglect and addictions, running with your voice in my throat, your calling of my name, your searching for father while I searched for mine, on your earth of many souls, craving the moon, the lunacy and warmth of these rocks covered in mud.

Maybe you got the prison sentence I should have gotten? I've thought of this many times. I escaped the long prison terms although I did the violence, drug use and robberies expected of my apprenticeship. The scars and tattoos testify to this. The pathologies don't go away. Neither do the addictions. I spent twenty-seven years on drugs and alcohol. I found my own prison, son, and now realize how it would help lead to yours. I'm in the sweat lodge with your name on my lips. I can take any heat the red-hot stones have to give—except when they say to me, "You should be there!" But I did my time. Society's gatekeepers may want more, but they don't know what they want. They imprison the body but not the spirit. And then there are those like me whose spirits have been caged while our bodies remain free. They don't know how this works, this giving, this taking, the reciprocity that Jesus named—the bottom will be the top, the top will be the bottom, the weak will rule, the poor in spirit will be strong. We're all blessed, even the sinners. You have to wake up to this truth.

Wake up, son. I slept for twenty-seven years. I dreamed I had a son. His name was Ramiro. He was a beautiful boy. He loved his father. He laughed and played and searched. I dreamed such a great boy. I woke up. And the nightmare of the reality told me I should be there.

The outlaw life, idealized, symbolized, even kids who've never truly lived are gangstas; it's in the rhymes, in the bass, in the rhythms from inside bouncing cars or yawning windows. Tattoos on faces—they're saying, you can't change this; you can't change me. Permanent pathology. But that's only the body. Inside the spirit sings a different song. Where's the place where people stop and listen to that song? Who will know these cries because they've languished here, too. The truth is we're all broken.

So you're "a danger to society," *mijo*, debris from the declining classes, a predator—that don't even begin to cover it. You're more and a lot less. There's no doubt you did what you did that cold winter day when you were twenty-one, when everything caved in on a moment of madness, when things quickly escalated from bad to worse to "fuck it all." A road rage incident—guns drawn, people shooting and shot, cars speeding down Chicago side streets. It got you three counts of attempted murder, including against two police officers. It almost got you forty years to life. But we had to fight that; it took us a year and a half but we stopped that noise. Although you shot the truck driver who had called you out, he lived. I apologized to him at your sentencing; he apologized for the long years they'd given you. That day you almost got killed yourself. But it wasn't "your time." That's what they say anyway: it just wasn't your time.

What regrets and longings must we carry, what clutch of inner fears forces our hand? What frenzy knocks on our door and then when we open it, darkness is swept in? Do we need more laws but less humanity? More punishment and less redemption? As Common asks, "High expectations but low patience?" Fear drives policy and then drives us from being human. It's time to understand, go open-eyed into ourselves, into our deepest fears, among our underground youth, into the futureless future, and then rise up. The time of sleeping is over.

Well, Ramiro, these are just some thoughts as you continue your isolation and years-long meditation. It's a long time to think. But, please, keep thinking. More people should do this, regardless of what side of the prison walls they're on. Heal, son, in a way that few can imagine. We'll be there. We won't let you go through this alone, although I've long ago told you this is your personal torment and challenge. The point is to get stronger, get smarter. We can help, but you have to get the teachings inherent in the circumstances. You have to take them to where they're supposed to go. Love is all we have. Love ties us together. Love is the bridge and the shore. We suffer for you being there, and I know you suffer being away from your family and children. But that's what love is—to suffer together. Let's just make sure it's the proper elegant suffering you must endure to find your path, your passions, your purpose.

Whether you're in prison or not—and as I said, we're all in some kind of prison—you still have to become vast in spirit, vast in art, vast in love.

The falling is so forceful, a gravity of soul to the bottom. The motion downward takes in reams of unwritten poetry, paintings with no canvases, notes without melodies. As a youth, I wanted somebody to stop me. To stop me from crumpling into the death surrounding me, the death that gives one life. I didn't seem to be able. Sometimes prison can work this way—most of the time it keeps you falling . . . further, deeper. The key to life is to have the words, the art and the songs as the barriers to all the great falls. Collapse into yourself; fold into the pages of your journals, into the chords in your head, into what your heart sees. Every other choice has a measure of death in it, so choosing your death seems empowering. Art, on the other hand, is about creativity, new breath and new birth. The only empowering course that resonates, that ripples, that takes on new shapes as it goes outward. Not down. Lateral to the rest of us. It took me a while, but I learned to fall sideways.

With Love—*Mexika Tiahui*,

Pops

LEAVING DEATH ROW
Reginald Sinclair Lewis
(#AY-2902, Death Row)

Fifteen years from home and I'm maxed out.
My stuff's all packed. Boxes bulge with
Tattered legal briefs and lost appeals
Stacks of tear-stained letters and the collection
Of haunting photographs of old girlfriends.

Can't leave without hollerin' at the homies
The brother with no TV gets my portable Zenith
The aspiring young rapper earned my radio
The George Jackson wannabe needs my books
And even though the old con downstairs
Ain't got but one leg left —
Let him have my scruffy old shoes
Because where I'm going I won't be needing them.

I went out like this and winged back
Plenty of times —
From the lush landscapes of day dreams
The deep blue infinity of madness
All the way from the last minute reprieve
Of the executioner's potion

One way or the other —
I'm leaving death row.

I AM/ I AM OUT
Rolando "Clever" Ortiz

Part 1. — I Am

I am the one pointing a gun at my enemies.
I am the one on the run from the cops.
I am the one on the late night news.
I am the one in the back of a squad car.
I am the one on the way to prison.
I am one of the 80% returning to prison.
I am the one caught up in prison politics.
I am the one to see a man in jail stabbed to death.
I am the one who hates prison.
I am the one who wants to change.
I am in no way returning here.
So why am I singing the same song
If I came for a second round.

Part 2.—I Am Out

Jr. high school dropout
drug dealing
good for nothing
Future cell living
watching your back 24/7 in here for 211s
And attempted 187 because of the way you live your life.
Stick to your own race or get a shank in the neck
When you're asked to ride
you ride like you've never ridden before
or get left behind so COs can put you on a gurney
And they could care less if you live or die.
Promise breaking parole
breaking on the run
a fool now
your life stays in the hands of twelve strangers
with two strikes and priors
. . . I'm out!

IV—THE POLITICS WE SEE

I have been bangin' all my life. Now, I'm bangin' for my People.
— Kalonji Jama Changa
(The Riot Starter from the revolutionary Hip Hop group, FTP)

The work and goal of the twenty-first century vote has been, and will continue to be, the education and mobilization of the African American voters, especially the youth. Whether the youth are aligned with the GDs (from Gangster Disciple to Growth and Development, or the Vice Lords or Stones or Crips or Bloods), my message is the same: Stay Focused and VOTE.
— Larry Hoover
(ex-gang leader [OG] of the Gangster Disciples, Chicago)

OLD LINES
Leila Steinberg

Old lines
on a young face
show signs of life
at an accelerated pace
define the stress
of the streets
& a pending case
a mind caged is a
terrible waste
blind to consequence
1 moves in haste

find a path or
lose your place
track your tears
trace 'em back
to the tragedy
both potent
& relevant

in my analogy
our shared reality
lives in my mentality
I trade places
in the casualty
at the hands
of my man's
brutality
I know
a black man's rage
& his insanity
& all the love behind the pain
that makes him hate
so passionately

I so tragically
pass the pain
2 my family
I had planned
to be the bridge
instead
was banished
because
belonging
means u can be
removed
and the loss
definitely costs
too much
such
that I
comprehend
an existence
more punishing
than death

that is why
I
like u
never rest
and the riddles
of an active mind
put comprehension
to the test
retention would b
best
if learning
didn't serve
and promote another's death

please manifest
yourself
into a new

existence
let the premonition
come to recognition
that our sum
is as great
as our
parts
and our possibility
is so much
greater
than just body
that our soul
exists Eternally
& infinitely
& thought
is as great
as our galaxy

sometimes
the brightest minds
are behind bars
blinded
because brilliance
misdirected
is lethal
so we attempt
2 contain them
as a way
2 save 'em
from criminal minds
2 criminal grinds
but the truth
about
beautiful minds
is u can't cage 'em
only disengage them

Did u ever think
words
would be the key
to the prize?
all u ever imagined
magnified
that language
would be your
liberty
and communication
would set u
free!

PARA LOS LATINOS Y FEDERICO GARCIA LORCA
Kent Foreman
(former member, Ace of Spades, Chicago)

. . . Well, welcome to the ghetto, Baby.
to the gesturing death
like the cancer
that terrorized gringos
and Lorca.
Bring with you your anger
on Saturday nights
and your beautiful children
their great eyes full of wonder
the hunger for learning
I understand.
Young man, with your outraged confusion
that smolders upon corners
go to the Walls
with your anguish!
Bear witness to sorrows
my fingernails screamed
in their bleedings.
To the Walls
where the prayers are scrawled

by the children
with spray cans
in coarse words.
To the Walls
where prayers are called
by the mothers
in sibilant Spanish.
Sleep on in the dungeons that tell of
that smell of the vomit of urchins
and derelicts
and rodents that nibble at infants

Welcome, friends!
Welcome to the roaches that molder like raisins
in repossessed pantries
then come you to hunt in the valleys
the alleys that glitter
the litter
of shattered amnesia containers.

Bring the young girls
who are ravishing women
so early
warm

To the Walls
of the tenement canyons
the outcasts deserted
bring them all
to the Walls
where I live.
I harbor but few harmless hatreds
Welcome, Baby
. . . welcome Home!

From the Gut
George Morillo a.k.a. Sen One
(The Fresh Five; La West Side Familia; Zulu Nation;
Black Panther Collective; Latin Kings; Netas)

Gangs, street organizations, crews, posses, political organizations—whatever names you choose to use to refer to any street group, the core reason for their existence is pretty much the same. The main purpose for the creation of a street gang/organization is to provide a base for what is missing in our lives, community, or in society as a whole. Most gangsters are products of what they see on TV, and because of that, Hip Hop and the gang life culture are being used to destroy us, instead of being used to move us to the next level.

True gang life is not a fad; it is a culture all in itself, a way of life, with its own laws, rules, and principles in place to guide us and to keep us in a certain behavior. Gang life, like everything else, has its good and bad elements. For me, the good outweighs the bad. Too bad that what I see today does not make me proud enough to say that I once belonged to a street gang, or a political organization for that matter.

One unforeseen tragedy in the gang lifestyle is that we spend a lifetime laying down our own demise, but I guess we would still do that anyway with or without gangs. Street gangs have to attack the source of their misery, not just what's in front of them, because every action has a reaction or consequence. We must learn to choose our actions carefully. If we continue to let our enemies divide us, they will continue to rule and conquer us.

Tattoo tears for all our Fallen Comrades. The struggle continues.

Introduction to Life
Malachi Daniels
(former member, Black Panther Collective, People Nation, Chicago)

As a slight introduction to life in its entirety
By the streets I was amazed and also raised so they inspire me
As I grew up I threw up liqas and gang signs to nickas

A ghetto game seeing who shoots quicka
And when I was small I knew shorties that didn't fear God at all
    at eleven
That's because heaven was about a million billion miles from here
But the neighborhood dope man was buyin' them new J's this year
Them displays new gear
And like them I was feignin' for a gleamin' diamond in my ear
But yea though I walk through the valley of a shadow of death
No evil will I fear
As the path of higher self becomes more clear
Now now now now
Instead of reaching for rocks I reach for stars
As my insight says, Malik, it ain't right to live life behind bars
But let me explain
We be lookin' for love in all the wrong places
Believin' the fake smiles on faces
And immitatin' the monsters that destroy races
But we betta leave them alone and deal with our own
Learn to build with our own
We'll know the race is won when we still with our own
So from a child to now peep how much I've grown
Now I understand that death and life is like man and wife
There can be no growth without strife or victory without challenge
The left and right make balance

ON THE LIFESTYLE OF GANG CULTURE
Rikoshey Ratchet a.k.a. OG Burner Blood

There are many misconceptions about what this lifestyle is about.
Some of us are well-educated, gainfully employed, and upwardly
mobile, but all of us are willing to sacrifice whatever we have to,
even our lives and freedom, to create a united movement amongst
the masses of the placated and stagnated People of the Black Nation
within the United States — a stolen country built and enriched and
drenched with the blood, sweat, and tears of our enslaved ancestors
who were never compensated, reparated, reimbursed, or restituted
for their 345 years of murderous wanton slaughter, genocide, all
sorts and forms of torture, rape, abduction, etc.

All problems have a history. Nothing happens in a vacuum! As Black Men, we are dealing with a 40–60 percent unemployment rate in every major city in the U.S., while Black Women's instances of unemployment are less than half that of Black Men. This directly corresponds with the 95–98 percent of Black People who were rendered "unemployed" by the end of the Civil War in 1865.

One important thing to note here is the fact that at this time in history Blacks had just come from under a set of specific laws that were particular to Blacks, the so-called "Black Codes." The Blue Dog Dixiecrats (mostly rich slave plantation owners in the South) and the Republicans (many of whom were Black before white folks began to abandon the Democratic Party, which opened up to Blacks after the Emancipation Proclamation was ratified and ended up becoming the New Republicans) worked together in setting up laws against such things as vagrancy (if you were homeless or didn't have $5, you'd be arrested, tried, and sentenced to go work on a chain gang).

After the Civil War, there were four million recently freed Africans with nowhere to live. So many lived their lives out as *new* slaves (known as *sharecroppers*) because this was better for them than death by starvation or exposure to the elements.

Sharecropping was used to create a Peonage system, which, in fact, was worse than slavery! It was worse because the "prisoners" oft times were worked to death. Plantation owners paid only a dollar a day for each body; during slavery, an owner would have to pay more than $500 for each body at the auction block.

At that time, white men outnumbered Black men in prisons more than three to one; conversely, today, Black men outnumber white men in prison six to one, even though more than 80 percent of all crimes in the U.S., including drug crimes, are committed by whites. The U.S. Constitution (Article 7; Amendment 13) states that slavery is legal for anyone convicted of a crime in the U.S. This is reflected today in the private prison industry and the contracting of manufacturing jobs to prisons. It is no wonder that while Blacks comprise only 13–15 percent of the total U.S. population, we represent 60–70 percent of the historically unprecedented 2.5 million U.S. prison population.

Our health issues have been ignored for more than 450 years here in the U.S.; only recently (since the 1960s) have about half of the Blacks in the U.S. been receiving any quality health care.

Today, in 2006, there are still about 45 million (mostly Black, Indigenous, and Latino) people without proper health care insurance. AIDS is running rampant in our cities and rural areas. The leading cause of death for Blacks, men and women, in the primary childbearing age group of 21 to 45, is AIDS. In fact, Black men are the most affected in 13 of the 15 disease categories that lead to death.

At the end of the Civil War, Blacks owned only .5 percent of the total land in the contiguous U.S., and today we collectively own only 1 percent (which is only a half of a percentage point gain in 140 years) while Black farmers are still losing acreage at a rate of 9,000 per year. All of these things, along with other very disconcerting statistical information, lead to a methodic and meticulous ethnic cleansing!

GANGBANGING THE AMERICAN WAY
Armen-Rah
(79th St. BGDN Boys Town Set)

Where all my thugs at with a nine millimeter Gat
On the attack can't wait to put a slug in your back
Wearing starter caps, beating up hippies with baseball bats
The sons of teachers and preachers afraid to face all of that
Drinking gin, beer, and Bacardi to chase all that
Vandalism ain't afraid to catch a case for all that
Influenced by *Goodfellas*, *Scarface*, and all that
How did it start, y'all? Let's come face to face with all that
Yo, who was the first to blast a fool over turf?
Who were the first gangbangers on earth?
Who was a thug since his date of birth?
The first to gangbang with religion in church
A thousand years before the Bloods and the Crips
The Knight's Templar had a gang and their sign was a crucifix
Murderers with the permission of their Lord, y'all
Cutting off heads, kids, their Uzi was a sword
Going toe to toe, fighting Turks and Moors
Blood fertilized the soil of Africa shore to shore
Islam and Christianity the origin of all gang wars

Jehovah Witnesses recruit for their gang door to door
A thousand years before these fools
The Romans gangstered Jerusalem from the Hebrews
They used spears to keep the Jews in line, not rifles
Till Jesus upset things with his gang, The Disciples
He upset their laws, rituals, and traditions
They didn't like it so they sent the Pharisees on a mission
They used propaganda to destroy Jesus' reputation
Because he had a prostitute named Mary in his organization
They said he was a warlock, said he was up to no good
Said he was a menace to the Jewish society and a thug in the 'hood
He gave wine to the Bloods, had Crips walking throughout the land
Until the Sadducees plotted at the caps program
They set him up for a 187
Because of his affiliation, he's now chilling in heaven
Before Snoop was a dog and P was a master
The master dog came from the cave, causing global disaster
With vengeance on his mind he was content to control the earth
This was evident when he bruised his brother's heel at birth
One of the first family Mafia wars started with Rachel
When two sons were battling within her womb prenatal
Or was it when Cain slew his brother Abel
Or Lucifer's jealousy because God made Adam so stable
See, gang wars are an international nation versus nation
The Bible and Quran are two books filled with gang confrontations
The father would assist his sons in every fight
He made the sun stand still so Joshua could defeat the Canaanites
What about Prophet Muhammad in the Battle of Uhud
In the 'hood where the original Black Stones stood
Back to back with the holy prophet against the gangsters in the
    quaresh
Well, the new Mecca is Chicago and Daley is the head of this mess
The same people who would tell you to love thy neighbor
Will condemn you to hell, if you don't accept Christ as your
    personal guide and savior
They didn't throw up the gang sign of the cross like the Catholics
Who, by the way, don't get along with the Protestants and
    Baptists
Who, by the way, don't get along with the Muslims
They say they read a Quran

Who, by the way, don't get along with each other because they are
Too busy fighting their own brother man
Warith Deen against the Minister, Sunni or Shiite
The Hebrews say all of y'all are wrong, you need to listen to the
    Levites
Some say A Salaam Alaikum, some say Shalom
Some say praise the Lord, baby, or just leave it alone
Some pray towards Mecca, some pray towards Jerusalem
With their hands up like Hebrews or make salot like Muslims
These are gang signs to the highest degree
The Lord could give a damn how you pray, just pray like us, see
From Iraq to Ireland, Rwanda to Kosovo
The end of the world is what we are getting closer to.

Original Garvey (OG)
Stic.man
(of Dead Prez, RBG, People's Army)

What is a gang? A gang is an organization
a formulation of riders with a common foundation
a nation, a tribe, unified by a common creed
dedicated, ready to bleed for what they believe
hard like the Mafia, but smart like Malcolm
only trues in the circle, squares unwelcomed

It's a comrade kinship, family friendship
when it's on, niggas swarm in an instant, on instinct
coordinated in sync with each other, same color
chain linked with ya brothers like in the hull of the slave ship

I let my bandana drip, for the Blood in my veins
for every Crip, we all one in the same
the daily struggle is the common bond we have
the police is the slob and the crab, the mob with a badge
they hate to see a squad of soldiers gang up
how the Bishops, Disciples, and Cobras came up

We turning this game up on you wimp ass busters
on the System, you got to be a pimp/slash/hustler
and to the young Gz that carry on the legacy.
show respect to the OGz 'cause that's ya history
the Sonny Carsons, Bunchy Carters, and Slausons
revolutionary but G'd in proportion
from the seed to the coffin,
putting in work, paying dues for the cause
staying true to the lawz.

KUN FIEYA KUN
Summer Hill Seven
(formerly with the Five Percent Nation)

Be and it is!
Kun fieya kun!

2 nuts away from you callin' me dad
now I'm bonin' ya sista—please don't be mad.

Don't rap much
but write it like such.

But when it gets real crazy
You please need just page me.

We don't roll with a click that
You can check with your physical;
Yes, my posse's invisible,
Yet my posse's more real than
You can steal with a digital.

The word is the power.
Kun fieya kun;
Be and it is.

I'll be there to elevate your soul
and through your mind reach ya.

I'll be there to elevate your soul
cuz I'm a poor righteous teacha

I want you to have life more abundantly
especially when you're alone — not listening to me.
Kun fieya kun:
The word is the power:
Be and it is.

When you listening to that tiny voice that says:
U ain't good enough —
I want you to look in the mirror
and assume a posture that's real rough,
Say: I'm whole and complete.
Daily snatching victory from the jaws of defeat!

What life means I'll decide right here — right now!
I'm getting my share of this world — I'll decide when and how!
All opposition must bow — right now,
Flee and retreat!

"Schweet! My neesy — yo!
That's easy — yo!
Why — because I said so!
Now Mountain move — go!"

Oh no!
Don't you dare deny
the power of your words to give life and bless.
Then listen and witness your destiny as you manifest!
The word is the power.
Kun fieya kun:
Be and it is!

2 nuts away from you callin' me dad
Now I'm bonin' ya sista — and she ain't mad.
40 acres and a mule, now that's a real joke
Spike's got fat stacks of green — yet he was born broke.
Don't look at the deficit in your bank account
Think about the defecation coming out of your mouth.

Kun fieya kun:
The word is the power.

"But I need loot, not a lecture or speech, sir!"
Well, go get your dough with what you now know.
cuz now you're a poor righteous teacher!

Don't do as I say or even as I do
Do as you say cuz that's what we all do.
Kun fieya kun:
The word is the power!
Be and it is:
The word is the power.
You didn't know!
Tell 'em, Brother Earl
They swine, throw 'em a pearl:
"The word is the power!
Poor Righteous Teacher."
The word is the power
Kun fieya kun
(That means be and it is!
True—for real that's Square Biz!)
Be and it is!

Now, my righteous teachers,
teach, don't become preachers.
Live—love, give—love!
The word is the power!

THE N WORD!
Kamal

"What's up, my nigga?"
was the term of endearment that he gave
I paused and looked around, like . . . you talking to me?
'cause, to me, a nigga is a modern day slave!
See, niggas is livin' in America with one foot in the devil's grave
but because you getting paid, nigga,

you think you got it made, nigga?
you think you got power 'cause you can pull a trigga, nigga
and kill your brothers and sistas, nigga.
'cause you irate and can show and prove that you can hate a nigga?

My father used to say, "The Black man is a coward,"
'cause he wanna act like a man
while real men are handling the affairs of the world.
Real men are trading diamonds, copper, gold, oil, steel, and uranium.
Real men are thinking long range
and manipulating the interest rates and the stock exchange
while niggas are playing games.
Niggas are playing games like "who shot ya?"
Niggas are playing games like, "who's darker?"
and who look like Beyonce and who look like Ms. Parker?
Who got the phatest prefabricated MTV crib?
Who got the fattest ass? Girl, what you mean?
You should be playing hopscotch—you only 13?
And whose pimpin' they ride?
Nigga, do you know what pimp mean?
Nigga, you bein' pimped by the establishment and the political
    machine.
Niggas are pimped by immigrant merchants in our 'hoods.
We got Arabs and Jews selling us swine, blunts, and cancer sticks
Koreans selling us Hip Hop clothes
and international niggas selling us what we put up our nose.
Parasites!
You ask them, "Yo, why you buy from these parasites?"
They be like, "Dog, it's all good! It's all gravy."

Niggas are being pimped by the army air force marines and navy.
Niggas are being pimped by the prison industrial complex
and you think pimpin' just got to do with money, cash hoes and
    sex?
Niggas need to study lessons
that Elijah, Malcolm, Louis, Clarence and them gave
and maybe niggas will realize that a nigga is a modern day slave!

POLITICAL POETRY
Rikoshey Ratchet

you're an immovable object; and i'm an unstoppable force
the cataclysmic upheaval will knock the earth's orbit off course
spinning, spinning out of control; on the event horizon of a black hole
like tyre on andromeda, i watch the debacle unfold
because the geometric rigors of retributive forces in the universe
    are cold
some a y'all haterazzi 'cause you hate everywhere you go
rest of y'all haternatti 'cause you hatin' on the low
we insurgent dissidents like the liberation front oromo
we protest the world bank, imf and wto
while puppet master billionaires and corporate ceos
pay off the politicians who orchestrate the fiascos
see mugabi in zimbabwe; fuck your quid pro quos
as a sport i was poor; as a loser i was sore
your status quo decorum is a bore
beat your ass with your protocol
you broke god's universal law
let's bring our past records to the fore
we the ethiopian and moorish kushites with isis black as nights
my people ascended to great heights; the asiatic black man owned
pangaea; in the beginning there were no whites
we built the first civilizations and wrote the oldest holy books
while your folks through history look like the point break crooks
vagabonds and marauders, pirates like captain hook,
sleaze balls and scuz buckets, give back everything you took
how you got the audacity to doubt my veracity
ya'll chester the molesters after 6-year-old chastity
prevaricator, americana is a menagerie
since this country's inception we've exposed the mendacity
from Africans to Asians, 900 years of traumatization
intergenerational reverberations; now examine the situations
people of color are facing; infant mortality rates in
our seeds need remediation; so ask the board of education
why schools that are caucasian get 3 times the money and legislation
then point out levels of graduation; slave wage jobs with no paid
    vacation
my peeps struggling: one meal from starvation

we subliminally trained for institutionalization
in the prison industrial complex nation
carnage and bloodshed will be the ramifications
if the rednecks and bluedogs don't give us our reparations
turn your white house red into one of total consternation
you're made in Lucifer's image; you're his personification
you a blue devil like duke; I'll block you like Antoine Jamison
i'm the 4th quarter go-to guy; i'll fill the stadium with elation
our championship history is our rock solid foundation
i'm the streets franchise player like the people's salvation
like uranium and plutonium, it's an explosive combination
so hold up and slow down 'cause this shit will have your heart racing.

GANGS R US
Word Engineer
(The Bloods of New York)

We are society's bastard child
overlooked
gate-kept
sanctioned
banned and abandoned
until we make noise
flash our toys
you see, we are watching
watching you clutch your bags
but our rags have the same value as yours
and if you look at our sores
you will see blood clotted
yet you'd rather us dearly departed from life
options — a gun or a knife
over turf
and for what it's worth
y'all are just the same
same shit different name
like Landlords and Owners
loan sharks and loaners
it's still a crime

and on earth we're doing time just like you
hate just like you
cry just like you
pray just like you
war just like you
like you are better
whether Swiss
American Cheese or Cheddar
we're chasing dreams
opposite ends of extremes
but no less than
and as long as there's oppression
we will set-trip to Heaven
for all have fallen short
we kill for rep
y'all kill for sport
for your crimes are Federal
for our 10 kills to your million
makes you a General!

BROOKLYN! DOWNED TOWN!
Joe PY a.k.a. Jose Irizarry

Brooklyn! Downed Town! Ghost Town!
Town of cold-hearted, gun-slinging, stick-swinging Marshall Dillons
roaming all around.
Roaming with cloaked, cloned dealings
for a multitude of natives going down in despair.
Natives! Both olive and brown,
suddenly being ghosted out from their own home grounds
from streets and corners once — now slowing growing theirs

Brooklyn! Downed Town! Ghost Town!
Space now combed and rented out right beyond our bite
While natives outpriced, stressed and tossed into a plight
that just don't seem right
a people unable to compete or fight the real fight
unable to see the split in we ain't right

Brooklyn! Downed Town! Ghost Town!
Turned on each other for a bite of pride —
a bite of something that's always in flight
while empty and caught, trying to survive —
chasing Illusions in a helpless plight
Don't we see we losing the fight —
Don't we see the split in we ain't right

Brooklyn! Downed Town! Ghost Town!
Full of cloned Marshall Dillons all around
Alien Ghosts occupying space out right beyond our sight
while the natives in plight fighting each other for a bite.

Where's God's Might in all this plight we fight
Were we always destined for this
Dissed for the carnal sin
of settling and trusting where we shouldn't have
given up homeland to foreign hands —
becoming have-nots in the sand
Living in Space — dignity erased —
Ghosted by a new bred master race
Doctrines Monroe and Manifest Destino in el Nido
where this side somehow their inheritance preordained

Oh when they get theirs — when they get theirs
when God comes down to Brooklyn Downed Town with theirs
wonder whose going upstairs
when God comes down to sort things here
right here at Brooklyn!
Downed Town! Town Ghosted of Olives and Browns!

BREAK YOUR CHAINS
Redstorm a.k.a. Dirty
(Gangster Disciple, Chicago, Eastside, 79th St.)

These chains I wear are a casualty of the game,
how quick things change chasing that transparent fame.
Got you locked up in your own flesh.

All my Folks plus narcotic smoke made life a joke,
plus you settled for less,
never knowing that you are blessed.
Never understanding you got a kingdom in your own soul,
never gaining the freedom that God knows,
mentally dead like a still-born child,
selling your soul, Homey,
for a big butt and a smile,
never realizing you're living life foul.
Out there strapped up against your own brother,
selling poison in the streets to your man's mother.
So where your head at?
You're walking dead black,
wake up and find yourself,
seek you a mirror and witness true wealth.

Break your chains . . .
Let your pain become your motivation to change.
Like two to the chest, your stress will never rest,
if you don't check yourself and save what's left,
break your chains 'cause it's life or death.
Stop thinking that when you open a bottle of beer,
you'll be like Billy Dee Williams
and some beautiful lady is going to magically appear.
See, it's all by design
to keep you hooked on a product and living a lie,
like Superfly . . .
Remember that late 70s hero,
a movie that promoted using and selling blow.
They called it Black Exploitation,
but I call it Black Degradation.
Just when cocaine started to hit the scene,
movie screens showed it like it was a cool thing
setting the stage for when the prices get cheaper
to introduce the Ghetto to the real Grim Reaper.
But that's just my view of the situation,
you've got to make your own interpretation.

Break your chains in your own way,
just don't waste another day.

Folks, I've wasted years,
my body and mind behind bars,
I watched my Mama die in there
and my heart is still scarred.
Watched my family go in different directions,
while I was on 79th Street with GDs searching for affection.
Never understanding the kingdom was in me,
not in some illusion manifested on TV.
I'm not a pimp, drug dealer or gangbanger,
just a spiritual being
created by a simple wave of God's finger.
A poet, a teacher and even a role model,
'cause I can definitely teach a lot of people
what path not to follow.

Folks, listen, whether you choose to believe or not,
if you do what you always did,
you're going to get what you always got.

So break your chains,
'cause after the knowledge has been given
you're the source of your own pain.
Find yourself and God will find you,
stop chasing Ghetto dreams that will never come true.

FEAR OF A BANDANA REPUBLIC
Malachi Daniels
(former member, Black Panther Collective, NYC)

My earliest years living in Bedford-Stuyvesant and Brownsville, Brooklyn, colored many of the beliefs that I still hold until this day. The basic tenets of street and family life seemed to shift and blend with each passing narcotics flood and repression tactic. The creeds and manifestos inhaled by ghetto children, like vapor, are absorbed through osmosis. The first rule: no one man is above the crew. So it goes in any family or tribe.

Urban warrior swagger and dark penetrating glares from beneath hooded jackets and fitted baseball caps were the armor of choice. Barricaded in the corners of America's great metropolises, we created culture from lack. We birthed expression from frustration and made a nation from nothing. It is these things that have earned us the envy and enmity of the world.

There are innumerable code words that politicians and media pundits have attached to African and Native youth in order to create patsies for almost every white fear and societal woe. Despite incidents such as the one that had occurred at Columbine High School, terms such as "youth violence" always translate as "non-white youth violence." We are also told that we should empathize with the young white perpetrators of their acts because they were "misunderstood." Suburban violence is painted with the broad stroked brush of "tragedy," while urban violence is shaded with primal descriptives, such as "wilding" and "rampaging."

There are those who would say that you are wholly responsible for your environment. These mouthpieces are usually in a position of affluence that makes shouting reactionary platitudes safer than concrete social analysis. The violence that takes place in the streets between crews is no doubt displaced. But what can never be overlooked is the African and Native attempts to reconstruct the familial in order to fortify what American colonialism and oppression has all but destroyed. The past 35 years have seen the American government's dismantling of the Italian Mafia through the RICO Act and COINTELPRO maneuvers. Although organized crime has claimed countless victims, historically the Italian Mafia served as the unofficial governing body of its community, meting out reward or punishment according to street codes and cultural standards of the time. And workers of all races can recall the days of Mafia-controlled unions in East Coast cities. My own mother is fond of saying, "At least the mob paid you on time." My mother's not a social scientist by any means, but I'd say her assessment was pretty sharp in this case.

Destroying the majority of the mob's infrastructure was a preliminary step in eliminating the competition and, more importantly, to further erode community sovereignty. The Harlems, Chinatowns and Little Italys of America must be destroyed because self-determination is no longer allowed. There is to be no confusion about who you and your family should turn to in times of need. All thoughts of self-reliance and street level organizing, whether legal or otherwise, are to be crushed. As a result of this design, the community as we knew it has been largely dismantled.

The American government and intelligence community has always served as supreme Godfather to organized crime. This being the case, there has always been a careful control of the tide of narcotics and disillusionment in African and Native communities. The drug surge can be most clearly observed whenever there's a great demand for social and political transformation. Critics have often said that we infiltrated our own neighborhoods with ships and planeloads of cellophane-wrapped cocaine and heroin. In truth, even at their most organized heights in the 1980s and early '90s, the Caribbean and Colombian street tribes were just foot soldiers in a "Drug War" against America's African and poor. This campaign has been the most protracted chemical war in the history of humanity.

In drawing these conclusions, we must also understand that the petty crimes that occur in our neighborhoods are the end result of unresolved contradictions of settler colonialism, white supremacy, and capitalism. What we are now witnessing with NAFTA, the World Bank, and IMF is the final consolidation of power and capital. In this final lockdown there can be no resistance by the masses on any level. What the street tribes represent is the last loosely organized armed resistance to final phase capitalism.

"Gangs," as they are termed, have always posed the greatest threat of becoming a true vanguard of the people—a group with no real ties to bourgeoisie thought or trappings—a set with no interest in wage slavery or institutional validation—an army with no allegiance to anyone but themselves and their beliefs. Given the right ideology and conditions, these gangs could become a wrench in the machine.

Finally, the gentrification and "population redistribution" that we are witnessing in our neighborhoods is happening all over the world. Indeed, what is local will become global and vice versa. Those who are committing thefts and acts of violence against this new, more affluent population usually belong to some kind of street tribe. We should never allow these incidents to be written off by the media as mere criminal acts. Our job is to use our own political and street level study to illustrate what is really taking place, because what is taking place is as plain as the lines in a grandmother's face. The sons and daughters of Africans and Natives are still to this very day resisting the colonial settler and slave master.

CAN YOU TAP INTO THE MENTALITY
Shannon Gross

Can you tap into the mentality:
"To protect and serve"
has many meanings in its reality
I know it helps, but I see the brutality
that's all around me
it's a daily occurrence
in my surroundings
while others find it profound
all they need to do is look around
from the Bronx to the Puget Sound
I know it doesn't take 41 rounds
to take an unarmed man down
19 shots ripped through Amadou Diallo
his murderers are free to walk around
I cried as they placed him in the ground
I can't blink, quicker than a wink
as fast as it's coming at me

Let me tell you about
Timothy Thomas
murdered in Cincinnati
shot down in an alley
where he took his last breaths
he was 19 years young
when they laid him to rest
another unarmed man
with a bullet riddled chest
murdered over 14 minor warrants

was it really that serious
about charges including
the lack of a seat belt
what did they tell his parents
a riot following was no coincidence

My screams are heartfelt
as I cry out for justice
for victims killed on an impulse
a criminal compulse
leaving victims with no pulse
like Crystal Grimes
shot by the chief of Tacoma 1 time
how many times
were there innocent crimes
erased like time reminded
claiming fear for their lives
as the reason why
the innocent were allowed to die

They were doing their job
when they pulled Tom Jones over
he was driving a car that was stolen!
It's a crime to take others'
hard earned belongings!
So they chose to teach him a lesson
59 blows in 28 seconds
I'm sure the 29th second was a blessing
to be scooped up
so they could clean up
the mess

Thomas Morgan, shot in Seattle,
had known mental illness
when a man can be raped
with a broom stick
and the offenders are acquitted
of all the pain and suffering
they inflicted

179

Put simply,
it makes me sick
more graphically, it makes
me want to vomit
over the atrocities committed

Equally, curiously, I wonder about
worried wives
sometimes innocently left widowesses
from other damsels' calls of distress
to their husbands who
vowed to protect
the innocent
and got caught up
in a situation that was
explosive
and the most they ever did
was stay dedicated
to protecting and serving
their communities
supporting unity
keeping the neighborhood
crime free
so we could
all have that
inner peace
from feeling
and knowing
you're semi-safe
in this crazy world
even if you forgot for
once to lock your door
he's the neighbor
you want next door

I try to empathize
with children
whose mothers lost their lives
in the line of duty
that's not a familiar feeling

but it's too real a shared feeling
by the 51 families
who lost a loved one in 2000

It's astounding
I don't know their names
stepping back I take a
long look and realize
I sympathize with both sides!

Everyone loses when
anyone innocent dies
even those guilty
sometimes
are only a product
of a previous victim
and a horrific crime
whose mind was
predestined to be a
genetically determined criminal
and who do we call when we need help
we call cops
who vow to protect and serve.

WHAT DO R.B.G. MEAN?

M1
(part of the revolutionary rap duo, Dead Prez)

What do R.B.G. Mean?
Red, Black, and Green,
We one team.
Struggling man versus machine.
Liberation Flag colors
Blood Brothers and Sistas, I'm witchu.
Marcus Garvey painted this picture
We rep that Bandana Style
Red, Black, and Army Green now
Dickie Suit down
Yellin' out Black Power!

BORN IDENTITY
Kalonji Jama Changa
(from the revolutionary Hip Hop group, FTP)

My words are laser guided missiles
That will pierce through ya' eardrums and rip ya' brain tissue
And reconstruct any unresolved issue
That you might have with me
That may cause you to stab at me
Don't touch or grab at me
The outcome could be mental or physical tragedy
As I step away casually
Ya' whole being and aura will disintegrate gradually
Writer's block could stop my flow
It doesn't have the authority
At the end of this poem
I will have more Sistahs stepping than a sorority

They say the majority rules
Now they putting cops in schools
Governor Roland cut education, now the teachers create fools
Break rules to be cool
Like a carpenter without tools
Useless
And the prison system is their residence
Truth is MCI made a billion dollars off collect calls
While mothers of Black babies shed tears
As their enslaved children lay in fear
These star spangled slaves saying let's support our troops over in Iraq
But who's gonna support our children
While the occupying armies are gunning us down for being Black
We are under attack

You could tell by the number of bodies these Gestapo pigs are bragging
While some cats in the 'hood on some Red, White, and Blue shit
False flaggin'-bangin' for a gang they ain't even down with
Rooting for a team of Klansmen
Our own demise we represent
We in the game but we on the wrong team
We need to rally round the flag on some Red, Black, and Green shit

What tickles me is when some liberal says
If you don't like it here, you should leave
But what's worse
Is my people was here first
And when you tamper on holy ground
Then man becomes cursed
I cripple concrete
A nightmare on Rhyme Street
Soon as the ink and line meet
The words my mouth secrete
Make you wanna rewind me
Or time me for the precision

Ring the alarm
Tell the children the Black Christ has risen!
Live and direct
That you might have with me not an abstract vision
From triple stages of darkness
Watch my light shine thru technicolor like a prism
Poetry's not a fad
When I pick up my pen and pad
Don't be mad
Nor take it personal if I insult you

You could tell by the words I speak
I'm a representative of my culture
And in and around my culture flies vultures
Vultures that scope ya'
With hopes to choke ya'
And they wait for the opportune time to attack
They come in all shades
From bloody redneck to house nigga black
Yes, even Black folks walk around comatose
With a overdose of global white supremacy
They full of shit like Colin Bowel
With criminal General Brooks tendencies

When I'm gone
I want the whole world to sip wine
Smoke a splif
And remember me
The riot starter
The man who escaped the matrix
With born identity.

GANGS
Abiodun Oyewole
(of The Last Poets)

I got to belong to something
To have something I ain't never had
I need a crew that can do
Whatever they want to do
A crew that be bad
I got to be a brick in this bitch
That breaks bones when I throw
I wanna be a part of runnin' shit
Wherever I go
You see I'm a real patriot
Flying on an eagle's back
Bootleg pimp extorts
And cancels you out like a bad check
America was a gangster killing for respect
You see it started back with Columbus
When they say he discovered this land
His disease-carrying crew
Tried to wipe out the Red Man
They gave diseases to the natives
And raped the women at will
Then they created a holiday called Thanksgiving
For the spiritually ill
Now they're the cops, the FBI and the CIA
And the little niggas in the street
Think they're the gangstas of today
It would be good if they cared and protected the 'hood

Like the Muslims and the Black Panthers
Looking out for us like they should
Then there's the Navy, Army, Air Force, and Marines
Being gangstas away from home
Destroyin' countries, taking lives
For the greedy pigs with hearts of stone
But it's just a matter of time
When all theses gangs will come to an end
And the world reborn will be made safe
For the real righteous women and men.

THE BROTHAS GUNNIN'
Commander
(Chicago)

Attention! Attention! This is NOT a test.
The injustices uncovered have erupted into social unrest.
The gangs are named for the innocent blood that's running.
The urban centers shut down because of the brothas gunnin'.
The governor's warning of such results fell on deaf ears.
The local cops were stopped, so the National Guards are here.
Whether day or night the gunshots take flight
while up, up in the sky ghetto birds engage for the fight.
The Folks and the Els are on one accord
In honor of Hoover. In honor of Ford.
Using war for pushing forward the Genocide UN Bill,
the nationalists unite for Karenga, Nkrumah, and Worrill.
The sounds from gats are sternly stating this fact:
No More Being Scapegoats For Political Maniacs.
With havoc and chaos raging throughout the city
the escorts for school children are few, if any.
In hostile terrain where truces have been strained
The armed clashes have officials asking that marshal law be
      proclaimed.
So after roars and flashes follow a projectile's burst,
ashes to ashes and dust to dust now thirst.

SinCity
(For Springfield, MA)
Jaime "Shaggy" Flores

Not your average
Municipality
A mob town
Managed by corrupt politicians
And cowardly community leaders
FBI monthly drug raids
And Drug Dealers
Yesterday's Channel 40
Evening News
Community award winning
Co-conspirators
South End
Godfather types
Playing God
With your future
Worthington Nightclub scams
And Baseball stadium shams
Your legend is infamous
Even beyond the shores
Of the mighty
Connecticut river.

SinCity
You got Solids
At High Street
Kings On the Main
Familia over in Jefferson
And Netas
In Franklin
And an army of
Disenfranchised youth
Flying cut sleeves
Real life Cartoon Gangs
With names like
X-men, Demonstrators, Whops, Playboys
Brothers of the Latin Race

And Guardian Angels
Warriors of yesterday
Killers of tomorrow
Creators of sorrow
Baby Makers
Death takers
Grim Reapers
And Soul keepers
Gunslingers
And Desperados
The West
In the Northeast
A Pioneer
In a valley
Covered with Black and Gold
Rosaries made of blood.

SinCity
How many have You claimed
In your rise to acclaim
When even the Big Apple
And Beantown
Turn their backs
On your killing fields
Where is your Soul
Kept By Downtown Political Thugs
and Poverty Pimps
Who Sell you at Harambee Bazaars
And Puerto Rican Cultural festivals
Greek Taste of the City
And Italian Fairs
Give yourself to the highest
Bidders
Turn your back on
The poor and penniless
Escape each summer
To public beachfront
Properties
On a polluted Connecticut riverfront
Crowded

By the Bilingual transients
And Gandara's
Mentally sane.

SinCity
We send You prayers
Wrapped in Voodoo rituals
And Holy Water
Let your Salvation
Come in the form
Of the youth
Let their innocence
Keep you from your
Daily Self-Destruction
Let the lives of those
That gave themselves
Give you purpose
Beyond your town lines
Bathe us
In your
Forgiveness
As we forgive
Those that dare
Trespass
Against you
Amen.

TUPAC
Ruby Dee

Tupac. Womb walked with
The warriors. The nation Builders who believed
They could make a difference who Made special rules who
Wore special hats who
Took special names who
Set up special schools who
Tried to feed some of the hungry Take responsibility
Take charge of their lives
Their communities.

Tupac. Came after
In aftermath
Tupac. Child of the self-made
Cut down warriors
Trails memories and sounds of
Death lessons tattooed in the
Buildings and in the foreheads of his Mamas and Daddies and
Big eyes swallowed some deep truths
Before brains got time to get in gear.
Grows up out loud
Sometimes wrong but searching.

Not knowing that the word's been out for years:
Okay. Grow up but quiet. Sing. Dance.
Do your weed.
C.E.O. it, even. Play ball.
But that revolution thing. We don't
Do that — no mo'.
Any number of ways to — like —
Get with it. Get over. Get down.
F — revolution. F — thinking.
Get yourself some money.
Get with a gang.
Be a star. Actor, rapper, athlete
Or the new town clown.
Revolutionaries don't get job security.
They compete with rats for cheese and
With strays for shelter after the
Big bullets make feet out of their knees.

Tupac.
Spelled backwards —
Caput. Meaning
Finished. Over. Ended. Done. Twenty-six was it?
Oh my God. So young
Mouths drop. Stop in
Unbelieving anguish and surprise And from dry eyes
Tears cascade inside.

UHURU
(a revolutionary carol)
M. Bonds a.k.a. Warrior Griot

black power
from the first to the 24th hour of each and every day
I wake up to speak
keep my soul dressed militantly
always thinking black, green

huey clothed and seated uncomfortably in these wicker chairs
mindset always black suited
pass the ammunition
like his mind
always cocked and
chairmen fred laced and
steel toed, thinking black booted

dr. khalid walking tall
looking like a malik zulu
still living in this concrete kenya with the cubs
and dubya-dubya-dubya.newblackpanther.comin'
for to carry assatas home
feeling exiled from bush country
skull and bones roasting on a pic-a-nigger fire
jim crow ripped up at his soul
revolutionary carols being sung by messiahs
black folk sheltered, fed, and clothed
everybody knows
them wickers make them guns and missiles blow
they're the reason why we fight

thugs, pimps, and gangstas got their dreams deferred
they're suited and booted now
armed and organized
for revolution come tonight
they know that satan is on top of his game
he's turning lots of boys in the hoodies into modern day slaves
and every bebe kid is gonna rise
to end his reign—dear mama, we ready to die

and so i'm offering this simple poem
to seeds from fetus to ancestors too
although we been bred to be psychological slaves
re-vo-lu-tion!

V—HARD LOVE

[L]ove is so desperately sought, and so cunningly avoided. Love takes off the masks that we fear we can't live without, and know we can't live within.

—James Baldwin
(author, *The Fire Next Time*)

WITHOUT PRETENSE

Jungle
(former member of the Kaos Crew, Bronx, NY)

Without pretense
I walk along your shadow
and introduce my foreground to your background
and in surround sound
auras blush childlike
while genuflecting to each other
we exchanged one part watercolor to two parts acrylic
to become fixtures in spirit
they can keep our leaves for we are rooted
irrespective of seasons and hormones
we keep growing
and bending
and breathing
and dressing
and breathing
and undressing
and breathing
and bearing
and bearing
and bearing fruit!

WHAT ARE WE HAVING

Anthony Graves a.k.a. Zoot
(member of the Killa Beez Crew)

"What are we having, doctor?"
"It's a girl!"

Da, da, da, da,
Daddy!
Farina and pampers . . .
Easy Bake and doll houses . . .

Cost of living turned baby
to latchkey kid
 . . . to crooked lipstick
 . . . uncles and lap-dances
 . . . cousins and finger-fucks
to innocence lost
at nine!

Escape to school numb
to get scraped knees and pulled hair
from jealous girls and precocious boys
missing teeth but still pretty
white stockings and patent leather
replaced by mini's mini and Gucci
Daddy's gone
and Mommy's here
but gone
eggshell rocks
purple haze and yellow submarines color pain

Mommy's boyfriend keeps landlords away
and bodegas in business
every nine months
every nine months
every nine months
until the pussy gets stale
and bruises look like makeup
"but that doesn't mean he doesn't love me"

Love equals pain
pain equals love and baby daddies
and final notices and hypodermics
and molars turned to dentures
and ex-boyfriends
 . . . turned cold-turkey then relapsed
half price on auction block
little girls for sale
souls for sale
da, da, da,
daddy!

Missing teeth and no longer pretty
daddy's gone
and never was
and never was
and never was there!

DANGEROUSLY IN LOVE
Philip Muhammad a.k.a. Senistar
(founder, God's Water Entertainment)

She thought about it
What is this?
He knew about it and already mastered it
She fell into the deepest romance with her wings up high
She lost her phone book and she kindly lost her mind
Her friends would call, "What's up, girl? Call me," and leave a
    message
They heard it on the streets and they never suspected
All of the sudden she appears with her new look
And a bold kick in her speech and a pink pocket book
Corsica's gone, and she's writing her own checks
Driving a new Lexus convertible and losing her good friends'
    respect
Her back is at the wall; her legs aren't secure
For her mind is at war and her gifts continue to pour
Kisses of a Drug Dealer; they fascinate her mind
A downward incline proven in scars soon to find
For her days have been shortened, and soon she will see
Why when some people get open, others always flee
Her hair is not done today, the side of her face in pain
She just got introduced to the sphere called the Hoe & Pimp Game.
Dangerously in love!

DANCIN' AT THE PRINTZ GRILLE
Alicia Benjamin-Samuels
(Wilmington, Delaware)

Israel just got out of Riker's Island,
wearin' a cross around his neck.
"God is the only man I fear," he says,

throwin' up his Brooklyn sign
wantin' me to be his savior
lead him to eternity.

"Be my lady,
Have my babies."

"Brother, you don't even know me."

"But I like what I see."

We dance and flirt with a dream —
Stompin' out the blues at the Printz Grille.

I want to pick him up
dust him off,
give him the Fruit of Islam.

The Egyptian sun rises in this Brooklyn Prince.
He's not the gangsta he pretends to be.
His smile gives him away.

His eyes dance hope
across my body.

SHE'S JUST MODELING
Philip Muhammad a.k.a. Senistar

She's Just Modeling! Naked? What, she's not? Naked, news or
    what?
The children look on at the ad in the paper
And wonder why She Is Naked
Smiling with no shame, hair done, lips painted
Destroyed is our world, and removed from civilization
A model, for what, in this sickened and rebellious nation?
She's NAKED, dressed in just a bra and panties
She's NAKED, say she's a model, but for whom but life's enemy!
The bottom line is that the woman has suffered
'cause if she wakes up, she'll request to be covered
Soon she will, soon she will, and without a pill
But the dosage of love is the strongest of wills.
"She's just Modeling, She's just Modeling," is what faggots say.
She's just Modeling, leave her alone," he only wants to get paid.

EYES OPEN WIDE
Redstorm a.k.a. Dirty Red
(GDN, Chicago, 79th St.)

Ever since my debut I've been inspired to give you
nothing but bloody raw knowledge
that you'd never find in some snobby ass College
unless they invite me
to give you straight heat
so clear a classroom for my street niggas to meet.

See, I'm trying to reach my people in the gutter
and every incarcerated brother
all the homeless in the winter time searching for cover.
That's who we need to think about.
I've been selfish much too long
it's time to help somebody else out.
My experiences make me a scholar

and it opens my ears to the victims who still holla,
victims like me.
I was caught in that same cycle too blind to see.
Can't nobody stop me on earth
some doing nothing.

Once you get up off them corners
and put your mind to something
the results you get will rearrange
no longer a peasant in the game
people respecting you now 'cause your attitude changed.
Done peeped now that talk is cheap now,
if you can't back up your talk with your walk
that's a conversation you can keep now.

The streets don't have nothing for you, Shorty,
nothing but a history of misery,
and I'm writing this realness hoping you feeling me.
The streets are wicked, sick and twisted,
they'll make thousands in front of your house
and watch you get evicted.

Set your mind to something real,
leave those streets alone before you get killed.
I'm living proof you can do it,
streets have taken me to rock bottom twice
now I just refuse to go through it.

INSIDE OUT
Monte Smith a.k.a. Super Tramp

Every member of my family has been locked up.
The educational process of scare tactics,
dehumanization and rehabilitation
quickly suffocated the innocence of six plus six.
These non-curriculum classes began after my Pops,
who by trade ran drugs, split

leaving my now mannequin of a mother
to fend for my sister and me.
He left us in one of those broken-down motels
you see littering rural highways and forgotten
neighborhoods the police would rather bomb than patrol.

With no transportation or immediate options,
Moms started writing bad checks to keep fast food
on the single, spring-exposed mattress
that somehow slept three,
until the night of June 15th 1983.

That night I traded in the fun of
hide-and-seek for the horror
of hiding in the bathtub, asking Momma,
"Is that the Boogey Man at the door?"
No matter how old I get, I still can't shake
the sounds of police rushing in.
Guns drawn, voices screaming,
"Everybody get the fuck down!"

I had never seen a gun, much less
had one shoved in my face.
How can a so-called trained officer of the law
hold his service revolver at the head of a child?
And Bush is telling me Iraq is wild.
Say word.

They led my mother out of the room into a
crowded parking lot to wait for a back-up cruiser.
She stood there for 15 minutes in her panties and handcuffs.
No clothes
No sheet.

Years later, she told me the officers
pulled in a McDonald's drive-through
just to add to the humiliation.
She served six weeks.

So you see, kids, my Boogey Man is the police man.
His abuse of the law has left me in and out of
mental institutions since I was 8.
When I arrived back at school later that year
Officer Friendly came to class one day
and needless to say
I stabbed him.

PROGRESS
Lonna Kingsbury

His red bandana served him well
catching up the blinding sweat
covering his nostrils
when winds came down so hard

He loved this life
his horse
his herd
forever cattle drives
sweet mystery of falling stars
surviving closest calls

His old harmonic
kept him sane
repeating songs he knew
where nights went on forever
and he slept all alone

His red bandana served him well
identifying turf
displaying colors proudly kept
when winds came down so hard

He hated life
his crib
his need

forever pushing more
remembering his fallen friends
he kept his head cock-sure

His throbbing music
ebbed away
beating with his pulse
nightfall covering his corpse
and he slept all alone.

THE DINNER
Lonna Kingsbury

BAM! the plate went
SLAM! the hand went
Better not react
no expression
eyes held downcast
maybe it will pass
before it gets real crazy
or maybe he will laugh
studying how quiet
the little egghead sat

Don't just sit there staring
you'd better eat your food
Breathing quickly, Thank You, God,
it could have been much worse
and what do you call this stuff,
something for a dog?
Crash! the chair went
Bash! the bowl went
thickening the wall.

FAMILY TIES
Carl Palmer

I love you, Daddy.
Sissy and I both love you.
Sissy didn't mean to be so loud.
I tried to get her to hush
but the tape was pulling her hair
and the plastic wire ties were much too tight.

Mrs. Temple's dog heard Sissy crying
and wouldn't stop barking at our garage door.
When Mrs. Temple came to fetch Queenie,
she heard Sissy crying, too.

She said she'd go get help.
I tried to tell her not to, Daddy,
but Mother had put tape on my mouth, too.
Mrs. Temple couldn't understand my screams.
I'm sorry, Daddy.
Sissy and I will miss you,
and we'll miss Mother, too.

UNTITLED
Amir Sulaiman
(of The Last Poets)

I wish I could just tell him that I love him
I wish I could tell them that we love them
but how could he believe me
when they are caught between
their enemies' prison systems
and their own families' criticisms
no one to council nor console
where does a young tortured soul find its home
where they are molested for being young
and punished for gettin' grown

our love for them is so conditional
our love for them is too conditional
but their condition is not conducive to our condemnation
picking at their faults like vultures
consuming the scattered leftovers once the beast has had his fill
our sons emasculated
and consequently overcompensating
and unbeknownst to them they are just waiting
for you to say, "I love you,"
not, "I love you, but . . ."
not, "I'd love you if . . ."

When love is missed
love turns to myth
why break your own heart waiting
on a myth
why break your heart waiting
for something that doesn't exist
our love for them is so conditional
our love for them is too conditional
I wish I could just tell him that I love him.

HOME STREET HOME
Dasun Allah
(DX 21)

Here is where cash is the golden calf
where a bloodbath makes children laugh

Where rats run like taxicabs down Fifth Ave
and the old lady's purse is a grab-bag

Young men pass green leaf
like Indian chiefs in a tipi
Train track Jack got smacked
now he's nodding back looking sleepy
This is Babylon!
The writing on the wall is called graffiti

Bad apples scream out to be bitten
A black alley cat
rummages through a garbage sack
to feed her kitten
Black, brown, and yellow with a smidgen
of red was its description
The smells of peppers, perspiration, and pork
drift out the window of a kitchen.

Vampires suck green blood after they walk a mile in
someone else's shoes and their bank accounts are smiling
The avenue's merchant crews make it look like Ellis Island

I'm profiling, as if I were a mug shot
Metaphors, similes, and melodies spread like buckshot
from the radio sitting on the stoop blasting Hip Hop
Middle finger with an itch to flick
at a rednecked boy-in-blue prick hick cop

Watch the children
leap over streams of urine
looking like melted butter as it runs towards the gutter
Instead of a shutter on her window, she has a sheet
on Sunday morning she'll go to church and be a sheep
waiting for the shepherd to arrive in his tricked-out Cadillac jeep
so he can pass around a plate from which no one can eat
Sometimes I find myself wallowing—it gets waist deep

But this is heaven, so I can bear my load
the pearly gates are the doors to my humble abode
and beneath all that trash . . .
every street is paved with gold!

ENGLISH ONLY SPOKEN HERE!
Roxanne Marie Pluas Hoffman

Veering to steer clear of my peers.
Muy Macho Muchachos! Latino blood brothers

carting boom boxes, Budweisers, and blades,
hooded in black satin fight jackets,
alcohol-breathing White Dragons emblazed,
backed up against the schoolyard chain link fence,
wielding clouded red eyes, wild and intense,
sneering and jeering at La Gringa Loca as she skirts by.
Giving her the finger, giving her the eye.

A crucifixed and medallioned battalion, swinging hips and bike
    chains,
they hang with squads of hops scotching,
bazooka popping, pony-tailed babes
bopping to the non-stop beat of Caribbean Conga waves.
Cuidado con la chica muy bonita! Watch the pretty mama!
(with the razors tucked in her braids!)
"Fea! Fea!" they cluck, "Ella es muy stuck up."
What a bunch of shmucks!

Another generation of already-boozing, soon-to-be using losers
I choose not to be confused with,
I say under my breath as I duck.
Not even twelve years old and already fucked.
Already up-chucked like stinky pink vomit onto mean city streets.
How long do you figure till you find one of these Latin Lovers
shot up face down on the concrete?
or his smart-mouthed eyebrow-plucked sista sucking dicks
turning tricks for her next fix of sweeter than candy pop treats?

Can these peers really have the power to persuade
me to live life on the edge of a razor blade?
Talking big, acting tough like they've got it made?
Getting ready to rumble, planning payback for a fellow Dragon
    filleted?
Can these peers really have the power to persuade
me to live life on the edge of a razor blade?
With one eye looking over that chip on the shoulder,
making out like they ain't afraid?
Can these peers really have the power to persuade
me to live life on the edge of a razor blade?

Thinner than the worn-down knees of my too-tight corduroy jeans
stretched out to last another year by letting out the hem,
extended with rows of rainbow striped ribbon Momma stitched
    onto them.

Thinner than the pancake flat heels
of Big Sister's too big hand-me-down shoes
or the toes of the white tube socks I double-up inside
to keep them from coming loose.

Thinner than the American cheese sandwich in my Barbie
    lunchbox
or the sweet pickle slices Momma tucks into the soft white bread
in her efforts to make sure I'm nourished and well fed.
Thinner than the postcards tacked to the walls of the doorless room
I share with Big Sis.
Picture postcards of parrots and condors and llamas from a tropical
    paradise
I've never been to yet miss. Ultra thin. Ultra sharp.
Like the pain in Momma's voice, hoarse from raging
against another winter without enough heat
and enough meat to keep us warm,
arguing with landlords and shopkeepers that cheat
and bill collectors and turn-off notices that
warn that soon they will have no choice but to cut us off.

Sharper than the pain in my gut
after throwing up a steady diet of Chiclets, Cheese Doodles,
Ring Dings, chicken wings, Twinkies, frozen pizza,
Sabrett hot dogs, and pistachio nuts
washed down with Kool-Aid, café Negro,
Alka Seltzer, and Hi-C Hawaiian Fruit Punch.

Sharper than the pain in my chest
after coughing up blood from smoking
back-to-back packs of Marlboro Reds.

Thinner and sharper than the line
Momma draws in the quicksand
between me and my peers

when she says,
"English Only Spoken Here! We speak English only here!"

Like the belt strap she swings when I forget and cross that line,
but I don't ever forget who I am nor the Latino Heritage that is
    mine!
Inside my gringa skin beats the wings of an Ecuadorian,
like the condor who soars over Amazon valley and Andean
    mountain,
I see it all. I take it all in.

And though I may rise above where I have been,
I keep these childhood memories tucked within:
of Momma packing me off to school with a sandwich and a kiss,
of the late night conversations and lingering longings I shared
    with Big Sis,
of a country and a culture our momma had dismissed,
of a people, Latino blood brothers and salsa sisters I loved and
    could not resist.
Me llamo Roxanna. I am Roxanne.
Soy Americana-Ecuadoriana. Forever Hispanic.
Forever Hispanic-American.
Forever White Dragon . . .
Cuidado con la chica muy bonita! Watch the pretty mama!
(With the razors tucked in her braids!)

IN THE NAME OF LOVE
Cierra M. Robinson

Here's a real life scene
which unfortunately goes unseen
the way a picture develops
in the crevices of a darkroom in photography
what's kept under wraps
like the mummy of ancient Egyptian history
that lies in the backs of books
so deep you couldn't dig it out with a treasure map

This is how the story unfolds
the way I was told
and the unfortunate facts I now uphold

Maybe her heart's too soft to say no
or she just don't know how to let go
but still I relay my opinion in hopes
she may grip it
and maybe not now but later run with it

I'm handing her clues like *Wheel of Fortune*
tossin' her vowels and the ABC's
of the way relationships ought to be
but she can't seem to see
the way he's damaging her inner being
playing with her mind like a game of Monopoly
as he jumps from female to female
making her a prisoner in a jail
created because she loved the wrong kind
who's daily on the grind
grinding all of womankind
trying to undermine her intellect
thinking he's just so slick
borrowing the car
to slip and slide in someone else's cootie cat
while she patiently waits for his return
so he can do the same thing to her
disrespectin' 'cause ain't no respect in her face
not in her place

So over and over
multiple times
he'll utilize
her body like a toy
doing as he pleases then walking out the door
careless without protection
nonchalantly having no knowledge of the direction
they could unfortunately be headed for
adding to another kid in her collection

In the meantime
predicaments, like annoying childlike nagging,
keep on intervening
revealing the truth
that's illegal to sell
but still she's so blind to what's right in her sight
letting him hit her night after night
or in broad daylight
without resistance
or a minute to use his common sense

Her common sense slips
and she forgets a woman's worth
her worth
how far she should let it go
all in the name of so-called love.

VISITING DAY AT ELMWOOD
Scorpiana X

I look at you through the glass
orange was never your color
your voice, static on the phone
as you talk the bullshit of possibilities

Orange was never your color
I picture you in your red Pendelton
as you talk the bullshit of possibilities
like this time is gonna be new

I picture you in your red Pendelton
as you say you will go to school, find work
like this time is gonna be new
but things always look different locked up

You say you will go to school, find work
quit leading la vida loca
but things look different locked up
outside, temptation owns your ass

"Quit leading la vida loca."
So now you're giving me advice
outside, temptation owns your ass
inside, your ass is all mine

You try to give me advice
asking for promises we can't keep
inside, your ass is all mine
and I think I like you better in here

Asking for promises we can't keep
your voice static on the phone
I think I like you better in here
as I look at you through the glass.

GHETTO HAIKUS
Hamza Atoi a.k.a. Beast

1. Roaches

Cockroach on my wall
stands waiting with his homeboyz
for insect drive bys

2. Food Stamps

Food stamp lines slither
as the hungry children wait
for chicharones

3. Shorty

Shorty is smiling
he got out of jail today
ready to raise hell

4. Weed

Fat azz blunt rolled tight
urbanized inhalation
peace comes in 3 hits

5. Drive By

Rat-a-tat-tat-tat
glass shatters and homegirls scream
exterminated

6. Why

Playing the man's game
for drugs, sex, and welfare checks
is this why we live?

7. Puta

Shygirl used at night
like a dirty bandana
by boys playing men

8. Homegirl

Lala had 3 kids
before she turned twenty-one
aged before her time

9. Crack

John sells drugs from home
to pay for his own habit
last night overdosed

10. Norteno

Red rag on forehead
he says it is por vida
in dreams of muerte

11. Warrant

The cops came for you
badges flashing destruction
run Miguelito

12. Santa Clara St.

Streets dressed in garbage
gray smile under the debris
its beauty silent

DEGREE OF SEPARATION (PART 2)
Karla "FyreMouff" Armour

I remember you.
Indian Summer.
Warm and sunny.
First day of fifth grade.
New school.
1980. September.

3:15 bell.
Menacing smile.
Frightening chase.
Spot singing
my name
like that!
Bully

personally
assigned
to me.

Moon runs.
Day catches her.
Bus stop.
I avoid your eyes.
A twig snaps
in the dark.
Quiet, adolescent
urgency calls my name.

College. The street.
Separate paths to
the same hard lessons.
Forbidden fruit is a
Newport-n-alcohol
flavored first kiss.

You're nothing that
I should want but
everything I need.
In my bed, your goatee
tickles my ear with
drowsy promises.

Love's imperfection
is flawless beauty.
Ugliness lies in action.
Sick of models.
Tired of foolishness.
I leave.

Telepathic phone calls.
Apologies. Pleading.
Your insistence.
My refusal.
I wasn't mad.
Just stubborn.

A gun.
A bullet.
A funeral.
An eternity.
Living for nightfall,
hoping to find you
in my dreams.
Do you miss me
on December 30th?

Seven years of solitude.
Faithful to your ghost.
I don't think that anyone
will ever love me
that much again.
I don't think that I
will ever love anyone
that much again.
My pain threshold
is too low.

Cutting my hair
does not shave time
off the grieving process.
Changing the color
does not alter my being
me losing you.

Transitions are
a spiritual choice.
So, you let go of me.
I tried to put you away.
Just in case.
It's time now.
So, on three,
I'll let go.

TRIBUTE
Chantay "Legacy" Leonard

I don't want to remember gun blast blues
or misty chronic memories
that shimmer in the pool of lost souls at my feet

These words shall be as passages from the Book of the Dead
for these are the names that shall never be written in the Book of Life
countless rubies encased in the crystal dripping from my cheeks
streak the broken concrete
where metallic shells once rang
leaving rotting shells of once warm, breathing bodies

One I called a friend
My brother, my sister
One until the world blows
taking me on wings of heart
to Ragtown
bury my pitchforks up in Gangster City
'cause I was down for you
true blue
kept that Love, Life, Loyalty close to my heart
like these thoughts of you
that beat on the barriers
I have erected against the furious flood
of memories that forces its flow through my brain canals
until I cry out in anguish
fall to my knees
your names slipping softly from my lips
as the tears rise in my chest
phantom faces float above my head
asking the question that I could never answer
the one God only answers with silence

"Why?
Why did we have to be the ones to die?"
I thought God respected these blue and black flags
that represented the struggle of the Black woman and man

We were a nation
developed from Gangster Disciple to Godly Divine
but I guess the yellow brick road don't exist
and I damn sure know King David isn't greeting us with open arms
at the pearly gates of Gangsta's Paradise
'cause that don't exist either
just the hell of awakening each morning
drenched in sweat
pillow soaked in tears
from missing those wind blown days so much

I never knew joy until
I sipped 5 o'clock in the frigid morning air at 7:00 am with you
or when the tendrils of blunt smoke curled up
and choked us in the heat of a Highland Park attic
while Pac crooned he'd Rather Be My Nigga
and we all swore that was a pink elephant
gliding across the McKenzie baseball field

I never knew joy until the night we stood outside and cried together
swearing it was just the rain running down our faces
I never knew joy until we made love to the vocals of Makaveli
you crowned me your thug missy
even from the day you were locked down
and we learned to make love through pen and paper

I never knew joy until I dragged you
from over the highway of self-destruction
even as I dangled one breath from Death
but you were my cousin
and we would hold it down for one more day

I never knew joy until the night our souls touched
for one moment
danced our bodies to the rhythm of love in the midst of our storm
knowing we would never be together,
but in the spirit we shall be one forever

I never knew joy until the day we united in arms
battling under the sharp rays of sunshine

fought in the darkness of gray alleyways
knowing even if we died in the struggle
it would be together

I never knew that this joy existed in those days of my youth
where a sip of gin
and a surge of violence
were the only reasons for my existence
until I opened my eyes
realizing that you all are gone now
materialized into the faded tapestry of my memory

Your flesh, your blood
are my flesh, my blood
your voices are as real to me
as the yesterdays we once shared
but I am a new woman now
no more Gangster Queen
I am politically correct now
corporately connected now
consciousness erected now
2000 seasons removed from the barren plains
where we once communed

Now I let go
remembering the G. I once was
still such a prevalent part of me
I could never bury this Conflict
that threatens to explode
every time I try to repress and fold
the reality of who she is
into the depths of Legacy
I am more woman now than the physical eye could envision
because of you

Now my third eye opens wide and sheds tears
as I pay tribute to those who taught me joy
yet the Book of Life will never know your names
so let this be as a passage quoted from the Book of the Dead
my silent tribute to the shadow souls of yesterday.

ELEGY: IN HOT PURSUIT
Louis Reyes Rivera
(former Marcy Chaplain, Brooklyn)

It could have happened
that the one we gather round
to bid this last goodnight
had been sunk or drowned
shot or lynched
or beaten down with baseball bats
& tree limbs splintered
chased onto a speeding highway
lurking with the stench of liturgies & last
rites ramming straight into the racist hoods
of windshields left for dead.

What can matter more
than seed rooted in the ground?

It could have happened
that a massive stroke
unwrenched this heart
of muscle tremble stomach pain
the thousand things we eat
from spray plane fields
of gnats & worms
chemically preserved
like butterflies & lizards
burnt into budding leaves
of wheat & corn
packaged & dis-served
on store stocked shelves of
 gimme
 gimme
 gimme profit margin range
bursting vessels shredding veins
like tumors spreading through a brain.

But matter more is breathing carbon
oxygating lungs in plants & trees
greening from the gleaming rays
of moonlit days sunning into night.

The things we may not pay much 'tention to:
each lifelong sense of birth & possibility
hunted down & crushed as easily as
a case of aids spreading sperm
    saliva's turn
    rock back
    stones thrown
against blood transfused
like manhood wasted misillusion
that never tamed the open scope
of life held dear/
    mobs of fists
    swat teamed guns
    drunken driving
    sniffing coke
    a doctor lame
a scalpel in his hand
claiming probe to test just how
quickly we can die
. . . be buried in an earth
that's half as hard
as these bones here now resting
while we who mourn our loss
must mourn ourselves
for the havoc we permit
in hot pursuit against
the pulsing breath of flesh alive.

VI—NEW LEAVES TURNING

Respect is the key to unity.

—Bmoredamu
(member of the Bloods)

Honor pa la gente—Poder pa' los reyes es que amor de reyes y amor de reynas
es como el cielo y el infierno . . . Intocable y immortal.
(Honor to the People—Power to the Kings: that the love we give to King
and Queens is like heaven and hell . . . Untouchable and immortal!)

—El Don Raul Juan
(Latin King from the 5TG in Switzerland)

They rather me have an UZI than a microphone.

—Mumia Abu-Jamal
(activist, author, former Black
Panther, political prisoner)

We are an organization of members who help each other grow.
We are gang members who still have a voice.
For those who will listen, we do have a message.

—from a wall mural of Memorial
Unit II, Bridgeport, Connecticut
Community Correctional Center

WHAT IS A GANG?
Shaka B. Shakur a.k.a. Sherrod DuBois

According to Webster's definition, it is as follows—a gang is a group of people associated or working together. Webster's also states that a gang is a group of people associated with some criminal activity.

Looking at current news stories, it is obvious that the lure of the so-called gangs is alive and well, but my question to the masses is that perhaps there is something to be learned from gangs. What if the very culture we seem to down is the only place that the youth find the one thing that seems to be missing from our communities. The thing nations are built from. The thing that makes all things grow. That thing is love and purpose. Some might ask, what kind of love and purpose can be found in these organizations?

Well, in a society where we isolate our own and make them outcasts, it is only natural for these souls to look to one another for acceptance. Hence, creating a gang. In this article, I hope to show a different view of the so-called gangs.

The standards for viewing so-called gangs are as two sided as Webster's definition. On the one hand, we as a society condemn these gangs; on the other, we turn around and make movies about them and even go as far as to give them awards and hail them as a historic part of this nation's history. Exactly what are we trying to say? Do we expect kids not to follow what we place in front of them? Will we continue to hide the truth behind the gangs?

There is a direct connection between gangs and past and present revolutionary movements. There is also a direct attempt to cut off the youth from that connection by forces that prosper off our destruction. The rivalry that has fueled so-called street gangs contributes to the ongoing genocide of our people. It appears as a well-thought-out plan by this government in its attempt to further divide, conquer, and oppress us as a people.

While researching the nation's so-called gang list, I once saw organizations such as the Black Panther Party, the Five Percent Nation, the Zulu Nation, and the Young Lords Party listed. These were groups that did nothing more than to help give direction to the people at a time when it was needed most. The Black Panther Party alone created many programs to benefit the masses. Most of all, it gave inspiration to many inner city youth and became the pathway to the formation of many of the same organizations that we view as criminal today. The Black Panthers further inspired the politics and principles needed to revolutionize many other so-called gangs, such as the Young Patriots in Chicago and the Young Lords in New York, along with several others around the country (like the Brown Berets).

As this new sense of self-determination began to grow, so did a full sense of unity, as well as the efforts of various government agencies to destroy it. We all know about COINTELPRO's [Counter Intelligence Program] efforts to destroy the more political groups, but it did not stop there, and it has continued to this very day. It is no mistake that most of the original leadership of many street organizations have either been killed or jailed in a calculated attempt to disconnect the head from the body and to feed the youth false information, henceforth creating the seed of disunity we deal with. The transporting of weapons and drugs to the inner cities of this country is all part of a continuing plot to ensure that these organizations will always produce negativity and destruction. This, in turn, helps to eliminate all hope of self-determination among Peoples of Color and guarantees that they never become a threat.

Don't get me wrong. I hate to see the level of self-hate perpetrated by these so-called gangs. It hurts my soul when I read about another young life lost in this war; however, I see the potential for what could be the very thing that could give inspiration back to the masses, if we embrace it and give it the direction it needs.

I like to look at things from a very clear and down-to-earth view. The bottom line is if street gangs were to realize the strength and numbers they have and their actual ability to fully control the very streets they live and die on, we would see the birth of something both wonderful and very intimidating to the system. We would see nations forged from the roots of oppression and the need to be self-reliant and respected. We would have an answer to the issue of police misconduct and brutalization. We would find a solution to the ills that plague our communities. It would make the 'hood more than a simple word in the middle of a Hip Hop verse. It would turn the 'hood into a real community, a place where love and dignity would be displayed in the hearts and minds of the same people who have been deemed as not having the ability to stand as one. There would be that sense of community envisioned by the late great Dr. Huey P. Newton, the founder of the Black Panther Party. We would have the start of the revolutionary spirit needed to free ourselves from the long and heavy shackles of this racist and decadent system of oppression.

This might seem far fetched, but it is a reality that those in power see and realize. That is why they work day and night in their efforts to destroy us. Therefore, we must unite and work diligently in our efforts to organize and bring this vision into a real state of being. It can be done. After all, wasn't this country formed around the same principles of self-respect and self-reliance that should be guaranteed to all? Was it not this very same country where groups of people associated and worked together in order to proclaim what the ruling class at that time considered to be antisocial activities? Weren't their acts labeled criminal in the eyes of the state, and doesn't that sound like the very definition of a so-called gang, according to Webster?

When the British came into their communities, much like the police do to us now, didn't this same group of people stand together to protect their communities (their 'hoods)? So, what is the difference between what we have now and what they had then? The only difference between then and now, them and us, is that they knew their origins and historical background, which gave them the ability to form a united front on which they could stand.

What I'm saying, in short, is that these so-called gangs are the victims of misinformation and massive propaganda that attempt to once again ensure that the masses remain divided and don't reach their full potential. Remember that the will of the people to be free will always override any obstacle placed between them and their goal. We have learned from history that the truth can be hidden, but if we push hard enough we will break through the walls of oppression.

We, The People, must not look upon these so-called gangs as the enemy, but as a vital part of our communities, the part that has been kept out in the cold for far too long; and it is time to bring them in. These are our young warriors and a true representation of our future leaders.

To these organizations I say: Now is the time to step up and organize your nations into a formidable force that will watch over and protect the 'hood from all who wish to contribute to our oppression. If the place you claim is truly your set and really worth killing and dying for, then take total control over all aspects of it. This includes ensuring the safety of our elderly, our women, and our children.

It is your duty to make sure that the people of our communities feel safe and that the children have an environment that will nurture them and help them grow. Most of all, it is your duty to make sure that whenever the police enter your set, they do so with the same respect they show the other half of society. You and I must learn to resolve our differences without shedding Afrikan blood. That is the challenge before us. We must dig inside our hearts and find the Afrikan that is trying to come out. When this happens, the rest will follow, I promise you.

With Love,
Your Comrade in Struggle

SCARFACE
Armen-Rah
(79th St. BGDN Boys Town Set)

In the beginning was the sword and the sword was God
And the sword cut flesh with precision 'cause the sword was
    sharp
The ugly truth of my life hurts when I think of it touching my skin
They want to know how I got this scar on my face. Sit back and
    I'll begin:
In the beginning when God created a ghetto heaven and hell
I was born in a garden, not Eden, more like Algal and Rockwell
A poverished community; there were no businessmen to till the
    ground
The soil was fertile but no positive male image could be found
My daddy was a gangster; on his belly he slid
Like a serpent living the life of crime until he ended up dead
As time passed, I got older, but before I was legally grown
I grew older and developed a child of my own
Working in and out of odd jobs that barely kept bills paid

I got fired once and my child was in need; I was afraid
With no fear for my life and no worry about doing time
I took fruit from the tree my father ate of and took a bite out of
crime
Hustling on the street, living that life-or-death game
Slanging those thangs, y'all know how I got my name
They call me cane, raw, uncut, pure and white
The lord wouldn't accept my offering because of how I made my
money, that's right
He scarred my face, gave me a mark on my record
That if any man saw me he wouldn't hire me because I've been
arrested
Why? Because I killed my Abel
Yeah, I killed my Ability to get a decent job and keep my life stable
They call me Scarface; my felony is my facial blemish
Every time I reach for success I can't get by the line of scrimmage
I don't want the whole pie; I just want a little piece
But I can't buy or sell 'cause I'm marked with the mark of the beast

Now I'm marked for death with the mark of the beast
No man who saw me wanted to hire me
So I fled to the wilderness, a land made desolate and waste
And met my wife there; she didn't care about this scar on my face
She fled to this world slinging rocks on her own
'cause she didn't know how to tell her mother her stepdad tried to
rape her at home
We got married, raised God-fearing kids; with love they were spoiled
Lower class trying to plant seeds in parched soil
That was dry rock with no sunlight
No water, just wine from the liquor store to drown our sorrows at
night
We got a few jobs here and there, but no benefits for retirement
We are products of a criminal environment
Mr. and Mrs. Scarface, the rejected and despised
'cause someone has a record don't mean that they are uncivilized
But I still can't get a city job or work at the post office, that's deep
'cause postal workers kill more at work than felons do on the street
My felony is my cross; I've carried it for ten years
Worked odd jobs, fed my kids through blood, sweat and tears
If I applied for a job to get a little more, they showed me the door

As if I committed the crime two days before
Ten years, no additional crime, you would think I paid my debt to
society
But social enslavement makes me feel like I'm back a few payments
There's no love, there's no forgiveness, that's the message you're
telling me
Well, say hello to my little friend, they call him Felony

See, you people need me so you could feel important
Every black man can't rap, sing, or play ball like Michael Jordan
So say bye to the bad guy 'cause I'll still persist
'cause this is the last time you'll see a bad guy like this
I carry my cross with no shame like when you stripped Jesus
naked
Damn a felony, I want low self-esteem expunged from my record
Pharaoh, increase your attack on me, double up on your mission
Like Bebe's kids in Israel we multiply from your affliction
We're trying to move up the ladder and reach a plateau a little
higher
How can I pay a debt to a society whose budget was balanced by
Nebuchadnezzar
So throw your stones at the Teflon don
I'm mentally bullet proof to all your firearms
Governor Ryan's staff sold bogus licenses and he's still free
You say, "In God We Trust," but you won't trust me
But you can forgive Bill Clinton and you can forgive Jesse
Jackson
But when it comes to us felons, it's affirmative we get no action
Well, at least I'm no longer part of the minority now
With a felony I'm part of the majority now
See, the majority of us are dead, the majority of us are in jail
A majority of us are unemployed 'cause a majority of us failed
Well, maybe we should get together and start our own nation
Create new government with a thug administration
But my request was denied by a government run by crooks in
politics
The U.S. had that idea patented in 1776.

It Seems Like Yesterday
Michelles
(Del Hendrixson of Bajito Onda)

It seems like yesterday it all began. I'm a twenty-five-year-old product of a single-parent household, raised in one of the richest cities when it comes to gang activity. I grew up with hardly any supervision, raised by my father who did what he could just to make ends meet. I didn't wake up one morning during adolescence and say to myself in the mirror, "Homegirl, you're gonna be a gangbanger." It just sorta happened. I was fourteen and going through all the awkwardness of coming of age, plus dealing with the hardships of being an only child and mostly feeling alone. I began to hang out with my clique. A close-knit group of people my age and older, all from the same 'hood, and all had similar problems. For once, I had brothers and sisters, la familia, that I could relate to and be myself around.

I was jumped on by my sisters three days before my fifteenth birthday. For most girls of Mexican descent, a girl's fifteenth birthday means a great deal. It's when they're finally considered a woman. Customarily, a huge wedding-like party is thrown. For me, there was no fancy party, no out of town relatives visiting in my honor, and no recognition that I was, in fact, growing up ahead of my time. I chose to be recognized in a different way. I wanted everyone to know I was with someone, that I was a part of something that stood for me and my neighborhood.

That Halloween I lost my first homie. My entire clique was celebrating at our park. The homegirls in circles talking about the usual chica stuff, and the homeboys shooting dice and talking about the chicas. A rival gang came by, booming their bass, and my brother, Gordo, with a 40 in one hand, lifted his shirt to show he was packing. It seemed like it all happened in slow mo.

I remember sitting on a swing in the park, smoking a premo and thinking I could almost swing high enough to touch the stars when shots rang out. I saw my homie grab his chest and fall. And it was all over. Everyone ran to him in shock. No one shed a tear. No one screamed. There was silencio. I accepted that night that this was how life was.

Nearly five years later, I entered a relationship with someone I considered my soulmate. I was still active in my clique, and the person I had hooked up with was also heavily involved in a clique. Sounds like a match made in heaven. However, there was one problem. I was in a relationship with another woman.

My partner and I were on our way to play pool one evening when, out of nowhere, a group of men showed and began beating me and my girlfriend. I passed out and regained consciousness in the emergency room. Although my body had no broken bones, I looked terrible and felt worse. My partner had a pair of broken ribs that punctured her lung.

A week later I had a house full of people ready to retaliate. I remember asking if anyone wanted coffee and hearing the people in my living room talking about ways of killing the people that had harmed me. I just zoned out. I felt numb and, as crazy as it sounds, I felt a presence speak to me. I knew I had to make a choice to change my life. I didn't go ahead with any form of retaliation. This angered my familia, but they had unconditional love for me and understood and respected my choice.

That one choice changed and probably saved my life.

Five years after that, here I am! Twenty-five years old. No longer living in the gang atmosphere that consumed so much of my youth, and volunteering to help those that have lost their way. I've taken several steps on my own to create the life I want to live, and I'm positive about my future. But there is one person I owe much love to.

Two weeks ago, I read an article that gave me an epiphany. The cover title of the *Dallas Observer* read, "Jesus in a mullet." It had an image of someone I instantly felt I could relate to—a strong female force to be reckoned with. I read the article, sent an email, and showed up on the doorsteps of Bajito Onda ready to give my time. I was given far more in return.

DIVERSE AND WILD
Kathleen Morgan
(Sydney, Australia)

Once there was a forest
diverse and wild,
it was watched over
by a little child.

He fell from the sky
into the canopy,
was taught by the trees
to be wise and free.

They told him man
has a power so great
with amazing ability
to destroy and create.

They warned him about
all the harmful things
which into the forest
man often brings.

The child grew older
began walking the ground
learning everything he could
about the species he found.

One day in the distance
he saw some boys
rolling in the detritus,
using sticks as toys.

They seemed to care
about the forest too,
they called him a man
he didn't know what to do.

So he ran and he ran
to the edge of the trees,
looking up to the sky,
he fell to his knees.

"If I am like them and
they are like me,
what can this mean
for my friend, the tree?"

In the depths of a forest
diverse and wild,
a man evolved
from a little child.

Just like a seed
dropping to the ground,
through taking things in,
looking around,

he became tall,
he became strong,
he knew how it felt
when things went wrong.

So he went to his friend,
the tallest tree, asking
"Did you know that
man looks just like me?"

THE PROCESS
Kathleen Morgan, Sydney, Australia

Opportunity called past one day
determined to be heard,
knocking hard on the door
at the rising of the sun.
Sabotage hid in ambush,

just behind the coat rack
waiting patiently for an opening.
Hesitation argued heatedly
with Anticipation, both
overwhelmed by Anxiety,
until Determination finally
woke up, quite startled
by the disarray.
Finding Awareness in the shower,
Enthusiasm dressed for the
occasion; accompanied by
Initiative, they went to meet
the persistent knock.
Organization was busy rearranging
with the help of Attention when
Ambition took control of the situation
opening the door, inviting
Opportunity inside to discuss
the next proposal.

ON SOME FREEDOM SHIT

Bruce George
(former member, Kaos Crew, Bronx, NY)

Believe what you heard while we take it there
cocked and loaded to blaze it there
like heavy mental
we are beyond just Z-plated rentals
with rims
for we Hip Hop in our Tims
as we spit shit
young, Black, and gifted
caps locked and shifted
to UPPERCASE
for we mastered inner space
with Deuteronomy
yet opposite to Gandhi
on some thug shit

jumped in like some Blood shit
or some Cuz shit
we have love shit
for struggle
and those who do the hustle
on the come-up
violators of code get done up
flashers of ice get run up
with the quickness
for the bling brings out the sickness
in the best of us
can't forget the rest of us
whose ribs touch
who live much
on the sideline
the grind line
is a fine line
and at time lines
seems hopeless
photogenic and photo-focused
we're beyond links and bezel shit
on some next level shit
we rise to the occasion
it's half amazing
how we do the damn thing
in spite of
to the right of
adversity
and at times it hurts to be
a target
but we Brooklyn Dodge it
on some Matrix shit
immune to the hatred shit
So we bring the drama
More like Osama
Save the Dalai Lama
for the aftermath
and if by happenstance
we gain Freedom
we're free!

MICHAEL JACKSON'S ACTIONS
Oscar Brown, Jr.

Down in the steel town of Gary
Indiana it is there he
Was born, one of five talented black sons
From the colored, nitty gritty
Depths of that industrial city
He became the foremost of attractions
When he was only eight years old
His genius began to unfold
There before a public he astounded

And as he grew up, for certain
He became a unique person
Who by controversy now is hounded
From where he started he went far
Beyond being a super-star
Blessed by talents nature generated
Once he's got into his groove he's
Doing concerts, TV, movies
Selling records; wildly celebrated
Premier artist, no denying
Performances electrifying
Over all others his talents looming
Earnings led him to establish
A lifestyle that's more than lavish
Never is it said he's unassuming

Michael Jackson's actions
Making him put up his fight
Michael Jackson's actions
Making himself such a sight
Michael Jackson's actions
Making like his rich is white
Michael Jackson's actions
Got America uptight

The childhood other youngsters had
Was not allowed this unique lad
His career was cruelly demanding
And what could properly prepare
Any parents to take care
Of the "property" his folks were handling?
Feeling much like Peter Pan who'd
Never grown up into manhood
As he enjoyed his enormous treasures
He would, in time, become noted
For the efforts he devoted
To recalling his missed childhood pleasures
He spent a fortune on a grand
Estate that he called "Neverland"
To recapture childhood as he missed it
With an amusement park, a zoo
Fantastic, fun-filled things to do
For children he invited to visit
Living a fantastic story
Dazzled by the blaze of glory
In which as a person he is tested
Wildly different he appeared so
Some start saying he's "a weirdo
Whose development has been arrested"

Michael Jackson's actions
Making him put up this fight
Michael Jackson's actions
Making himself such a sight
Michael Jackson's actions
Making like his rich is white
Michael Jackson's actions
Got America uptight

Discontent being a Black son
He did not find satisfaction
As one of the world's most gifted creatures
Damns the color he was born in
Straightens his hair, bleaches his skin
And then surgically alters his features

Seems for all the joy he gives us
Of some truths he is oblivious
If of the adult world he was conscious
He would see what he is reaching
For cannot be got by bleaching
And some plastic surgery appears monstrous
Seeing how he fantasizes
And has delusions of whiteness
In his personal and business dealings
Many who at first adored him
Began finding they abhorred him
As he went through several racial ceilings
Bedded Elvis Presley's daughter
Altogether out of order
Making her a Colored fellow's spouse
Can anybody possibly
Imagine the hostility
Marriage to Lisa Marie would arouse

Michael Jackson's actions
Making him put up his fight
Michael Jackson's actions
Making himself such a sight
Michael Jackson's actions
Making like his rich is white
Michael Jackson's actions
Got America uptight

He bought The Beatles' catalogue
That's "eatin' high up on the hog"
Checks are written with too many zeroes
Having all that much of plenty
Cannot be permitted any
Son of Gary, Indiana Negroes
He causes constant consternation
In a world of his creation
They offer an inch, but he takes a mile
So interest in little children
He had always taken till then
Foes now use to charge he is pedophile

Occurring in America
This causes wild hysteria
Critics who attack can be convincing
Through press, TV, and radio
It's on they come and off they go
To a big public relations lynching
He was exalted as a boy
But the man they must destroy
It is genuine Americana
He has grown to be much bigger
Than is allowed any "nigger"
Ever born in Gary, Indiana

Michael Jackson's actions
Making him put up his fight
Michael Jackson's actions
Making himself such a sight
Michael Jackson's actions
Making like his rich is white
Michael Jackson's actions
Got America uptight

From the brilliant mind body
With which he has been begot he
Has begotten fable, fame, and fortune
Anybody who's so unique
Must be regarded as some "freak"
Whose entire life is a great distortion
He was raised to be related
To a world that he created
So his education was informal
By great talent he was powered
With great riches he was showered
Nothing in his world could be called "normal"
People do not make allowance
For one with all his endowments
Heavy dues are paid by one so gifted
There is much he's misconstruing
Up where he does all his viewing
From the pinnacle to which he's lifted

He sees himself as "Peter Pan"
He sees himself as a white man
He sees his fantasies now being spoiled
He sees the outcome had to be
This American tragedy
In which he will forever be embroiled

Michael Jackson's actions
Making him put up his fight
Michael Jackson's actions
Making himself such a sight
Michael Jackson's actions
Making like his rich is white
Michael Jackson's actions
Got America uptight.

PATIENCE OF THE SPIDER (An Interview with Spider Loc)
Adisa Banjoko
(Bay Area)

With all of the drama between Game and 50 calming down, the rap world can move onto bigger and better things. One of those things is the ascension of a former Crip turned ice-cold MC by the name of Spider Loc. He's locked and loaded to represent the G-Unit later this year. Of all of the rappers I've had the pleasure to interview in recent times, he sounds like one of the hungriest on the scene. One of the characteristics of a spider is that it can sit patiently on its web for hours, perfectly motionless until ready to strike. The following interview took place while Spider Loc was recording his new LP, The West Kept Secret, *due out soon. In this interview we talked about how he got into Crippin', how he got out, what we can expect from his new LP and if 50 and Game really squashed that beef.* —AB.

Adisa Banjoko: You seem to have gotten into gangbangin' at an early age. But what is the process of a cat going from just being affiliated with dudes, 'cause maybe you live in the same 'hood, to gettin' down to *real* Crippin'?

Spider Loc: My situation personally, and it's not identical to anybody else's situation . . . I'm from a broken home. There are many others. It's not a big deal. It's not a sad story. My mother happened to live in Compton, and my father lived in South Central. My mother being a single mother—I have four brothers, actually—my mother was a real strict lady. She forced me to go to private school. She made every effort to make a positive environment for me.

Even though I did not live under the same roof as my father, from his house to my house was a ten minute drive. Growin' up, I had three brothers over there that were close to my age. My father was real big on having us together a lot. It wasn't just on the weekends or once a month. Often, during the week, I would find myself at my father's house. It was kinda like living in Compton and South Central at the same time. It was so close, and I'd go back and forth so many times. Even today, I might drive to the Eastside of South Central to Watts, back and forth to Compton ten times in the course of my day. My mother was working as hard as she could to make a positive environment for me. My father, on the other hand, was not religious at all. He had all boys and we basically ran kinda loose on that side of town.

I can't describe to you the origin of my desire to gangbang. But I can reflect upon the fact that I had a brother who was four years older than me. He actually took those steps [of becoming a gangbanger] before me. Although he might have taken those steps, I'm pretty positive I would have ended up fuckin' around [and getting into a gang]. My name is Spider, but I'm behind him. He's Big Spider. A lot of my activity was because of my brother. It made it a little bit more accessible to me.

I can't really speak on what makes the next nigga turn the set. A lot of people live right in the 'hood. Some people are semi-involved. Whatever gets you to the point where you are around these people and you around this set—it gets to a point where you're not just hangin' anymore. Either niggas is gonna hit you up 'cause you hangin' around too much and put you on. You gonna ask to be put on. Or you gonna act in a manner where people don't wanna put you on, and you'll just be from the set.

Once I started running around with the set, I just assumed my position. I happen to be a leader. So I went from being a young homey to a G homey. Basically, any circle I'm involved in, I set the tone for that circle. Everywhere I go, it's like that.

AB: How old are you?

SL: I'm twenty-six.

AB: One of the things I like about you is that you openly downplay the gangster life. Since you don't bang anymore, how did you get out?

SL: A lot of the gang traditions that used to be in place are totally down.

AB: Back in the day, you got jumped in, and you got jumped out.

SL: That used to be the way niggas used to push their line. But nowadays it's like the game on a lot of levels has gotten weak — soft. On the Eastside, I'm tellin' you, there are certain ways to bow out. Like if you a nigga that got a job, you start carrying yourself positive. You don't fuck around at all . . . You might slide through and holla, maybe not. But niggas respect that type of shit. But if you not doing anything else positive, you don't fuck with the homies no more — you scared to gangbang. But you still sag, but you still wanna come in and out the 'hood — but you don't wanna fuck with the homies.

When I was actively in the circle, that type a nigga got dealt with. But if you been in for some time, and you experienced some prison, niggas know that you 'bout it. But you come to the realization — "This is some bullshit," or, "I'm getting' too old for this." Niggas respect those kinda niggas.

AB: Tell me what you feel you bring to G-Unit. It's already such a powerful crew.

SL: There's more than one thing. But the main piece of the puzzle . . . them being perceived as being the G'est group in rap . . . if you look at each individual and look into their background, when you get away from their image as rappers and look at them, they are about the G'est shit that ever happened yet. We all know that Hip Hop originated on the East Coast. The G shit — this mentality originated on the West Coast. As well, my niggas represent that mentality and all that. It's only right that a West Coast nigga pay homage to the East Coast. It's only right that the East Coast G mentality pay respect to the West . . . I feel like the whole picture is not actually complete until you get a full representation of that.

I learned a long time ago that the top of the rap game is saved for the best poetry talent combined with the best street-credible person. Once I learned that, I realized the top of the game had been waiting for me. 50 Cent is a wise man for noticing that nobody can represent him in the West on the G level, on that lyrical level, on a gentleman level and intelligent level . . . I'm just as intelligent as I am ignorant. Nobody can represent that as well as myself.

AB: You do come off quite intelligent. Let me ask you, are you a reader?

SL: No, I've never been a reader. I learn more by listening and observing. I can learn a word by listening to the context it's used in. If I hear a word more than once and it's used in the same context, I got the definition. I'm a real absorbent person. Reading is kinda boring for me. I read quite well, I'm literate. But it moves too slow. So I live it and soak it up.

AB: Who or what is the greatest love of your life?

SL: My daughters.

AB: What so far has been your lowest depth of misery?

SL: Being in prison and finding out the woman I loved was cheating on me. You wake up in the middle of the night, and you don't *know* it's true. But your gut tells you it's true before you really find out. You can't get out that cell—the cell is six by nine. That's one of the sickest feelings. Not just because she did it, but you can't go to nobody else to try and console yourself.

AB: What has been your greatest joy so far?

SL: I've never had a happy feeling like the feeling of being paroled from prison. That's an excitement that's hard to compare. The only thing I can compare it to is the birth of my daughters. That and the anticipation of this career. Those three run about neck and neck.

AB: What did you go to prison for?

SL: Initially, I went in for robbery. I was paroled and I was out in about six months. I returned for ex-con with a firearm. I did thirty-two months, that's eighty percent. I haven't returned to prison [since then]. County jail—a couple times on miscellaneous shit. But I have not done any time.

AB: Who can we expect to hear on this album production-wise?

SL: The keepers we got so far are Sha Money, the Megahertz, Hi-Tech, Neckbones, Nephew, a couple of up-and-coming cats. A portion of my album came from a stack of CDs and the beats had no names on them. So, I'm not familiar with some of those tracks.

AB: What about MC-wise?

SL: Only G-Unit's MC.

AB: How did you meet 50?

SL: I met him at the "Short Wanna Ride" video shoot. It was September 2004. I walked into a trailer, and I did not know he was inside the trailer. He was in there discussing some serious issues with Youngbuck, but there were quite a few other guys in the trailer. I walked into the trailer and kinda invited myself into the conversation. It was a pretty heavy conversation. But he respected my opinions without even knowing who I was. It turned into a three-way conversation [50, Youngbuck, and Spider Loc].

In the midst of that conversation I took the opportunity to start rapping a capella. He asked me where I was from. I told him. Next thing he said was, "Why put off for tomorrow what you could do today?" He walked over to the cameras at the video shoot and said he had a new West Coast artist named Spider. He said he had to go overseas in two days for about a month and some change. While he was overseas, we talked quite a bit on the phone. As soon as he got back, he started making it right. It's been right ever since, and it's been getting more and more right.

AB: I don't wanna talk about the Game and 50 situation too much because it's kinda been beat over the head. But I gotta ask one question. A lot of people feel like one of two things happened. Either the beef was phony or the peace was phony. Tell me your thoughts on that.

SL: I'm just glad that it cleared the air and we're moving onto other shit. I think it was real unnecessary activity. I'm glad it's under the rug, and I hope it doesn't stick its ugly head back up. I just want everybody to eat and get money, man.

AB: Do you converse with Game at all?

SL: I do from time to time. I holla at him now and then when I bump into him. The other day he was doin' a cameo in a Snoop video. There was a lot of Black Wall Street cats there. It was just me and a friend of mine. Me, him, Jimmy Henchmen, and Big Face. We didn't talk about the politics that's going on. But we chopped it up real quick.

AB: That makes me feel good because I like to see real peace between real cats.

SL: I'm a ex–gang member. I have learned to make relationships with my former enemies. Niggas from Swan, Mainstreet, Avalon, Crenshaw Mafia, and Bounty Hunter Watts. Even with Suge Knight—him being a Compton Piru. I was able to deal with him and get along with him for quite some period of time. And the BooYaa Tribe. If I can get that type of long lasting enemy situation that can somehow be muffled and maintained . . . There's no way any real nigga that went through that is gonna let some rap shit get outta control.

AB: Any last words for the young Gs out there?

SL: Be more smart than hard.

TRUTH AND HONESTY
Afiba Allison
(age 15, 1997)

I seek the truth to set me free
These mental chains have been set to detain me
My ancestors were hung when they opened a book
Now I glance in the mirror and take a closer look
I see my ancestors' same brown eyes
I feel their open hearts that led to their demise
Police used their cuffs and bounded me
Oh please, dear Truth, please set me free.
Malcolm X believed in honesty;
An assassin's bullet put him deep.
These lies I believe have become my truth —
How misguided and lost are today's youth!
Violence rules our minds, drugs cloud our eyes
Money towers over the tallest mountain's size.
Misguided minds seek to oppress me
In the end Truth wins and we all weep.

AN OPEN LETTER
Kublai Toure

Greetings:

In The Name of Allah. The Beneficent. The Merciful. My name is Kublai Khan Muhammad Toure. In Chicago, I'm called Brother Kublai. I'm the Executive Director of Amer-I-Can Illinois. I have a positive mindset to help my brothers and to get them to stay focused. I look for ways to help change a brother's life, in hopes that he will accept his responsibility as a Black Man in this society, because "I-Can."

I was very much involved in a push for the Gang Peace in Chicago after my stepson was shot in the back in August 1991 (a case of mistaken identity). Since losing my son to gang violence, I have dedicated myself to preventing the senseless killing of the youth of Chicago. On many occasions, I have placed my life between warring gang factions and I have achieved successful mediation and negotiations. I'm of service to The Almighty, The Most High. Peace. Love & Happiness.

Youth and Community
Carlos "Chino" Garcia
(ex–gang leader, Lower East Side, NYC)

Growing up in the ghettos of New York City in the 1950s and '60s, my peers and I became gang members for protection against discrimination by other nationalities and races. As a disenfranchised but clever streetwise population, we created our own economic opportunities, and, as time went by, crime became a major part of our daily lives.

We learned in the mid-'60s that the same type of organization that the gang had for illegal actions could be structured and organized towards legal interests. One of the realities that I learned as a young man was that when you unite with other people of the same needs, you have the opportunity to actually accomplish goals that will benefit the community. I have been involved in many community and political actions in relation to the needs of our people. We have seen that this energy we put out has been tremendously beneficial to the areas where we live and serve.

(*An Action.*) When a group feels strongly about an issue in relation to their own life (for example, bad housing, poor quality education, general lousy services to their/our community), it needs to organize and implement a force to deal with the problem. This could be a demonstration, media event, a meeting with or strategy to put pressure on political leaders. The goal is to implement change to benefit them.

(*The Individual as a Community Member.*) People always have to remember that they are part of a community, so they must set aside their selfishness and work as one body in order to achieve a common goal: to institute positive changes. Their deeds will make them role models for future generations of youngbloods.

(*Apathy.*) Apathy is one of the most dangerous things that the people of a community will face. It is important that one recognize when youth and adults feel powerless they cannot do anything to solve the problems that face them.

One should never feel that one's involvement is a waste of time. Every little thing that you do at some point will add up to a major development that will benefit the 'hood. For example, in my experience in political work, we have won and lost elections with a margin of 30–80 votes. Therefore, in the long run, a loss could hurt us for years, and a win could be to one's great advantage.

(*A Strong Future.*) A good education is very important for one's personal enrichment. It's like the foundation of a building. It cannot stand up without the strength of the bottom that's holding it up. I would encourage any youngblood or adult, no matter where they are located, neighborhood or prison, to make education a main priority. This would help you to better deal with many of the other situations in your life that occur, and create new opportunity for yourself, your family, and your community . . . and believe me, time goes quickly, so don't waste it.

THE THOUGHTS OF A MAN, THE WORDS OF A CRIP
Maxwell Houser a.k.a. Boss Blu
(Original Westside 83 Gangster Crip)

I am Boss Blu of Original Westside 83 Gangster Crip. I am not a gangbanger or gang member. I am a Black warrior of the ghetto, protecting my neighborhood. The Crips is my Black army, my Black tribe. The blue wardrobe is my uniform. I am Crip, in and out, whether or not I stand alone. This is not a trend. It is more than just an image. This is a way of living. It is a culture. I bleed and die for this. I live for a cause. I live for the struggle. I do not bang or kill over colors. I do not hate any members of the Bloods or any other gang. We are all equal. We are all a part of the same struggle, whether or not we acknowledge it. As long as your skin is the same as mine's, you are my brother.

This culture has become corrupted by the system we once fought. It has been exploited by the mainstream media. The focus of the cause has been lost. These Artificial Gangsters who we call rappers have tampered with it. They use it to fabricate and build a reputation for themselves. It has become a major gimmick. Now, you have young teens joining for acceptance; they think it is cool. They join for the protection. They join as followers. They hear the raps, they admire and idolize the wrong things. You have these so-called OGs who take advantage of their willingness to prove their loyalty and use it for their personal reasons.

We need change. I am tired of having to hurt and harm my own kind to survive another day. It is genocide. The place we once swore to protect and uplift we have turned into Warzones. I'm tired of seeing my own kind, my own race, behind those prison walls. I'm tired of writing letters to my homies in the pen. I'm tired of the funerals. Our enemy is playing an old game in a new way. They pressure us into the system. We take the easy route of the streets and succumb to their plan. I call it "Physical Reverse Psychology."

We need more militant soldiers. We need more leaders. The message needs to be pushed once again. We need more of the OGs teaching the true movement of improvement instead of How to Flip an Ounce of Coke or How to Kill or Rob Another Brother. We need more Crips and Bloods becoming doctors, lawyers, teachers, and politicians instead of just another statistic or prison number. The streets are not ours anymore. The minds of many are poisoned so early.

We need to learn to cherish our own kind as a whole. To do that, the Crips and the Bloods have to come together. For that to happen, you need the Crip-on-Crip wars to cease. Let's stop being lazy and blind; let's stop hating each other. Our nation of brothers and sisters seems to be suffering from the Willie Lynch Syndrome. It seems we hate to see the next brother or sister succeed. We have no values. We do not cherish life. We are our own worst enemies these days. Everybody wants to be the King of the Block, the boss of the streets.

The streets are not ours anymore. We have our own people snitching for money, helping to incarcerate their fellow brothers. The government supplies most of the drugs. We are killing each other over turf, but we do not own one thing in the entire area or city. We are at war with our Brown Brothers even though we all are in the same hole, trying to dig ourselves out. We are at the bottom of the food chain, and we are eating each other to stay alive. They do not care about us. We have to take care of ourselves. When they look at us, they see dollar signs. They only care about the green we bring them from prisons and rap music. They are taking away our cultures the same way they took America from the Indians, the same way they took land from the Mexicans. Let's bring it together.

These are the thoughts of a man, the words of a Crip. Let's get the movement going!

TO WHOM IT MAY CONCERN
Malik Yoba

When will we brothers learn
that the true definition of a man is not defined
by how much money we earn
by how much pussy we get
by how many niggas we wet
but something of a deeper concern
something that lurks just beneath the skin
something that takes great concentration
something that only the third eye can discern
something that exists within the Spirit
hear it
feed it
we need it
believe it
cherish it
even though we can't see it
nurture it
please don't hurt it
understand it so you can work with it
it keeps our blood warm
so that we may have sustained life
it carries with it our greatest purpose
it's the inner voice that tells us wrong from right
from my heart to yours as we all fight through our struggles
Stay Strong, My Brothers, Stay Strong.

ON DAVID
Lord Cashus D, Fifth Universal
(Universal Zulu Nation)

I was in the store the other day when I overheard two young brothers, both about 15 years old, talking. They gave each other dap and one replied, "On David"—and I had to ask, "What David are you talking about? King David Barksdale, the founder

251

of the Black Disciple Street Nation, who has been deceased over 30 years, or King David of the Bible, who was King of Israel?"

They both looked at me kind of dumbfounded, not knowing the history of either. This goes to show you that many of today's youth who follow the so-called gangs or street nations have no history or enlightenment as to what they belong to. I began to explain to them about their symbols. Did they know who created them and where the origins of the street nations actually came from? I asked them if they knew anything about Larry Hoover, chairman of the GDs (Gangster Disciples), who has been incarcerated since the early 1970s, before many of them were even born.

They are on the streets committing crimes and selling drugs, calling his name with phrases like "On Chief," but what many of them don't know is that Larry is about growth and development, and talks of us being politically strong and protecting and building the community. See, originally, when many of the gangs in Chicago started out, their origins were in the Black Power Movement. Groups like the Blackstone Rangers, who were created by Eugene "Bull" Hairston and Jeff Fort in the mid-'60s, wore as their colors the Red, Black, and Green (the colors of the Pan-African flag, created by Marcus Garvey for the UNIA, in 1919).

There were groups like the Vice Lords, considered one of the oldest Black street gangs in the nation. They were responsible for the protection of the late Dr. Martin Luther King, when he took residence on the Westside in 1966. Founded in the late 1950s by King Pep as a social club for youth, the Vice Lords is the first street nation to be incorporated as a business. Under the leadership of Bobby Gore, the Vice Lords created businesses, such as Teen Town (ice cream parlor) and the House of Lords (a community organization), and were a major political force in the building of the North Lawndale community on the Westside of Chicago. At its height, the Vice Lords had members ranging into the thousands.

By the late 1960s, after the riots sparked by the assassination of Dr. Martin Luther King, several of the street nations came together in unity to create organizations such as YOU (Youth Organizations United) so that they could create social programs for the community. Many of the street organizations were crippled by government interference, like COINTELPRO and Operation Weed and Seed. These organizations were neutralized so that they would never grow too politically strong and hold the keys to empowerment.

By the late 1970s, a large number of these organizations were wiped out due to the influx of heroin, the Vietnam War, and the rise of the prison industrial complex. Due to cuts in social programs in the early 1980s, some of the groups tried to hang on by forming political organizations that created a united political front. These efforts marched hundreds of youth to the polls to vote, resulting in the historic landslide victory for the first Black mayor of Chicago, the Honorable Late Mayor Harold Washington.

The emergence of crack cocaine ripped the lining out of the political street movement and set the community on a course for total destruction. The street nations became involved in this deadly transition, no longer moved by the spirit of social change and uplifting the community. By the late 1980s and early '90s, the street nations had become major drug cartels. Today, our youth are soaked into the popularity of being thugs and the glorification of drug dealing and violence through a multibillion-dollar entertainment industry. This industry dictates today's style, trends and culture, which, in turn, feed the newly privatized prison industrial complex, pharmaceutical companies through behavior modification drugs, and even state-of-the-art funeral parlors.

Through mass media, the glorification of organizations like the GDs, Blackstones, Crips, Bloods, Vice Lords, Latin Kings, etc., has taken the image of drug culture and thuggism all across the globe.

Do these young people really know the history of these street organizations that they live and die for? The answer is NO! All they know is what they watch on television and listen to on the radio.

During the late 1980s, movies like *Colors* and music videos that promoted so-called gangsta rap began to emerge, glamorizing this image, and through mass marketing began to promote this image all across the world in places like Johannesburg, South Africa, where you can find young people imitating these organizations. When South Africa emerged out of the darkness of apartheid, it stepped into a ready-made nightmare. During the late 1990s, crime had become so bad in South Africa that people began to invent such things as flame throwers placed on the side of your car to prevent carjacking and robbery. If someone walked up to your vehicle, you could press a button and burn them alive. Now, in this new era of supersized images of pimps, hos, gangsters, and cranked-out-of-control youth whose morals seem to have been ripped from them, we must find a way to regain control of our minds and our image.

One way is to study the history of the street organizations. You'll find that most of them started off as social clubs that gave the young people things to do. Today, we must find a way to pool small groups of us together to create private social clubs that are not government funded, but financed by neighborhood businesses and community contributors. These will be social clubs that will offer more than just basketball. These will be schools of thought and action that will teach trades, technology, arts, and entrepreneurial science from an African-centered perspective. They would service the needs and issues of today's youth. These centers can work if we learn to do them on small scales, meaning starting in storefronts, basements, garages, etc.

We've been tricked into thinking that we need multi-million-dollar centers to help our youth, when all we really need are multi-million-dollar ideas to instill in their minds. These centers would teach the true history of our people and our struggle through Hip Hop culture, which young people today use to express themselves. This would build better character, self-esteem and a positive image.

It is imperative that we remain in control of these centers, financially and culturally. So many times, when we take government funds, we wind up getting caught in red tape and politricks. This gives the system power of censorship and control over the programs so that they become watered down and young people never receive the essential teachings of our culture.

So the next time you see and hear our youth saying and doing things that *you know* they know nothing about, don't criticize. Remember, it is *our* job to educate, uplift, and motivate them into greatness. It is only us who are going to save us. Peace.

50 CLIP REINCARNATION
Victor "Gotti" Cherry
(OG Gotti Valentine SMM Blood Gang)

Big brother Shakur, I wonder myself if heaven has a ghetto
Maybe, maybe not, greetings, 'cause
we was taught that hell is low
u inhale thug air exhale thug air
Represent from Harlem 2 bell-air legendary
Jealous enemies envy 'cause their thoughts was scary
Hail Mary, they feared u and now they fear me

PAC, u was a self-made millionaire
Baller, true shot-caller, revolutionist thugged out
I loved u, player, no doubt
My brother, I've shared your pain
from the 5 shots 2 the jail cell of
Clinton fools claimed friendship
but reality answered they wasn't
u honored the people like a revolutionist suppose 2
royalty loyalty busters robbed u from it
50 clip tattoo.

America, I inherit it
don't be mad at me 'cause I'm a shot from that clip
revolution retaliation revelations
I spit soldier's death, never perish

Snitches, go tell this
2pac is well alive,
take a look
can u see him in my eyes
am I clear 2 y'all
still rolling reincarnation
still haven't found salvation
searching for 49 others across the nation
traveling mentally from place 2 place.

SIMPLY GIVE
Jauqo III-X
(ex–Gangster Disciple)

I have danced throughout the sphere of truth at micro
increments of disillusioned time while maintaining a
grasp onto where existence may take me while the
journey of self travels the depths of my soul
whispering in the just right ear of my heart, only to
kickstart my complex simplified life pulsing vessels
shipping out onto the shores of my co-induced reality
that it is I who choose the life that I live and it
will be I who change the life that I choose to not
live. While the journey of my deepest inner core
reminds me that your embattled mindset is mine, was
mine, will always be mine, and thru it all I have
received multiple gifts simply to bring back to share
upon those who are heartfully willing to accept I and
it is thru I that I welcome with the warmth and
openness of my experiences thru my deepest growth's
essence Caress and multi-particles of all that I not
only have to offer but the very rare ability to simply
give.

THE DEAL IS DONE
Monte Smith

So what do you do when you've
Lost all space for the sun to shine upon?
The deal is done
The wheel has been spun

Say, who is spinning the wheel?
I want their address
The end result is always degrading
To those who are belittled
In the first place

The deal is done
To the youth
I say,
"Hold on to your mind
when the pigs strut by.
Main street whispers hints
it's only a matter of time."

The expectations the rich
have set upon us are
twenty light years away from
the common worker obtaining
two percent of the great American swindle.

I want to kill rich people, even though it's wrong
I want to drink their blood
then throw up in their leather Lexus seats
and write about it in a song:
Just Because I'm Poor, I'm Still a Man
will be the title
the deal is done
yet life is so vital to the
killing of itself
Evil has won
Humanity has lost
modern world creates slavery
and famine
so global business like
De Beers Diamonds
can keep mining no
matter how many Africans keep dying

So think about that the next time you flaunt your ice
the deal is done
but don't you look nice?

GANGS
George Tavarez
(12 years old, J.H.S. 50, Brooklyn)

In the city that never sleeps, there's lots of gangs
gangs that can end your life in a bang

Gangs carry their guns and knives
those are just tools to steal lives

These gangs, they think they're so hardcore
they try to show it by killing and robbing stores

These gangs think they're so cool
but they're just acting fools

Using guns and doing drugs
they're nothing but a bunch of thugs

Why don't they leave us alone
then the world would be a big safe zone

AMERICA DOESN'T HAVE A GANG PROBLEM
Kwame Jamal Teague #0401897

America doesn't have a gang problem. We don't have a gang
problem when three, four, or even five hundred men and women
wearing the same color, talking the same language, and reppin' the
same principle get together. That's not a problem, that's Unity! After
all the marches, speeches, and rallies, gangs have done what some of
our greatest leaders have failed to do. How is that a problem?

The real problem is the psychologists, sociologists, and all the
other open mouthologists who do this so-called research, seeking
only to isolate and quarantine The Problem, making it seem as
though it is the cause, when it's only the *effect*. Then they go and
get funding and grants to start programs that aren't designed
to work or meant to solve The Problem, because if it did, they
wouldn't get any funding for the next year!

The Problem is the "Talented Tenth" subscribing Black elite, who think a Harvard/Yale/Duke education gives them the right to tell us what we need to do, and their apparent Blackness makes them the voice of authority for us to their white colleagues.

And, of course, The Problem is the politician who needs A Boogeyman to scare the vote out of people, administrations that need their Budgets Boosted, and Police that need an Indian to Cowboy. All creating disturbed images of us, and then using them as criteria for community relations. Who has the right to Define? Them or us? That is The Problem.

Let's not forget many gangs began as community action groups, inspired by or spun off the Black Panthers and the Young Lords. Their purpose was to *Empower*, not *Devour* the community. Then what happened to *our* Definition?

Crack happened, and it redefined *Everything*, bringing the paradox of capitalism to our threadbare infrastructure paradox, because it gave us the ability to be "successful" individuals at the expense of our communal destruction. With Crack came terror, like Black-on-Black crime, gang violence and drive-bys, and in these terms we find a whole generation defined.

To see The Problem we must get beyond The Game, beyond the Sociological Studies, scholarly rhetorical and political scapegoating, and see our lack of self-determination and absence of ownership translated into misdirected initiatives.

We fight on corners we don't own because we don't have a right over them; therefore, we must prove our right to them. We can't take the streets to court, so we hold court on the streets. Like Bonz Malone once said, "When Freedom is outlawed, only outlaws will be free." So if we aren't respected by the law, then we make our own. Any man would or he isn't a man. And before there were any colors, sets, or flags, we were/are Men representing the same principles from dangerously different perspectives. So where do we go from here?

Where did the Jews, Italians, and Irish go, after standing on corners gangbanging? They went into the Mayor's Office, the Governor's Mansion, and even the White House. Ask Giancanna.

So we must use our resources and the networks we have established across the country to put the OGs in the Mayor's Chair, in corporate positions and scholarly circles. This is the way of a true Gangsta because we'll take our slice of the pie instead of being the pie that's sliced up by police, courts, politicians, and social services that get rich and powerful off our backs!

If the Jews, Italians, Irish (and every other ethnic group) can define themselves in relation to this country, then we can too. And if we can't, that's not a problem, that's a motherfuckin' Shame.

To the Fallen Soldiers, God Bless the Dead.

To the Soldiers at War, God Bless Your Life!

WE SHINE
Daniel J. Class a.k.a. King Almighty Wizdem

We are the sun
And our shine is bright
We shine all day long
Plus we glow at night
We got rich royal blood
Flowing through our veins
And the glitter of gold
Still remains
The light that shines bright
Illuminates our crown
Skin color be brown
While our robes are red
Like the blood of ancestors
For the cause they shed
In the black of the night
Our gold crowns shine bright
We are the Almighty Kings and Queens
Among knights, bishops, rooks, and pawns
Battling against injustice
Until a new day is dawned
We are political prisoners
Royal rebels, freedom fighters
Fighting like a mutiny
Until minorities are truly set free
With true justice and true equality
Until then we struggle
Lion hearted, Kings of the jungle
Through knowledge, wisdom and, overstanding
We gain love, respect, and unity

Having pride in our culture
Remembering our heritage
And giving back to our community
Is our righteous duty
Giving all praises to the Almighty most high
Because just like the son in the sky through time,
Yesterday, today, always and forever,
We Shine!

THE GHETTO MANIFESTO
Lil Chairman Fred Hampton, Jr. (P.O.C.C.)

So Let This Be Heard.
Pull your patna', grab your girl and leave nothing behind.
This is a universal call through geographical lines.
Stones, Ds, Crips & Bloods
Bangers and ballers, Hustlers and Thugs.
From the ghettos, the barrios, the strips and sets.
From the packed prisons and back to the projects.
From the crews in Compton to the hoods in Harlem
Once politicized—what can stop 'em?!
Throughout the North and the South, the East and West
Cats in college, and don't forget the roughnecks
Let the Soldiers in Seattle stand and shout
To the Mississippi movers way down South
To the cores of the caves and the souls in the hole
To the dedicated Diehards held on Death Row.
From the OGs to the peewees, from beginners to vets.
This is a call to the wild! So let it be heard.
From the city dwellers and back to the 'burbs.
Bros in Boston and Sistahs in D.C.
To the Mean Magnolias in New Orleans.
To the captives in Colorado, to the fighters in Folsom.
To the Bros in Brittany battling across the ocean.
From Angola to Atlanta, potential warrior tribes.
This shit's so intense, it transcends those lines.
Sleeping Giants who can't afford to rest.
Descendants of slaves who shouldn't forget.
Deep down in Detroit and in the gut of Gary.
Get wise to the guise of your adversaries.

261

I'm still with you soldiers standing strong in the 'ville
Through hard times, lockdowns, and the rest of the deal.
Send a signal to the Super Max that we send 'em our love
From Sanyika in Pelican Bay and back to Tamms with Gov.
From the boot camps, the juvees, and the women in jail
I feel yo' pain. I know it's hard when you livin' in hell.
Through the veins of Virginia, in the alleyways.
To the ridahs in Richmond, redirect that rage.
Legends of Lucasville, let me know if you're listening.
Let 'em know on Riker's Island about this type of resistance.
On the up! All bullshit set aside
Got to get it together, for the stakes are high.
As a matter of fact, Word to the warriors in Wichita,
Wave the clenched fist
From San Antone to Sacramento, let 'em feel this shit!
From the Boogie Down Bronx to the forces in Philly,
To the cats in Cleveland to the Windy City.
Libertád! To my Esés in East L.A.,
Bring the sounds of the Browns in the spirit of Ché.
Let the spirit of the Panthers once again be redeemed.
Bring the Hueys and the Huttons once again to the scene.
They say we facing extinction but I refuse! To lose 'em.
Yell Yeshitelism! To the 'hoods in the heart of Houston.
For those who missed the message, wake 'em up, let 'em know
That it's past time they realized: No more games in the Ghetto!

CODE OF CONDUCT
Akua Njeri

Prisoners of Conscience Committee's Code of Conduct:
If you bang, Bang for FREEDOM.
Africans, claim the set that is rightfully yours, Africa.
Don the colors of the Red, Black, and Green
To the colonized that ride wit' the red, white, and blue.
Let those star spangled slaves be recognized as false flaggers
Who rep a set that they can't even claim.

THE DIRECTIVE
Dasun Allah a.k.a. Krazo Schizophrenik
(CMM / 21 GUNZ! member of the Five Percent Nation)

Some try to floss Hip Hop like a diamond and platinum necklace
thinking it's all about the videos and all about the records
when in truth, the only ones who can really wreck it
are the ones who live and breathe and rise to eat Hip Hop for
    breakfast.
It's a way of life, a movement, the gravy's what the rest is
It's time to play Chess
The game's the same it's mundane Checkers
So let's play Go, go elevate your perspectives
We were young, gifted, and black,
but now we're just the young and reckless
It's time to say, fuck that!
and be the young progressives
This one goes out to all my natives getting restless
Let the tribal beats direct us like Spike Lee or Zemeckis
Be disciplined warriors, not ignorant aggressives
If you a real nigga' and your bitch is the best bitch
it don't mean you ain't gulley if you get with this message
It's gangster to own the jail, not to get arrested
These are words that you can step with
and blast off your Intratec with
Words to live your life and fight to the death with
But we don't have to have a death wish
It's just the little bits and pieces of my heritage I'm left with
says I won't have peace until Babylon is intercepted
The South Bronx and South Africa are deeply connected
That's why Africa for Africans is still the directive
It's self-determination when it comes to the methods
But community control is the immediate objective
No time for cowards, it's the hour of the intrepid
The ends justify the means will be our only ethics
And we don't want platinum plaques,
we'll build empires with our efforts
Rise, my nations, and be the inspirations of epics.

Image Credit: Jenny Mie Lau King

Poet/essayist **Louis Reyes Rivera** remains among the more respected underground poets, having assisted in the publication of over 200 books. Known as the Janitor of History and a living bridge between African and Latino Americans, he has taught courses on Pan-African, African-American, Caribbean, and Puerto Rican literature and history, as well as Creative Writing. In addition to solo recitals and lectures, he has worked with jazz bands (Sun Ra All Stars Project, Ahmed Abdullah's Diaspora, Ebonic Tones, and his own, The Jazzoets), appeared on HBO's DEF Poetry, and hosts Perspective on WBAI, 99.5 FM (www. wbai.org) Thursdays at 2 p.m.

Other Works by Louis Reyes Rivera include *Scattered Scripture, In Control of Spelling* (Four Editions), *This One For You*, and *Who Pays The Cost*. His CD and cassette releases include *Live @ Sistas' Place—A Jazzoetic Jam* (anthology with Atiba Kwabena), *Ahmed Abdullah's Dispersions of the Spirit of Ra: Traveling the Spaceways*, and *YO!* (cassette). He has also edited the following anthologies: *Bum Rush the Page: A Def Poetry Jam* (withT. Medina), *Portraits of the Puerto Rican Experience* (with Adal Maldonado), *Womanrise, Love: A Collection of Young Songs*, and *Poets in Motion*.

Bruce George is a visionary, executive producer, writer, poet, and activist. He was born and raised in New York City. He has written poetry/prose and articles for over 38 years. His work has been published in major magazines, anthologies, and literary publications. He has written testimonials for the likes of *Essence* magazine, *Emerge* magazine, *Class* magazine, *Harlem River Press*, and others.

Bruce is the co-founder of the critically acclaimed, award-winning *Russell Simmons's Def Poetry Jam*. He has won multiple poetry and talent contests as well as several awards including a Peabody Award and a Milky Award for *Russell Simmons Presents, Def Poetry* (HBO), an Upscale Showcase Award, a Trail Blazer Award, and others for his outstanding vision, production, writing, and performance.

As an activist, Bruce has been and currently is associated with major grassroots organizations that foster and uplift people in struggle. Bruce comes out of gang culture and is committed to anti-gang-violence initiatives. He has served on numerous panels (Hampton, Harvard, The New School, Fordham University, Medgar Evers, Schomburg Center for Research in Black Culture) and has judged hundreds of poetry/spoken word competitions.

For more information, check out these websites:
www.brucegeorgemedia.com
www.myspace.com/brucegeorge
www.myspace.com/thebandanarepublic

Printed in the United States
By Bookmasters